The Only Man for Her

KRISTI GOLD

D0001829

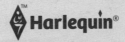

™ **Harlequin®**

TORONTO NEW YORK LONDON
AMSTERDAM PARIS SYDNEY HAMBURG
STOCKHOLM ATHENS TOKYO MILAN MADRID
PRAGUE WARSAW BUDAPEST AUCKLAND

Recycling programs
for this product may
not exist in your area.

ISBN-13: 978-0-373-60709-9

THE ONLY MAN FOR HER

Copyright © 2012 by Kristi Goldberg

www.Harlequin.com

Printed in U.S.A.

ABOUT THE AUTHOR

Kristi Gold has a fondness for baseball, beaches and bridal reality shows. She's always believed that love has remarkable healing powers and feels very fortunate to be able to weave emotional stories highlighting love and commitment. As a best-selling author, National Readers' Choice winner and a three-time Romance Writers of America RITA® Award finalist, Kristi has learned that although accolades are wonderful, the most cherished rewards come from networking with readers. You may contact Kristi through her website at http://kristigold.com, Facebook or through email at kgoldauthor@aol.com.

Books by Kristi Gold

Other titles by this author available in ebook format.

To my amazing children, Ashley, Kendall and Jordan, who've taught me that it's the little things in life—and love—that matter most.

PROLOGUE

As THEY TRAVELED the winding roads threading through the Smoky Mountains, Rachel Wainwright sent a sideways glance at Matthew Boyd, the boy who'd been the center of her existence for the past six years. Threads of gold glinted in his light brown hair, complementing his bright blue eyes that he kept trained on the road ahead. She'd left her home and financial security behind to make this ultimate journey with him, defying her father and, as some would say, the odds.

But before they went any further with their plans, she had to know if he was truly ready to take the next step—marriage. "Are you sure you want to do this?"

Matt turned down the radio and gave her only a quick look before returning his attention straight ahead. "Only if you'll promise me one thing."

She would promise him just about anything. "Okay."

"You won't ask me again if I'm sure." He topped off the comment with a grin, the one she'd fallen in love with in the second grade, even if she hadn't fallen completely in love with him until five years later. That in itself had posed a problem. She was the daughter of a millionaire, and he the son of a mill worker. Her daddy had never accepted her relationship with Matt, but she hadn't let that stop her. Still, he'd be furious if he knew she was eloping, not attending freshman orientation at the university. When all was said and done, he'd have to learn to live with it—provided Matt didn't change his mind.

"I know I keep asking if you're ready," she said. "But everyone's been saying that eighteen's too young to get married and we should wait until after college. Do you wonder if maybe they're right?"

His smile dissolved into a frown. "Are you coming down with a case of cold feet, Rachel?"

She shook her head. "No. I just don't want you to have any regrets."

He reached over and pushed a loose strand of hair away from her cheek. "I only regret that I couldn't convince your dad that we're meant to be together. That way you could've had the dress and the cake and the church wedding you've always wanted."

"None of that matters." And it didn't. Being with Matt—marrying Matt—was the only thing that mattered.

His smile returned, but only halfway. "Glad to hear it. I reserved a honeymoon cabin that's got a king-size bed with our name on it. And since you've made me wait all these years for the lovemaking, I plan to put that bed to good use for the next two nights."

Despite her excitement over finally being with Matt in every way, she pretended to pout. "Then you're only marrying me for the sex, huh?"

"I'm marrying you because you're the only girl for me."

And he was the only boy for her. Always had been, always would be.

"Okay, then," she said. "We're going to do fine, as long as we stick to our plan." The plan that had been two years in the making. "First we finish college."

"Then we buy the clinic," he added.

She wholeheartedly supported Matt's

dream of becoming a veterinarian, even knowing it would require compromise on both their parts. "I'll run the office while you're becoming the best vet Placid, Mississippi, has ever seen."

"You bet," he said. "And when we've saved enough money, we'll build that house on my grandfather's land."

Then came the most important part, at least to Rachel. "Don't forget the babies. I'm thinking two or maybe three." A boy first, with dark eyes and hair like hers, and then a girl, with Matt's sun-streaked light brown hair and blue eyes. Or they could both look like Matt, as long as they were happy and healthy.

He tugged at his tie, as always looking uncomfortable when the subject of kids came up. "Let's not get ahead of ourselves. Right now we have to get married, and it looks like we're almost there."

Matt navigated the pickup to the right where a sign pointed the way to the Wayhurst Wedding Chapel, two miles ahead. Rachel could see only more rugged, wooded terrain and a few remote cabins peeking out from the thick grove of trees. "How did you find this place?"

"I went to the library in Memphis before school let out," he said. "The reference librarian helped me find it, then I gave them a call and made the arrangements."

Rachel worried Matt had spent too much money when a simple courthouse wedding would have been fine. "How much did it cost?"

"Not a lot. I told the lady named Helen who runs the place that we're kind of strapped for cash and that it's only going to be us at the wedding. She booked us this evening for a fourth of the normal rental fee. They also had a wedding earlier in the day, so we'll get to take advantage of the decorations."

More than likely he'd earned the discount using his trademark charm. "That's very nice of her, but I have my trust fund. I could've taken some of it and told my dad I needed it for school."

"You know how I feel about touching that money, Rachel."

Oh, yeah, she knew. And sometimes his pride grated on her nerves like sandpaper on cypress. "You might as well accept it. We're going to have to use part of my trust to get through school."

"You can use it for your tuition, but I'm going to pay for everything else."

Obviously he didn't mind starving, she started to say, but withheld the comment in order not to spoil their special day.

As they rounded a hairpin curve, their destination finally came into view. And what a view it was. The sun had begun to set behind the hazy mountains, the emerald valley beyond serving as a breathtaking backdrop to the white chapel with ornate stained-glass windows and a heavy wooden door.

Rachel was both awed and appreciative as she stared in disbelief at the scene. If only her friends and family were there to witness the ceremony, the day would be perfect. "Oh, Matt. It's beautiful. It looks like a postcard."

"It sure does," he said as he pulled the truck into a parking space in the empty lot. "Only the best for my bride."

My bride.

In a matter of moments, she would be a bride. A bride with a typical case of butterflies in her belly.

Matt shut off the truck and shifted to face her. "Looks like it's time to make it official."

Rachel swallowed around a little knot of nerves. "Looks like it."

He gave her a soft kiss. "Then let's do this."

Without hesitating, Matt slid from the cab, rounded the truck and opened the passenger door to help her out. Once her high heels hit the pavement, Rachel adjusted the knee-length white linen dress and smoothed a shaky hand over her hair. "Do I look okay?"

"As pretty as a Mississippi moon, darlin.' I'm the luckiest damn man in the world, and you're the most beautiful bride to ever walk this earth."

She straightened his tie and the sports coat's lapels. "You're not so bad yourself."

"But I am forgetting somethin' important." He leaned into the truck, opened the glove compartment and withdrew a small black box. "We can't get married without this."

She lifted the lid to find a silver wedding band circled with tiny diamond chips. "I can't believe you did this!"

He cleared his throat. "It was my mom's. My dad told me she wanted me to have it to give to my wife. I know it's not the nice set you deserve, but I promise someday I'll buy you a new one."

"It's beautiful, Matt, and it's special. I couldn't imagine ever wearing another ring once you put this one on my finger. But I feel so bad because I don't have a ring for you."

He slid the box into the pocket of his slacks. "It's okay. We can get one later."

Rachel couldn't fight the sudden melancholy. Couldn't quite hold back the tears. This was her wedding day. A happy day. The most important day of her life to this point. But a few things were still missing.

When she lowered her eyes, Matt framed her face in his palms, forcing her to look at him. "Even if I'm not wearing a ring, that doesn't mean I'm any less married to you. Besides, I'm left-handed, and when I start vet school, I wouldn't be able to wear it anyway."

She drew in a deep breath and let it out slowly. "It's not only the ring. I was just thinking how nice it would have been to have my mom with me." The mother who'd died shortly after giving birth to her daughter. "I know that sounds crazy, since I never had the chance to know her, but I still miss her. Don't you wish your mom were here?"

He studied the pavement beneath his boots. "No use wishing for things that can't be."

She wasn't exactly surprised by his attitude. He'd never been one to open up about his mother's death, ironically the event that had brought them together. In fact, revealing the wedding ring had belonged to Meg Boyd had been the most he'd said about her in years. But his bravado didn't fool Rachel. She was certain that not a day had gone by during the past five years that he hadn't thought about his mom, or felt guilty over not being there the day she'd died. "You know, I'm not sure what's worse. Losing someone you've known all your life or a loved one you never knew at all."

He took her hands into his and gave her a heartfelt look that he reserved only for her. "I don't know, Rachel. But I do know you're never going to lose me."

She prayed that always remained true. "And you're never going to lose me, either."

After he hugged her tightly, Matt stepped back and hooked a thumb over his shoulder. "Can we go in now, or do you want me to ask if we can be married right where we stand?"

"Since I want to walk down the aisle, we should probably go inside."

He pressed a kiss on her forehead. "Then let's go get hitched so we can get to that honeymoon."

She gave him her smile as easily as she'd given him her heart. "Let the hitching begin."

Matt offered her his hand. "Shall we, darlin'?"

Rachel laced her fingers with his and held on tightly. "We shall."

As Matt guided her up the walkway, Rachel prepared to pledge her future to the love of her life. For better or worse. In sickness and health. Through good times and bad.

At that moment she simply couldn't imagine anything but a lifetime of good.

CHAPTER ONE

I'M NOT SURE what's worse. Losing someone you've known all your life or a loved one you never knew at all.

After thirteen years of marriage, Matt Boyd finally knew the answer to the question Rachel had posed on their wedding day—both were equally bad.

Steeped in despair, he sat alone in the barren nursery with his back against the wall, a miniature baseball glove in one hand, a glass of smooth Kentucky bourbon in the other. He visually tracked the multicolored wild horses that ran along the pale blue wall, each one carefully painted by his wife. Then his gaze came to rest on the black letters stenciled above the empty space where the crib had been.

Caleb. His son.

He'd known him for only a few short hours. He'd known his son's mother much of his life. Now both were gone. Four months ago his child had left this world at the cruel hand of nature. A month ago Rachel had left because he'd given her little choice. Or so she'd said the day she walked out on him.

Since that time, he'd awoken every morning in their bed and reached for her. The space beside him was always empty, exactly as he felt right now. He'd tried to convince himself her absence was only temporary. After all, most of her clothes still hung in the closet, and her shoes still lined the shelves. Everything in this house that they'd built together reminded him of her.

Turning to the bottle had been the only thing to help tune out the memories of her bitter accusations. Maybe he was an emotionally closed-off bastard. Maybe lately he did drink too much. Maybe he was unreadable. Unredeemable. But disposing of their marriage like yesterday's news made her pretty damn unredeemable, too.

After coming to his feet, Matt set the glove on the vacant shelf, left the room and stood in the hallway outside the master bedroom. He raised the almost empty glass for a toast to his estranged wife. "Congratulations on running home to your daddy, darlin'."

After he downed the rest of the whiskey that burned as badly as the unshed tears, Matt hurled the tumbler with the force of his fury. Shards of crystal rained down the closed door in splinters and shattered the silence. He stared at the scattered glass, hating his total lack of control. He had a good mind to leave the mess, but Rachel would be madder than a wet hen if he did. Like she was there to notice.

He gathered the largest pieces of crystal in his open palm and headed down the hall toward the kitchen, muttering a few oaths aimed at his stupidity, followed by a few indictments of his wife. So what if she'd left for good? He could get by without her. No use having her around if she didn't want to be there. Goodbye and good riddance.

Still, when the doorbell chimed, the same old hope came calling again. Hope that she'd come to her senses and wanted to reconcile, canceling every negative thought he'd entertained only moments before. His fist automatically tightened, jabbing a jagged glass edge into his thumb. The cut stung like a scorpion bite, but he didn't care. He cared only about getting to the door before she turned and left.

Then again, he didn't want to seem too eager, so he tossed the fragments into the trash, turned on the kitchen faucet to rinse the trickle of blood from his finger and finally made his way to the front door after the third ring.

But he didn't find Rachel waiting on the threshold—only a good friend he hadn't seen in a while.

Sam McBriar had always been the serious type, and he seriously looked as if he might be on a mission. "Got a few minutes to spare?" he asked.

Matt mentally ran through a laundry list of excuses not to let him in, but the questions about his and Rachel's recent breakup were inevitable. Might as well get it over with. "Sure. Come on in."

He stepped aside and guided Sam through the great room to the dinette adjacent to the kitchen. "Sit," he said as he gestured toward a chair.

Sam grabbed a seat and surveyed the take-out boxes from the local diner and the crumpled beer cans spilling out from the overflowing garbage can. Then his gaze came to rest on the open whiskey bottle set out on the counter. "Did you tie one on last night and fire the maid in the process?"

Matt pulled out the chair opposite Sam and collapsed into it. "Yeah, I know. I'm a freakin' cliché. Wife leaves husband. Husband wallows in self-pity and garbage."

"And booze?"

No sense in denying the obvious. "I have a couple of beers after work, just like I always have."

"But you've been hittin' the hard stuff today." Sam posed the comment as a statement of fact, not a question.

"It's Saturday." The only legitimate excuse he could come up with. "I don't have any calves to pull or colicky mares I have to treat. Besides, I only had one drink."

Sam made a show of checking his watch. "It's barely past noon."

Matt's anger began to simmer right below the surface. "Who died and made you my guardian?"

"I'm not telling you what to do, Matt," he said. "I'm just questioning why you feel the need to drink whiskey after what you've been through with your dad."

His friend could have gone all day without mentioning that sorry subject. "Look, I'm not my dad. I'm not hanging out in the bars every night and getting so drunk that I can't work. I still put in ten-hours-plus a day down at the clinic. I see no harm in having a drink now and then. Nothing better to do."

Sam shook his head. "Man, this isn't like you at all. You've always been a scrapper, ready to fight for what you want. You're never gonna get her back if you just sit around feeing sorry for yourself."

The chance that Rachel was going to come back grew slimmer every day. "I can't make her do something she doesn't want to do. And right now she doesn't want to have anything to do with me."

His friend sat quietly for a few moments before he said, "Tell you what. Chase gets off patrol at seven. We'll pick you up and do a little night fishing at Potter's Pond. That way you'll have something to do, at least tonight."

Matt could see several flaws in that plan. "First of all, Rachel's dad owns that place, and if he knows I'm there, he's going to have me hauled into jail. Secondly, I can't imagine your fiancée and Chase's wife letting you take off for a fishing expedition without them. Lastly, I'm not interested in fishing today."

Sam held up his hand and counted down, one finger at time. "First of all, Wainwright isn't going to know we're there, and if he finds out, we'll have the law with us. Secondly, Savannah's making an afternoon trip to Memphis with Jess and your wife to take care of some wedding stuff. Lastly, you need to get out of this house even if you don't want to bait a hook."

Matt could just imagine the conversation going on between Rachel and her friends. No doubt he was the featured topic. "I'll think about it."

Sam pushed back from the table and stood. "I'm not taking no for an answer. We'll be here around seven-thirty. Just bring your pole, and Chase can take care of the bait. I'll bring the hot dogs."

Maybe getting out of the house for a little male camaraderie wouldn't be such a bad idea after all. It did beat trying to find something decent on TV, or staring at the ceiling, wondering how everything had gone so wrong. "Okay, but I'll meet you there on the chance the fish aren't biting."

"It's April. They'll be biting."

"I'm still going to bring my truck." In case his friends took it upon themselves to lecture him about saving his marriage. "And I'll bring the beer."

Sam frowned. "Are you sure that's such a good idea?"

Damn if the guy wasn't treating him like some worthless reprobate. "We've always had beer on hand before. I'll only bring a six-pack. That's two apiece. No one's going to get drunk on that."

"Fine. Only two apiece. That'll keep us all out of hot water."

Maybe for Sam and Chase, but not Matt. He'd been up to his ears in hot water with his wife for weeks. Tonight he planned to relax and forget all about his problems. Forget that Rachel had left him high and dry. Forget that he harbored a four-month-old secret that kept him drowning in guilt. A secret that could destroy everything, especially the woman he loved.

BABIES EVERYWHERE SHE TURNED.

Even in a wedding salon, Rachel Boyd couldn't escape the reminders of what she'd lost four months ago. A woman pushing a stroller down the sidewalk had just stopped before the picture window, leaned over and picked up a precious baby girl. The infant appeared to be around the same age Caleb would have been had he lived. But he hadn't, and each day without him renewed her pain. Every moment without his father had been just as painful.

This was also the last place to forget her faltering marriage. The small boutique was filled to the max with giddy brides-to-be looking forward to their future. She, on the other hand, had no idea what her future might bring. But for the sake of one of her best friends, she pretended to be enjoying the outing.

Rachel glanced at the dressing-room door, anxiously awaiting Savannah's appearance in her newly altered wedding gown. After a few more minutes ticked off, she regarded Jess, her other best friend and former sister-in-law, who seemed to be nodding off in the purple paisley chair. "What is taking her so long?"

Jess opened her eyes and hid a yawn behind her hand. "I have no idea. I swear it took me less time to plan my whole wedding."

Considering Jess had pulled the New Year's ceremony together in just short of three days, Rachel had to agree. "If she doesn't come out soon, I'm going in there."

Her friend yawned again. "I'm right behind you."

She wouldn't be surprised if Jess fell asleep on the way to see about the bride. "You need to tell your husband to lay off and let you get some rest."

Jess grinned. "Why would I do that when I'm married to a gorgeous, sexy guy like Chase? But seriously, my fatigue has a lot to do with the school year ending in less than two months. Try containing twenty-two second graders who have summer vacation on their minds. It's a good thing I like kids."

Rachel liked kids, too. A lot. Yet it didn't seem to be in the cards for her to have one of her own. As usual, the soul-deep sadness returned, and the nagging tears weren't far behind.

Fortunately, Savannah emerged from the dressing room, providing a much-appreciated distraction, and a little nip of envy. Rachel had worn a simple Sunday-best white dress on her wedding day, not a formfitting, satin, halter-style gown with a silver beaded sash at the waist. Funny, that hadn't mattered way back then, so it certainly shouldn't matter now. For some reason, it did.

Savannah stepped in front of the three-way

mirror and twisted her blond hair back at her nape. "So what do you two think?"

Rachel managed a generous smile around the memory barrage of her own simple wedding. "You look dazzling, girlfriend."

"Sam is going to have a stroke when he sees you in that," Jess said. "Guess I better brush up on my CPR skills."

Savannah turned and looked over a shoulder to study her reflection, then frowned. "Are you sure it doesn't make my hips look too wide?"

Jess rolled her eyes. "What hips? If you want to see a butt, step aside and let me in front of that mirror. We'll make a comparison."

"Enough about butts," Rachel said. "Are we finished with everything here?" She hadn't meant to sound so cross, but she truly needed to get away from "wedding central."

Jess checked her watch. "It's almost six and I'm starving. We should have dinner while we're in Memphis. They have some fantastic restaurants on Beale Street."

Rachel only wanted to go home, not wade through the masses out for a good time on a Saturday night. "I'm wearing jeans, which isn't really appropriate dinner attire. And isn't your husband expecting you to be back by now?"

"We're all wearing jeans," Jess said. "We don't have to go to a four-star restaurant, and my husband is on deputy duty until seven, not to mention we haven't been apart since we married. You know what they say about absence and the heart growing fonder."

"Dinner works for me, since I told Sam we might be late," Savannah added right when someone's cell began to ring.

After Rachel and Jess checked their phones, Jess lifted Savannah's purse from the floor and held it up. "It's yours. And if that sappy love-song ringtone is any indication, it's the groom."

"It is." Savannah took the cell from Jess, flipped it open and smiled. "Hey, honey. I was just about to call you…I know, I miss you, too…."

Savannah disappeared back into the dressing room to talk to her fiancé, leaving Jess and Rachel alone to wait it out again.

Rachel wished she'd brought her own car so she could make a speedy exit. Wished she didn't feel so ready to jump the bridal-party ship. "Let's hope this conversation doesn't detain us any longer than necessary." When

Jess didn't respond, she glanced over to find her looking somewhat pale and slightly alarmed. "Are you okay, Jessica?"

Jess muttered, "No," slapped her hand over her mouth and rushed into the nearby ladies' room.

Rachel hated that Jess might be coming down with something, but on the other hand, it could mean the evening would be cut short. She truly wasn't in the right frame of mind to endure a lengthy dinner. And some friend she was—worrying about her own mental condition when Jessica was obviously in distress. Just as she was about to check on her fellow bridesmaid, Jess came out of the restroom looking as jubilant as she'd been most of the afternoon. Her auburn hair, pulled back in a high ponytail, bobbed in time to her peppy gait. The former head cheerleader had returned.

"Something you ate for lunch?" Rachel asked as soon as Jess reclaimed the seat beside her.

Jess kept her eyes trained on the row of gowns to their left. "It probably has to do with not eating. My stomach doesn't like being empty these days."

Funny, they'd had lunch less than five

hours ago. Rachel could think of only one explanation for her friend's intestinal distress. "Are you pregnant?"

Jess still refused to look at her. "What makes you think that?"

She released a frustrated sigh. "Come on, Jessica. You've been yawning all day and now you're throwing up. All signs point to morning sickness."

Jess looked more than a little sheepish when she finally met Rachel's gaze. "It's afternoon."

"That doesn't mean a thing. When I was pregnant with Caleb, I hurled morning, noon and sometimes night. So are you or aren't you?"

"Hungry?"

Heavens, this was like passing a bill through Congress. "Pregnant. Knocked up. With child."

Jess looked apologetic. "All the above. I'm sorry I didn't say anything sooner, but I didn't want to upset you."

Rachel had grown weary of being treated with kid gloves, and she certainly expected more from her friends. "My own loss doesn't mean I can't be thrilled for you and Chase. I am happy, Jess. Honestly." She could only hope she sounded sincere. Yes, she was happy for her friends, and slightly jealous. She absolutely detested her petty feelings and vowed to keep her personal issues in check.

A few moments of awkward silence passed before Rachel went for a subject change. "How does Danny feel about having a new brother or sister?"

"We haven't told him yet," Jess said. "He's been through so much over the past few months. Dealing with causing Dalton's injuries, Dalton going to prison for trying to kill me, learning Chase is his real dad. Do we sound like a soap opera or what?"

Rachel hated what her brother had put Jess and her son through. A twenty-five-year prison sentence might not be long enough atonement time for Dalton. "High drama or not, that's a lot for an adult to handle, much less a nine-year-old boy."

"Yeah, but he's been working through everything with the counselor. Luckily he loves Chase so much, the transition hasn't been bad at all."

Just one more loss Rachel had endured. Learning Danny wasn't her biological nephew had been tough, but he was much better off with Chase than with her worthless brother. "I'm glad he's doing so well. I'd love to see him at some point in time."

"He's mentioned a few times that he wants to visit Uncle Matt and Aunt Rachel. And speaking of Matt, when are the two of you going to call a truce so you can move back home?"

Her gal pal was nothing if not blunt. "Until he's willing to talk about our problems and stop drinking, I'm staying right where I am." Living alone at her father's guesthouse in a constant state of confusion, crying herself to sleep most nights.

Jess laid a hand on her shoulder. "Don't wait too long before you work things out. Take it from me, time is a precious resource that once it's gone, you can't get back. Just think of all the years I wasted."

"That's different," Rachel said. "Chase was off fighting a war, and you were married to my brother. It wasn't possible for the two of you to be together during that ten-year span."

"If I hadn't stayed in a marriage that was a dead end in the beginning, I wouldn't have squandered that time."

The comment threw Rachel. "Are you saying I should divorce Matt?"

Jess looked appalled. "Heavens, no. Dalton was a jerk and Matt is a great guy. I'm saying life's too short to let pride or fear or stubbornness keep you from being happy. You and Matt have so much invested in your marriage, I know you can work it out if you try."

Rachel understood what her friend was saying, but lately she hadn't been at all pleased with her husband's behavior. She hadn't been happy with much of anything since the day she lost her child and hadn't been given the opportunity to say goodbye. Oddly, when the tragedy should have brought them closer together, it had only driven them apart.

Savannah returned once more, fully clothed with her wedding dress bagged and draped over one arm. "Change of plans for the evening regarding dinner."

"I have to eat soon," Jess said, sounding borderline desperate. "This baby is determined to be fed on a regular basis."

Savannah's eyes went wide. "Jessica!"

Jess waved a dismissive hand at Savannah. "Calm down, Savvy. She figured it out after I tossed my cookies a few minutes ago."

"Oh." Savannah sent Rachel a sympathetic look. "Are you all right?"

She wished everyone would stop asking her that. "Yes, I'm fine. Life goes on and I'm excited for Jess and Chase."

"Good. We were worried." Savannah dropped her cell into her purse and slid the strap over her shoulder. "Anyway, after we stop by the bakery for the wedding-cake tasting, which shouldn't take more than an hour or so, we're going back to Placid. Sam's making dinner."

Jess scowled. "What about us?"

"The cake samples should tide you over," Savannah said. "And Sam is making dinner for all of us."

Rachel had never known Sam to be much of a cook. "Mac and cheese?"

Savannah grinned. "He says it's a special dinner in a special place."

A special place? Rachel didn't like the sound of that. "Then we're not going to your house?"

"Who cares where we have dinner, as long as we have it?" Jess came to her feet. "Right now I could eat this chair, so let's go."

Rachel stood and followed her friends out the door, a multitude of concerns bouncing around in her brain. Surprises weren't always good, and her instincts told her that could very well be the case with this one.

THE GUYS HAD PULLED a fast one. Matt realized that the minute he heard the car doors slam and the sound of feminine voices. So much for a simple fishing trip down at Potter's Pond.

When Jess and Savannah entered the clearing alone, Matt figured Rachel had bowed out when she'd learned he'd be there. Then he caught sight of her standing beside the old oak tree where they'd met in secret during their youth. She balled her fists at her sides as if she wanted to punch someone, glanced at the beer in his hand and sent him a glare hotter than the fire pit.

She'd obviously been blindsided and probably assumed he'd had a hand in pulling this little shindig together. She was dead wrong, and he planned to set her straight if she didn't turn tail and run before he had the chance.

Matt came to his feet and waited while the other two couples delivered hello kisses and endearments, the same way he and Rachel used to carry on not all that long ago. Now they remained yards apart, in a virtual standoff that wasn't lost on their friends.

After a round of uncomfortable quiet, Sam gestured toward the portable table holding all the food. "There's hot dogs and some wire to roast 'em. You'll find beer and sodas in the cooler. Help yourselves."

To Matt, Savannah's and Jess's mad rush to the table, with Sam and Chase trailing behind, looked more like the result of discomfort than starvation. Not one of the foursome even sent him or Rachel a passing glance. Served them right. They should've known better than to try to play mass matchmakers.

When Rachel failed to move, Matt set his beer on the ground beside the lawn chair and approached her, keeping his distance in case she decided to throw that punch.

Before he could say a word, she clenched her teeth and spoke through them. "Did you have something to do with this?"

Exactly as he'd predicted. "Nope. I was as surprised as you were. Sam invited me to a guys-only fishing trip and said you and the girls were in Memphis. I just figured you'd be there most of the night."

"You figured wrong." She wrung her hands like an old-time washer. "One of us should leave, and I think it should be you. Don't you need to go inoculate a cow? Or maybe that dive on the county line is calling to you?"

That just plain pissed him off, even if she did make a valid point about the bar. But when home was no longer a haven, a man had to do what he had to do. "No, sweetheart, I'm free for the evening. But I wouldn't mind taking you home."

"No, thanks, but you can take yourself home."

With that, she brushed past him and joined the others at the table.

As usual, he couldn't leave well enough alone. When he walked right up beside her, the others scattered like crows and returned to their seats around the fire.

Rachel's refusal to look at him spurred his determination to tease a smile out of her. In order to garner her attention, he reached in front of her, speared a hot dog with a wire and held it up. "Could I interest you in a—"

"Don't say it, Matthew."

"Hot dog?"

"That's not what you were going to say."

So much for that strategy. "Didn't know you could read my mind."

"I'm no mind reader, but I know you. You're an expert at double entendre."

Time to bring out the big guns—a little soda with a side of seduction.

He moved behind her, rested a palm on her hip and leaned over to withdraw a drink from the cooler set on the end of the table. Then he straightened and touched the can against her neck where her blouse opened right above her breasts. "Here ya go, sweetheart. A nice cold cola to help cool off your temper."

She took the can and gave him a sugary-sweet smile over one shoulder. "Here's a news flash. I've become immune to your charms."

She spun around, leaving him holding an unwanted hot dog and the urge to prove her wrong. He left the speared hot dog and went back to his chair that had conveniently been positioned next to Rachel. She didn't hesitate to pick hers up and move it to the opposite side of the fire pit and him. If their friends hadn't gotten the hint that this was a bad idea, they'd surely figured it out now.

Sam cleared his throat around the awkward silence and smiled. "This reminds me of old times. Remember when we ran off to Nashville that Sunday for the football game without telling our folks?"

"Who could forget?" Chase said. "We

didn't have the money to buy tickets, so we spent the day in the parking lot, tailgaiting."

"And Matt was the only one who didn't get grounded," Savannah added.

Because his dad hadn't given a rat's ass what he did. "We should have all gotten our stories straight and then none of us would have been in trouble."

Rachel gave him an accusatory stare. "I believe it was Matt who told Chase's dad we went to the lake right after Chase had told him we were at the fall festival in Yazoo City."

"Just one of my many shortcomings," he said. "Do you want to go ahead and recite all of them while you have the chance?"

Jess jumped in quickly like a marriage referee. "Savannah's diary got us into the most trouble."

"Sorry," Savannah muttered. "I had no idea my mother would read it and that she'd have the audacity to call everyone's parents."

Sam chuckled. "Best I recall, your dad wasn't too happy, either. I wasn't allowed to come over for two weeks, although that didn't stop me from sneaking into your bedroom."

Savannah smiled. "No, it didn't, and we almost got caught then, too."

"Wasn't that the first time you two did it?" Jess asked.

Savannah's cheeks turned red as a robin's breast. "Yes, I believe it was."

Sam reached over and patted her thigh. "Took me two years to convince her, but I managed to climb up that old trellis one night and sweet-talk myself right into her bed."

"It took me five minutes to convince Jess to let me in her bed," Chase said with a grin.

Jess rolled her eyes. "Oh, please. We didn't plan that whole dorm-room incident. I just thought you were pokin' fun."

Chase leaned over and kissed his wife. "You can't deny that was some mighty good fun."

"A little too good," Jess said. "That's how we ended up with Danny. But I'm glad we did."

Matt wasn't too keen on the current course of conversation. Hopefully they had enough sense not to mention his and Rachel's first time.

"When was your first time with Rachel?" Chase asked Matt.

Great. Just great. He looked at Rachel, and Rachel looked at him, right before they simultaneously said, "Our wedding night."

Sam shook his head. "No way. To hear you tell it, Matt, you'd been doing it since the two of you hooked up in the seventh grade."

That earned him another glare from Rachel. "Not true," he said. "Whenever you asked, I always said that it's disrespectful to a lady to kiss and tell."

"He's right," Chase chimed in. "He was always evasive. He just let us assume they were doing it."

"I think it's remarkable," Savannah said. "I can only imagine how special your wedding night was because you waited."

Rachel shifted in her seat, a sure sign of discomfort. "It seemed like a good idea at the time, but things aren't always what they're cracked up to be."

Matt could think of several responses, none of them very nice. He picked the least caustic one. "Sorry I disappointed you, sweetheart."

Jess shot out of her chair, nearly knocking it over. "I think this hot dog's done, and after I've finished this one I just might have another, since I'm eating for two now."

That was news to Matt, but Rachel didn't seem all that shocked by the announcement. She also didn't seem too pleased, or maybe it was that ever-present sorrow he'd seen in her eyes for a while now. Under different circumstances, he would've gone to her, consoled her. But for the past few months she'd made it pretty clear she didn't want or need his consolation. No reason to think she'd welcome it now.

She did put on her happy face, but she still couldn't fool him. "How far along are you, Jess?"

Jess returned with a plateful of food and lowered herself into the chair. "Twelve weeks. I suppose you could say this is a honeymoon baby."

Sam frowned. "You two got married four months ago, not three."

Chase winked at his wife. "It was a long honeymoon."

"Yes, it was," Jess added. "And we wanted to wait to tell everyone, just in case."

In case something happened with the pregnancy. Matt had been told that problems usually occurred during the first trimester, only his son had been born later in Rachel's pregnancy. He'd been informed after the fact that having a baby always posed some risk to mother and child if something went wrong, which it had. That was a risk he didn't care to take again. A risk he *wouldn't* take again.

Rachel suddenly stood and rubbed a temple with her fingertips. "I'm sorry to cut the evening short, but I have a headache. Savannah, do you mind taking me home?"

"Not at all."

Rachel didn't hesitate before she took off through the trees, heading for the car at a fast clip. Matt rose and brushed past Savannah before she could move. "I'll handle this," he called over one shoulder, although he had no idea *how* he'd handle it. He only knew he had to try.

He found Rachel standing by Savannah's luxury sedan, arms folded across her middle, her head slightly lowered. He figured she could be crying, but he also knew she'd do her best to hide it from him.

"You okay?" he asked as he approached her.

She swiped at the moisture on her cheeks with her fingertips. "No, I'm not okay. I'm tired and I want to go home."

He saw an opportunity and grabbed it. "I'll take you home."

"That's not a good idea."

Stubborn woman. "It's just a ride. I won't ask to come in or pressure you into anything. We don't even have to talk."

"That wouldn't be a first." She lifted her chin and sent him a determined look. "I'd rather have Savannah take me."

He intended to keep prodding her until she gave in. "No reason to inconvenience her when it's on my way."

"I appreciate the offer, but no thanks. If you want to help, then please go back and tell Savannah I'm ready to leave."

Apparently she wasn't going to budge, and he decided not to waste his time. He backed away, hands held up in surrender. "Fine. At least you can't accuse me of not trying to give you what you need, although lately I damn sure don't know what you need from me."

"I need…" Her gaze drifted away. "Never mind."

He did mind, but he sure as hell wasn't going to beg her to spill it.

Matt turned and headed back to the group, scraping his forearm on a wayward branch on his way back, adding injury to insult. Now he had a cut finger and a chunk of missing flesh. As soon as he appeared in the clearing, the crowd stopped talking and stared at him as if he'd sprouted a second head. "She wants you to take her home, Savannah."

"Okay," Savannah said. "I'll be back in a few minutes."

Jess stood and handed Chase her plate. "I'll go with her. See you guys later."

After the girls hurried away, Matt sat back in his chair and took a drink of beer. Hot beer. He emptied the rest onto the ground, crushed the can in his fist and tossed it into the fire. "Looks like your plan to throw me and Rachel together backfired. Hope you're both proud of yourselves."

Sam eyed him a long moment. "Man, I didn't realize things were that bad between the two of you."

"Yeah, they are." Real bad. "According to Saint Rachel, I drink too much and I don't talk enough about my *feelings*. When I do try to talk to her, she doesn't give a tinker's damn about what I have to say. I can't win for losing."

"And you're giving up on working it out, just like that?" Chase asked.

Matt shrugged. "She doesn't want me near her, so I'm going to give her space. Lots of space."

"Like I told you earlier today," Sam began, "you're traveling down the wrong road if you don't do something and soon. Anything worth having is worth fighting for."

He'd grown pretty sick and tired of the ongoing war and the advice. "If you're so damn wise, how do you propose I change her mind?"

Chase forked a hand through his sandy hair. "Be persistent. Use every trick in the book to get her to come around."

"Seduction usually works well," Sam added. "Worked wonders for me and Savannah when she came back to town."

Hard to mount a seduction when Rachel wouldn't let him within five feet of her. "You can't seduce an unwilling woman."

Chase grinned. "You can if you play your cards right. Have you been married so freakin' long that you don't remember how to charm the pants off a girl?"

Sometimes he wondered if that could be the case. "I don't take too kindly to rejection."

"Here's what I think you should do," Sam said. "Give her a while to cool down tonight, then march over to Wainwright's grand estate and politely convince her to let you in the house. After that, do your best and let nature do the rest."

Easy for Sam to say. He didn't run the risk of getting booted out on his ass. "And if she doesn't let me in?"

"Then try again tomorrow," Chase said. "Try every day until she finally listens to you. She's bound to get tired of you hounding her."

Maybe in a year or so. But his friends were right. He had to keep pushing until they hashed everything out. Otherwise he might never get her back home, and that wouldn't do. "Fine. I'll pay her a visit in a half hour or so. But right now I'm going to have another beer."

Before Matt made it to the cooler, Sam blocked his path. "Didn't you mention that Rachel thinks you drink too much?"

He could use a little liquid courage if he planned to see this through. "It's only one beer. I didn't even finish the last one."

"Doesn't matter," Chase said from his chair. "If you're going to get anywhere with your wife, then you better go there stone-cold sober. And since I'm the law, I can't let you drive if you've had too much to drink."

He'd been waylaid by the booze police. "Okay. You win. No beer."

And no expectations. Matt had a hard time

believing Rachel's attitude would change in less than an hour. That she'd suddenly decide to hear him out when she'd done nothing but close him out of her life since after the first of the year.

Only one way to find out, and he would in a matter of minutes.

CHAPTER TWO

"Do you want us to come in?"

Rachel appreciated Savannah's offer, and she loved her friends dearly, but at the moment she needed solitude. "I'll be okay. I'm going to take a shower and go to bed. I'm sure I'll be asleep as soon as my head hits the pillow." And that was a colossal lie. She'd be lucky to get any sleep at all after the disastrous day.

"You should eat something," Jess said from the backseat.

Her appetite had diminished the moment she'd laid eyes on Matt. "Don't worry about me. I'm going to be fine."

"Are you sure?" Savannah asked. "It seems you and Matt have a lot of issues to work out."

"That's an understatement," Jess muttered.

Yes, it was. "I agree, and I plan to tackle that in the near future. Right now I need some rest."

Savannah reached over the console and laid a hand on Rachel's arm. "Let me know if you need anything. Anything at all. Just pick up the phone and call me."

"Same here," Jess said. "Even if you only need to talk. And if you need someone to verbally beat some sense into your husband, I'm your gal. Ask Chase."

Jess could talk all day to Matt and it wouldn't make a difference. Rachel had learned that the hard way. "I do have a favor to ask. Make sure someone takes Matt home if he has too much to drink. He's been doing a lot of that lately." One of the major issues with their marriage.

"I assure you neither Sam nor Chase will let that happen," Savannah said. "But we'll serve as backup, just in case."

"Thanks."

After doling out hugs to her friends, Rachel left the car and walked into the house alone. She flipped on several lights, hoping to make the place seem a bit more warm and inviting. But even though the two-bedroom, two-bath guest bungalow was nicer than many people's houses, it still wasn't home. It had afforded her some independence, at least until her father returned and insisted she move into her old bedroom, not the guest quarters. Maybe by that point she'd be back in her own house with her husband, though that seemed highly unlikely under the current circumstances. Maybe she should find a place of her own. She didn't have enough energy to worry about that now.

Rachel set her purse on the counter, walked to the large picture window and made sure the main house was completely dark. Zelda, the maid, always went to bed with the chickens and awakened with the roosters. Meeting a millionaire's demands was tough business.

Still restless and somewhat tense, Rachel decided a dip in the hot tub might help her relax. On that thought, she went into the bedroom and, after a brief consideration, bypassed the drawer containing her swimsuit. Normally she wouldn't dare go outdoors in the buff, but the remote estate allowed enough privacy to stay concealed from prying eyes. Besides, she highly doubted anyone would come calling this time of night, and even if they did, they'd have to get past the security gate.

She stripped out of her clothes, wrapped an oversize towel around her torso, pulled her hair into a clip and headed toward the deck.

Just to be on the safe side, she flipped off all the lights before she opened the French doors and stepped onto the deck. She stopped at the control panel mounted on the wall and turned on the jets and heater. Then in a fit of daring, she tossed the towel onto the nearby chaise and lowered herself into the tub.

After she settled into the swirling water, she leaned her head back to study the host of stars and the three-quarter moon partially concealed by the wisp of cloud. But she couldn't fully appreciate the night sky or the country quiet. Not with so much turmoil spinning around in her brain.

She closed her eyes in an attempt to block the childish scene she and Matt had caused back at the pond. Forget that the remarkable, caring man she'd always loved had become almost a stranger and that she didn't particularly like who she'd become in his presence.

Yet she couldn't quite forget everything that had transpired earlier. The talk about first-time lovemaking had definitely generated more than a few memories, and not only those having to do with their wedding night. She considered all the years they'd spent together and the passion that had always existed between them, no matter what, until recently.

Even during those days when she'd been too tired, or not in the right frame of mind to make love, Matt had always had a way of wooing her right into his arms. She recalled the times he would receive a late-night emergency call, and before he left their bed, he'd always given her a kiss. A few suggestive touches. A promise to finish what he'd started. When he'd returned in the early-morning hours, he'd made good on those promises. And during those instances when she'd beaten him to the clinic, he had no qualms about locking doors and putting an end to her anticipation right there in his office.

She shivered in spite of the heat and craved what they'd once had. She longed for the past and, sadly, her husband. She couldn't have any of it, at least not unless things changed. That didn't keep her from wanting it back, wanting Matt....

"Is this a private party or can anyone join in?"

Practically startled out of her skin, Rachel's eyes shot open at the sound of the deep drawl. She could barely make out his features now set in shadows, but she didn't have to see the owner of the voice to identify him.

She immediately sat forward and hugged her knees to cover her bare breasts. "What are you doing here, Matthew Boyd? And how did you get through the gate?"

"I know the code."

Of course he did. "I can't believe I didn't hear your truck."

He leaned a shoulder against the wall and hooked his thumbs in his pockets. "I parked at the end of the drive and walked up here. When I was on my way home from the pond, I thought, I wonder what Rachel's doing now. I just bet she's in the hot tub, taking it easy."

What a load of bull. "Oh, sure. You think you know me so well."

"That I do, sweetheart." He crouched down and swirled a finger around the water, slowly, purposefully coming only inches from her bare thigh. "I probably know you better than you know yourself. I definitely know your body better than anyone."

The movement of his hand, although innocent enough, generated some fairly warm sensations that ran from her forehead to her toes, pooling in unseen places. At the moment, she could boil the water with her body temperature alone. And if she didn't insist he go away now, she could make a major error in judgment. "Would you please get back in your truck and leave me alone?" Heavy emphasis on *alone*.

"Am I making you nervous?"

Definitely. "No. You're making me mad because you can't take a hint."

"I just want to talk for a while."

For weeks she'd tried to get him to talk, to open up about their shared tragedy. If by chance he'd finally decided to honor her request, she shouldn't pass up the opportunity. "The whole reason I'm in this tub has to do with stress relief. I don't want to ruin that by covering the same ground with you and getting nowhere. However, if you're willing to finally have an honest discussion about our marital problems, I'm willing to listen."

"I didn't come here to get into that tonight, but I do have a couple of questions."

Rachel's patience began to wane. "Questions about what? The weather? The stock market? Whether Foy Lowry's prize hog is going to win this year at the county fair?"

"Whatever floats your boat, babe."

So much for thinking he might actually want to have a serious dialogue. "I have no intention of getting out of this tub to talk about nothing with you."

"I didn't ask you to get out of the tub. In fact, I'd be glad to get in there with you. I could use a little stress relief, too."

Oh, no, no, no… "Don't you dare."

He released a rough sigh. "What are you afraid of? That I'm going to see you in your bikini?"

That might be a problem, were she wearing one. "No, I'm not worried about that. I just don't feel it's a good idea for us to be in such close proximity."

He straightened and hovered above her. "Fine. You stay there and I'll stay out here. But I want to see you while I'm talking to you."

Before Rachel could issue a protest, Matt strode to the panel and flipped the switch that turned on the underwater lights. When he returned to the tub, she automatically tensed and hugged her knees closer to her torso. "Do you mind?"

He didn't even try to conceal his blatant perusal of her body. "I don't mind at all. You look pretty damn good, all wet and naked. But I imagine your daddy wouldn't approve of you skinny-dipping on his sacred property."

As usual, he never missed an opportunity to throw her father's rules in her face. "It's none of his business what I do."

"Then I guess we better not tell him, huh?"

Rachel had several things she'd like to tell her husband, but he rendered her speechless when he pulled up a deck chair and sat without an invitation. "What part of 'I want to be alone' do you not understand, Matt?"

He stretched his long legs out in front of him, boots crossed at the ankles, hands laced atop his abdomen. "I'll leave you alone as soon as I get what I came for. If you won't let me come in there, and you won't come out here, I figure we can just continue our conversation right here."

Clearly he had no intention of leaving, at least not anytime soon. "Fine. You have five minutes to say what's on your mind."

"First question."

Rachel was already dreading that question. "Go ahead, but make it quick."

His expression turned solemn. "Do you regret that I'm the only man you've ever been with?"

She hadn't expected that. Truth was, she'd

never even thought about another man. "No, I don't regret that you're the only man I've slept with. Do you regret that I'm the only woman… Oh, wait. I'm not the only woman. I almost forgot about that buckle bunny you met during that summer you and Chase ran all over the state, team roping."

"You mean that summer you broke up with me, per your daddy's orders?"

He had her there. "You still couldn't wait to sow your wild oats when the first pair of tight jeans and exposed cleavage presented itself."

"And when I came clean about that, you didn't hesitate to take me back."

Another point scored in his favor. "I was young and stupid back then."

He leaned forward, arms draped loosely on his knees. "Young, yeah, but not stupid. You knew we were meant to be together. We still are."

Uncomfortable over the course of the conversation and her waterlogged state, she felt the time had come to end the soak and the exchange. She could ask Matt to toss her the towel, or she could just exit the tub and get it herself. She could request he turn his back, or she could just go for it. Going for it worked. After all, they had well over a decade of naked between them.

As soon as she rose from the tub, he sized her up with pale blue eyes that looked translucent in the soft glow reflecting off the water. She knew all too well the slow, sensuous grin that followed. Those attributes had proved to be her downfall on more than one occasion.

She didn't want to experience that same old desire for him, yet it crept along her flesh like a firebrand, leaving a blanket of goose bumps in its wake.

If she knew what was good for her, she'd head for the safety of the house as fast as her wet feet would allow. Instead, a primal force took over, a sense of power. She grabbed the towel and slowly began to dry herself, starting with her legs and working her way up. She didn't have to look at Matt to know he was still watching her, maybe even wanting her. She confirmed that when she took a quick glance to find him shifting in the chair before she lowered her gaze to his fly.

Yes, he definitely wanted her, but he couldn't have her. Not tonight.

After she cocooned herself in the towel and tucked the edges between her breasts, she faced Matt to discover he'd come to his feet. "I'm going inside now," she said in a voice that sounded grainy and unsure.

He took a few guarded steps toward her. "You know what you just reminded me of? That morning last spring, when I'd been out most of the night tending to the Fielders' gelding. I came home and sat down at the breakfast table, and then you did that little striptease, shocking the hell out of me. Best I recall, we had one wild ride right there on the ceramic tile floor."

A flash of heat slapped Rachel in the face when she thought about her lack of inhibition. She was almost positive she'd become pregnant that very morning. "I'd prefer to forget about that, thank you very much."

As Matt took another few steps, she immediately backed up against the brick wall. "Are you blushing because you're embarrassed, sweetheart?" he asked. "Or because you're remembering how good we are together?"

A little of both. "A lot has changed since then."

"Not everything." He moved closer, leaving only a scant few inches between them. "You're still sexy as hell. And we can still be good together. I'll be glad to prove it."

She was so, so tempted to take him up on

his offer, until reality took hold. "Sleeping together isn't going to solve our problems."

"But it might make us forget them for a while." He braced a hand above her head and pushed a wayward strand of hair behind her ear with the other. "Besides, who said anything about sleeping? I'm not tired. Are you?"

She was tired of fighting and almost ready to give up and give in. But she had to stay strong or suffer the consequences of her actions. "Again, I'm going inside. Alone. Have a nice night."

Rachel ducked under Matt's arm and opened the French doors, only to have him follow her inside. When she turned to protest, he reeled her in for a kiss. A sultry, suggestive kiss. She couldn't remember the last time they'd kissed this way, deep and provocative. Couldn't remember the last time they'd been this close. She did recall all those nights over the past few months when she'd needed him this badly, but anger and resentment had prevented her from acting on that need.

That anger still existed and should be enough to stop her now, yet her resistance began to dissolve when Matt rimmed a fingertip beneath the edge of the towel, immediately above the knot. He didn't release it but

Rachel sensed he wanted to. He was simply waiting for her permission. If she told him to stop, he would. If she demanded he go away, leave her be, he'd back off. Her husband might be determined and stubborn to a fault, but he'd never force her to do anything she didn't want to do. Unfortunately, she wanted the intimacy. She needed the intimacy, right or wrong. Wise or not.

And in one defining moment, when feeling something other than angry and sad and resentful mattered more than wisdom, she released the towel. It fell to the floor, leaving her completely exposed, both physically and emotionally.

From that point, everything happened quickly. They headed toward the bedroom adjacent to the living area on a rush of desperate kisses. Matt guided her to the mattress's edge, and while she watched, he yanked his T-shirt over his head and tossed it onto the floor. Then he fumbled with his fly and shoved his jeans and underwear down without even bothering to take off his boots. Somewhere in the back of her mind she thought she should say they shouldn't be doing this, but she was already too far gone.

Matt nudged her back onto the bed and

eased inside her with more restraint than she'd expected. But the sheer intensity in his blue eyes that he kept trained on hers, the tight set of his jaw showed his struggle for control. Normally he would take his time coaxing a climax from her, but Rachel didn't need any fancy foreplay. Just the feel of his damp skin against her palms, the powerful movement of his body, coupled with a few descriptive, sexy words he whispered in her ear, proved to be more than enough.

Matt had always prided himself on making it last, but like her, he couldn't hold out any longer. The spontaneous and ill-advised love-making had driven them both over the edge in record time. And with one more thrust, he collapsed against her.

Their ragged breathing echoed in the silent room as Rachel's heart began to slow and awareness settled in. She'd forgotten how good he felt in her arms. Truthfully, she hadn't let herself remember. But now it all came back to her, all the things she'd come to appreciate over the years. The way he'd always held her in the aftermath, making her feel secure and cherished. Loved. Yet in light of their recent troubles, she could no longer rely on that love alone.

If a person really loved his wife, he wouldn't bury himself in work to avoid her. He wouldn't exchange coming home to her for frequenting seedy bars on the outskirts of town. He wouldn't ignore her grief because he refused to deal with his own.

And as the moments ticked away, and once again she mourned what used to be, what might never be again, Rachel did the only thing she could possibly do at the moment. She cried.

MATT WOULDN'T BE SURPRISED if they'd felt the explosion in the next county.

Maybe he hadn't lost his touch after all. Here he was, with his wife in his arms following some mind-blowing sex. Maybe now they could get back on track, and she'd come back home where she belonged.

Then he felt the dampness against his shoulder, heard a soft sob and realized he'd jumped on the optimism train way too soon. The euphoria he'd felt only seconds ago disappeared as quickly as it had come.

He raised his head and found Rachel with her eyes tightly closed, tears streaming down her cheeks. Tears he'd seen quite a bit over the past few months, some he'd been responsible for. No matter what he'd said or done to try to make it better, he'd failed. Tonight was no exception.

He brushed a kiss across her forehead. "What's wrong, Rachel?"

She released a broken sigh. "I don't understand how this can be so right between us when everything else is so wrong."

He should've figured she'd see it that way. Should've known that his plan to woo her back into his life had fallen flat.

Matt rolled over and draped his forearm over his eyes, blocking the light they hadn't bothered to turn off. Hell, he hadn't even bothered to take off his boots or his jeans. Hadn't bothered to...

The thought stopped him cold. Asking the next question could throw fuel on the conflict fire, but he had to know. "Are you on the Pill?"

"No. I haven't had any need for birth control."

Damn. Exactly what he'd feared. "How much of a risk did we just take?"

When he felt the mattress bend, he opened his eyes to see Rachel seated on the edge of the bed, putting on a robe. "You mean could I get pregnant?"

"Yeah. Is it possible?"

She stood, faced him and cinched the sash tightly around her waist. "Now, wouldn't that just thrill you, Matthew?"

He couldn't ignore her sarcastic tone or cynical look. "What is that supposed to mean?"

"You know exactly what it means," she said. "You've never wanted any kids."

He worked his jeans back into place and came to his feet. "I never said that." Even if he had thought it at one time.

She crossed the room and took a seat on the frilly blue floral chair in the corner. "Maybe you never said you didn't want a child in so many words, but your excuses have sent the message, loud and clear. First we couldn't have a baby until after you finished vet school. Then it was establishing the practice and building the new clinic and finally the house. After that, you ran out of excuses—"

"And you got pregnant anyway."

"Not by your choice. Sometimes I wonder if you're relieved that you don't have to worry about being a father anymore."

Her accusation hit him with the force of a left hook. If she only knew what he'd been through when she'd given birth to their son, she wouldn't be so quick to judge. But if he revealed the truth, provided any details, she'd hate him for the decision he'd made. "Nice to know you have such a damn low opinion of me. I never wanted anything to happen to the baby, if that's what you're getting at."

"Caleb," she said, her frame as stiff as a two-by-four. "His name is Caleb."

She didn't have to remind him of that. He'd chosen the name from her list of prospects. He wanted to move past this topic before he made a few confessions that would serve no purpose now. "What happened to us was unthinkable, but we have to move on. Otherwise we'll never get over it."

She leveled her dark eyes on him. "Maybe you can get over it, but I never will. I carried him in my belly for seven months. I felt him kick. He was a part of me. A part of us."

They'd covered this territory before, and each time the rift between them got a little bit wider. He'd rather focus on the step they'd taken only minutes ago. A step in the right direction. "Look, Rachel, I know we've got a lot more ground to cover, and if you'll let me stay, we can talk about this again in the morning when we've both had a good night's sleep."

She rose from the chair, looking every bit the regal princess her father had insisted she was. "You're right. I'm too tired to continue this. But you can't stay the night."

She could be pretty pigheaded at times—not that he'd let that deter him. "I'm your husband, dammit, and if what we did a little while ago doesn't prove there's still something between us, something worth fighting for, then I don't know what does."

"It was sex, Matthew. Sex alone does not a good marriage make."

He released a sarcastic laugh. "I thought we were making love. But then again, maybe you don't love me anymore."

Her gaze momentarily faltered before she brought it back to him. "As they say, love isn't always enough."

"I don't care what anyone says. We belong together." Hell, he sounded almost desperate. Probably because he was. "What can I do to convince you of that?"

"You could start by agreeing to marriage counseling or at the very least go with me to the grief-support group on Monday nights in Trimble Oaks."

That was asking too much. "I'm not like you, Rachel. I can't spill my guts to anyone who's willing to listen. You knew that when you married me. How I handle my emotions is my business and no one else's."

She sighed. "I realize everyone grieves differently, but you don't seem to be dealing with your grief at all, and that includes grieving for your mother. Talking about your feelings is the only way you'll ever come to terms with loss."

Another sad subject he didn't want to address. "My father talks about my mother all the time, even after eighteen years, and look where he is now. Living alone and unable to work because he's drinking himself into an early grave."

"Lately all signs point to you heading right down the same path, Matt."

Overcome with searing anger, he snatched his shirt from the floor and yanked it over his head. "I don't have to listen to this."

He headed out of the bedroom and opened the French doors with so much force, he rattled the glass. After he stepped onto the deck, the porch light came on and he glanced behind him to find Rachel standing in the doorway, looking as frustrated as he felt. He stopped and turned to present his ultimatum. "The ball's in your court now. As soon as you decide what you want, give me a call. Until that time comes, I won't bother you again."

With that, he strode back down the path leading to the gate, only managing a few steps before Rachel called his name. He almost kept going, but die-hard habits brought him around to face her again. "What?"

She lowered her eyes. "I already know what I want."

Her somber tone told him he might not want to hear it. "Then tell me, Rachel, because I swear to God, I don't know anymore."

Finally she brought her attention back to him, her dark eyes again filled with tears. "I want a divorce."

Those were fightin' words, and he wasn't ready to wave that white flag just yet. "Well, princess, here's a first. You just might not get what you want."

CHAPTER THREE

"ARE YOU ABSOLUTELY SURE you want to do this?"

Rachel regarded Savannah from across the mahogany desk, on the verge of saying no and leaving the law office immediately. But her inability to resolve her marital problems kept her planted in the chair. "I'm not sure about much of anything these days. I only know I have to do something."

Savannah leaned forward, her hands laced together atop the desk, looking every inch the serious, successful attorney. "Does Matt even know you're contemplating a divorce?"

"I told him I wanted a divorce two weeks ago," she said. "He came by the night we all got together at the pond, shortly after you and Jess dropped me off."

"And his response was?"

"He said that I might not get what I want. But I haven't heard a word from him since, so maybe he's accepted it." And that made her incredibly sad. She'd expected an ongoing battle, more effort to win her over. Perhaps he didn't see any reason to fight. Perhaps he was right.

Savannah straightened a few files and set them aside. "First of all, I can't represent you in a divorce."

Not the news Rachel wanted to hear. "I thought you decided to practice general law, not just corporate law, when you moved here from Chicago."

"I did, and I am, and that unfortunately includes the occasional divorce. But you and Matt are my friends, and if I represented you, I'd be taking sides. I won't do that."

Savannah's loyalty didn't exactly surprise Rachel. It did disappoint her. "What if Matt agrees to the divorce and it's only a matter of filing the appropriate paperwork?"

"That would depend on whether you and Matt can equitably divide your assets on your own. That's going to be impossible if he isn't on board with it."

The assets wouldn't be a problem, at least as far as she was concerned. "I don't plan to ask him for much of anything. He can have the house and the clinic. I have my own money."

"Have you thought about calling him and discussing this?" Savannah asked. "Better still, you should consider meeting with him face-to-face."

The last time they were face-to-face, they'd ended up body-to-body. She couldn't let Matt sweep her off her feet and back into bed again. "The thought of seeing him is too painful. We keep going around and around and we never seem to get anywhere."

"Do you still love him, Rachel?"

"Yes," she answered without hesitating. "But that can't be all there is to it. I wish it could be."

Savannah sighed. "I'm getting married in less than a month and I'm watching the most solid couple I know fall apart. If your marriage isn't going to last, I wonder if the rest of us stand a chance."

She reached across the desk and patted Savannah's hand. "If you and Sam didn't fall out of love after being apart well over a decade, then you're meant to be together."

"I hope you're right."

So did Rachel. "And I hope you'll agree to my next request."

Savannah narrowed her eyes. "Something tells me I might not care for it."

Probably not, but she had to ask. "Would you at least file the papers and have Matt served? Maybe then he'll realize I'm serious."

Savannah frowned. "Are you using this as some sort of a wake-up call?"

"I suppose you could say that. If he's not willing to work on our marriage after he has the proof in hand, then I'll go ahead with the divorce."

"Let me just caution you, Rachel. When you bandy about the word *divorce,* it's always going to be hanging out there. You can't take it back, even if you and Matt decide to reconcile."

A chance she would have to take. Matt might be too stubborn and had too much pride to agree to her terms for reconciliation. He didn't believe he had a drinking problem, nixed counseling altogether and he couldn't commit to having another child. "I realize this is extreme, but he hasn't given me much choice."

"I still can't represent you," Savannah said after a brief pause. "But I will agree to file the preliminary documents, as long as you are absolutely positive this is the right thing to do."

Right, maybe not. Necessary, definitely. "I'm as sure as I can be. It's do-or-die time for Matt."

Savannah removed her glasses and pinched the bridge of her nose. "All right. As soon as I have the paperwork finished, I'll call you in to sign the forms. I should have everything completed by this afternoon, and I'll have them served to Matt on Friday."

Only two days away. She hadn't expected it to be so quick. "There's no waiting period in terms of how long we've been separated?"

"There's no statutory requirement in this state that requires you to be separated at all prior to filing for divorce. And since you have been apart for a few weeks, I'm going to assume you haven't done the deed. And if you haven't done the deed, then there's no reason to believe you'll be involving a child."

Rachel couldn't issue a denial, nor could she look at her friend.

"Rachel? Is there something you're not telling me?"

She shrugged. "Matt and I did have a little post-separation sex, so I suppose it's possible I could be pregnant, but not very likely."

Savannah's mouth momentarily dropped open. "When did this happen?"

She felt like an errant teenage girl who'd gotten caught parking with her boyfriend. "The night I asked him for the divorce."

"And if you are pregnant, when do you plan to tell him?" When Rachel again failed to respond, Savannah added, "You would tell him, right?"

"I don't know what I would do." And she truly didn't. "But I don't see any reason to borrow trouble right now. There probably won't be anything to tell."

"I have something else I want to ask you." Savannah tapped a pen on the desk in rapid succession before putting it down. "Do you remember that night we got together at Rudy's, not long after I came back to town?"

How could she forget? That was the night she'd made the pregnancy announcement to her friends. "I remember it well."

"You said something that's been bugging me for almost a year. You said *you* decided to get pregnant, not *we* decided. I've wondered if you took matters into your own hands."

That secret had been a burden she'd carried for months. One burden she'd like to ease among all the others. "I might have forgotten to take a pill or two."

"Forgotten?"

"Okay, I intentionally forgot to take them. I thought that if I let nature take its course and I got pregnant, he'd get used to the idea. I even hoped he'd be happy about it." And she had been so very, very wrong.

"But Matt still doesn't know it wasn't an accident?"

"What would be the point, Savannah? It's done. I got pregnant and I lost my baby." Logical or not, she'd worried that losing Caleb was some sort of karmic punishment for deceiving her baby's father.

"But Matt knows you aren't on the Pill this time," Savannah said.

"Yes, he knows." His reaction was still fresh on her mind. "And that's part of the problem when it comes to our marriage. I want another baby, and he doesn't. In fact, I'll never know if he really wanted Caleb."

"Of course he wanted him, Rachel. Matt's a good man."

A good man who had no desire to be a father. "None of that matters now. I have to focus on the future, with or without him."

"And you're prepared for a future without him?"

She might never be prepared for that, even if she was capable of making it on her own. "Let's just take it one step at a time and file the papers. I'll decide what I'm going to do after that."

Yet her biggest concern involved Matt and his reaction when he learned what she had done. She would simply hope for the best—and expect the very worst.

"HEY, MATT, ARE YOU in here?"

The question echoed down the barn aisle at the same time he slid the needle into the mare's neck. Startled more by the voice than the injection, she tossed her head and sidestepped to the left, nearly throwing Matt off balance. Only years of experience and well-honed skill saved him from going down and being trampled by a skittish horse. A pregnant skittish horse. Being put out of commission was the last thing he needed. Right now, his job happened to be the only thing keeping his mind off his problems.

He managed to calm the mare enough to withdraw the needle, keeping a firm grip on the halter with his free hand in case she decided to bolt again. Fortunately the hay bag gained her attention just as his friend showed up outside the stall.

"Got a minute?" Chase asked.

The question irritated Matt to no end. Then again, everything irritated him these days. He capped the needle, opened the stall door and set the syringe down on the supply cart until he could properly dispose of it. "A minute's about all I have. I've got to get out to the Bailey farm and vaccinate some heifers."

Chase peered into the stall at the mare. "Nice little bay. Who does she belong to?"

"Sam. She's bred to his stud and due to foal in the next few weeks."

"I thought Sam stopped breeding that old stud a few years ago."

He really didn't care to get into this right now. "This one's going to be the last in the line, and Rachel's birthday present. If my wife ever comes home. I'm not sure that's going to happen."

"You could be right about that."

The comment threw Matt, considering his friend's "fight for your wife" speech delivered only days ago. "Thanks for the vote of confidence. Did you come all the way out here to chastise me about that little scene me and Rachel made at the pond?"

Chase suddenly became preoccupied with the ground. "Actually, I'm here on official business."

That explained why his friend was dressed in his uniform, but it didn't explain what that official business entailed. He'd bet the ranch that it involved his dad. "Let me guess. My father's back in jail and you're looking for someone to bail him out."

"This isn't about Ben." Chase offered him a tan legal-size envelope. "Savannah asked me to give you this. Right now I'm supposed to say, 'You've been served,' but I'm going to make an exception and just say I'm sorry."

Matt stared at the envelope a few seconds before taking it. Maybe some disgruntled animal owner had decided to sue him for no good reason, but he couldn't think of one person in Placid who had ever threatened him with legal action. He could think of someone who had threatened him, but not over his practice. The possibility that this could be Rachel's doing made him sweat.

He undid the clasp and opened the envelope to end the suspense, only to discover his worst fears had been confirmed. Divorce papers—signed by his wife.

The anger began to build, coming from a deep, dark place that made Matt want to put his fist through the stall door. Instead, he held the documents up and turned his fury on his friend. "Did you say Savannah had something to do with this?"

He hated the sympathy in Chase's expression, in his tone when he said, "She decided to bypass the usual process server and let me do the honors. She was worried about how you might react, and she figured I could keep you calm."

A fifth of whiskey couldn't calm him, although he wouldn't mind trying it. But first things first.

Matt took off down the aisle and headed straight out the barn door, not even bothering to stop when Chase called, "Don't do anything stupid, Matt."

Stupid would be to do nothing. Stupid would mean lying down and letting Rachel run over him. The least she could've done was to inform him before she dropped the divorce bomb. He deserved that much. But she had told him that night at the guesthouse that this was what she wanted. And like a fool, he'd chosen not to believe her. He'd also decided to give her some space for the past two weeks. Enough time to realize what they'd been missing since they'd been apart. Obviously she didn't give a damn about the lovemaking. Well, all of it mattered to him, and he planned to tell her that immediately.

He jumped into the truck, tossed the papers onto the passenger seat and tore down the drive past Chase's cruiser, spewing dust and gravel in his wake. When he reached the highway, he planned to turn left and head to the Wainwright estate to confront her. Instead, he took a right toward town when he realized she wouldn't let him into the guesthouse, provided she even answered the door. Or she could have her daddy standing guard at the gate. A confrontation with his father-in-law would definitely send him over the edge. He decided having a sit-down with the architect of this whole mess might be a good place to start.

He made it onto Main Street in record time, whipping into the parking space in front of what once was the old five-and-dime store, which now served as Savannah Greer's law office. After grabbing the papers, he left the truck and pushed through the wooden door, expecting to find a receptionist waiting to receive him. Instead, he discovered Savannah leaning against the reception desk, not looking at all surprised to see him. Apparently the deputy had called ahead and given her fair warning. Traitor.

Matt held up the papers now fisted in his hand. "Want to explain this?"

She glanced to her left where Ike Wilkins was kicked back in a chair in the corner, hands folded on his big belly. "Mr. Wilkins, I'll be right with you. Matt, you come with me."

"Not a problem, Savannah," Ike said. "Looks like the doc's got bigger fish to fry than me."

Great. Now the whole town would know about the vet's legal issues and start speculating. But they'd never guess in a million years that a divorce was in the works. A divorce he didn't want and planned to fight.

He followed Savannah into a small corridor, where she showed him into a room containing a conference table lined with four chairs. As soon as she closed the door and faced him, he made her the target of his wrath. "How in the hell could you let Rachel do this?"

"First of all," she began, "Rachel has a mind of her own. Secondly, I tried to discourage her from proceeding without discussing this further with you. And you and I both know that if you push too hard, she'll only dig her heels in and push back even harder."

How well he knew that. He bcgan to pace with restlessness, helplessness, and paused to stare out the window onto the street. "This still isn't fair, blindsiding me like this."

"I know. I'm sorry, Matt. I wish there was something I could do to make this process easier on you."

He turned back to Savannah. "There is something. Call Rachel and tell her to come here and tell me to my face why she's so damned set on throwing away a thirteen-year marriage. She owes me that much."

Savannah planted both palms on the table and leaned into them. "It's probably a good idea you calm down before you talk to her. You should go home and give her a call to-morrow."

He pulled back a chair, sat and folded his arms. "I'm calm enough. Since she probably won't take my calls, and my father-in-law wouldn't take too kindly to me camping on the doorstep, I'll just wait here until you call and get her down here. You don't even have to tell her I'm here."

She looked away. "She knows you're here, because she's in my office."

That just made him mad all over again. "And you didn't say anything?"

"She asked me not to unless absolutely necessary."

He released a cynical laugh. "Is she hanging around, expecting a show?"

"As a matter of fact, yes. She assumed you'd probably come here first and she's worried you might react badly. She insisted on running interference if you gave me a hard time."

He wanted to give only one person a hard time, and she was in the next room. "Let her know that I'm not leaving until she sees me."

Savannah sighed. "I'll ask if she'll see you, but I can't guarantee she will. And if she does decide to meet with you, you have to promise not to go ballistic. I'd hate to have to call Chase to haul you out of here."

Since he could dig in his heels just like his wife, it would probably take Chase and half the sheriff's department to remove him. "I'm not going to cause a scene. I only want a few minutes of her precious time."

"Okay," she said. "I'll be back, either with or without her."

After Savannah left the room, Matt got up and paced some more. He didn't have a clue what he would do other than demand an explanation. But he didn't require one. He already knew what she would say, because she'd already said it. And as Savannah said, she wasn't going to give in, especially if he pressed too hard.

And that gave him an idea. He sank into the chair again. She expected him to fight her on the issue, so it was high time to do the unexpected. He had no intention of letting her go, but he sure as hell could pretend to be going along with the divorce. Maybe that would shock her back to her senses. If not, he'd figure something out.

As the door opened, he did the gentlemanly thing and stood even though he didn't particularly feel like being polite. Savannah walked in first, with his wife trailing behind her. Rachel wore a leopard-print silk top that hung off one shoulder and a pair of black pants that showcased her butt when she turned to close the door. Her dark hair had recently been cut into long black layers and she had on more makeup than he'd seen her wear in quite some time. The fact that she looked so damn good only made him more determined to put an end to this nonsense.

As Rachel took the chair across from him and centered her gaze on his, Matt sat back down and stared at her until she looked away.

Savannah cleared her throat. "Since Wilma's out today, I have to have Ike sign some papers. I'll be back in a few minutes, and while I'm gone, I expect both of you to play nice. Can you do that?"

Rachel finally brought her attention back to him. "I will if he will."

Oh, he'd play nice, all right—for now. "Not a problem."

After Savannah left the room, a long bout of silence passed before Matt decided to break it with a backhanded compliment. "Nice outfit. I've never seen you in animal print before. Looks like you're ready to go out on the prowl."

She folded her hands together on the table and gave him a good eye rolling. "Believe me, that's the last thing on my mind."

He sent a pointed look at her white-tipped, freshly manicured fingernails. "Then I guess you're all ready for the divorce party."

"Look, Matt, I know you're angry, but I did warn you two weeks ago."

"I'm not mad." And that was one of the biggest lies he'd told in recent history.

Her eyes went wide. "You're not?"

"Nope. Just disappointed. I thought after I left the house following our little reunion, you might've given it some thought and changed your mind. But hey, if this is what you want, I'm not going to stop you."

"Then you're not going to fight the divorce?"

"What's the point? You've made up your mind, so I'm not going to try to change it." The second biggest lie.

"Good," she said quietly. "I'd like to think we can handle this civilly."

"I do have one condition."

"What would that be?"

"Because you didn't warn me before you dropped this little divorce grenade, it's only fair that Savannah's my lawyer."

She narrowed her dark eyes. "She's one of my best friends, and besides, I was here first."

If she wanted to play dirty, he'd play right along. "I met her before you did way back when, so I get first dibs on her."

"That's the most ridiculous thing I've ever heard come out of your mouth!"

He sat back and smiled. "I figure we'll have to divvy up our friends along with the property anyway. We might as well start with Savannah."

She looked like she was about to blow a gasket. "Is this how it's going to be, Matthew? Are you going to give me grief during this whole process?"

You bet he was. "Hey, you wanted this divorce. Guess you'll just have to deal with whatever comes your way from now on."

"And you are the most stubborn, infuriating person I have ever met."

When she got ticked off, she had to be the sexiest woman he'd ever seen. "Right back at ya, princess."

"Stop calling me that!"

Savannah rushed into the room looking fit to be tied. "Would the two of you keep it down? The entire town can hear you."

"Sorry," Rachel muttered. "He started it by claiming he should be able to retain your services instead of me."

He didn't appreciate being painted as the bad guy in this situation. "Like I said, it's the least you can do after your little surprise."

Savannah formed a T with her hands. "Time-out."

Rachel went from angry to ashamed in five seconds flat. "I apologize and so does Matt."

When Rachel kicked his shin beneath the table, Matt winced. "Yeah, sorry for letting it get out of hand."

After Savannah took a seat, she sent both of them a hard look. "First of all, as I told Rachel when she initially met with me, filing the petition will be my only role in the process. I'm not going to represent either of you because it would be a conflict of interest. You'll have to hire your own attorneys, and heaven help them both if this is the way you're going to act when you get within five feet of each other."

"But you did mention you'd handle the divorce as long as we agree to an equitable division of property," Rachel said.

Savannah rubbed her temple with her fingertips, as if she had a major headache. "I don't think you two can agree on what day it is, let alone who gets what."

Rachel shifted her attention to Matt, her expression all sweetness and light. "I personally don't want to hire an attorney, so I don't see why we can't call a truce and sort through the division of assets."

Matt personally didn't see why any of this was necessary. But he'd pretend to agree, for now. "Works for me."

She turned a fake smile on Savannah. "See there? We can be mature, congenial adults."

"You'll have to prove it," Savannah said. "If you can come up with a list and let me look it over, and if you don't disagree on any points, then I'll consider finalizing the divorce for you." When Rachel opened her mouth to speak, Savannah held up a finger to silence her. "But if it appears you're going to contest anything, and I don't care if it's a DVD, then you're both on your own."

Matt didn't mind going over the assets. This course of action afforded him the opportunity to be with Rachel and wear her down a little at a time. Before he was done, he planned to have her home and in his bed.

Savannah scooted her chair back and stood. "Call me when you're ready to iron out the details. In the meantime, I'm meeting my future husband for lunch to talk about the wedding. You can see yourselves out when you're ready, but please do not resume the brawl until you're outside."

After Savannah turned on her heels and headed out the door, Rachel regarded him with an all-business look. "I suppose the next step would be to pick a day and time to go over the property. Tomorrow's out because I'm volunteering at the fire department's rodeo."

Matt saw an opportunity and grabbed it. "Just so you know, I'm going to be there, too."

"Doing what?"

"I'm always on call in case someone's horse pulls up lame, and someone's always does."

"Of course." She folded her hands on the table, looking as prim and proper as a spinster. Or as proper as she could in that leopard top. "As long as we both live in this town, we're going to run into each other now and then. That doesn't mean we have to be anything but cordial to each other."

"Then you're prepared to let everyone know we've split?"

She seemed to mull that over for a while. "That's probably not a good idea, at least in the short term. My father doesn't know yet."

That made no sense to Matt. "You're living right under his nose and he hasn't noticed?"

"He left for Florida the day before I moved into the guesthouse. He won't be back for another week or so."

"And you've managed to keep it from the hired help?"

"I told Zelda we've been painting the house and the fumes were getting to me."

His wife had become a pretty little liar. "Must've been one hell of a paint job, since you've been there for almost a month. Or maybe I should say a snow job."

"I'm just not ready to deal with my father."

"Afraid he's going to tell you 'I told you so'?"

"I'm afraid to hand him more stress. He's had enough of that with Dalton's trial and sentencing."

No one deserved to be in jail more than his former brother-in-law. And he frankly didn't give a damn about his father-in-law, either. "Well, sweetheart, you're going to have to deal with your daddy sooner or later." He stood, planted his palms on the table and leaned forward. "Maybe you should've thought about that before you started this mess."

Without saying goodbye, Matt left the office and climbed into his truck. As bad as being blindsided had been, at least now he had a goal. Come hell or high water, he'd figure out some way to get her back.

CHAPTER FOUR

"NEXT UP IN the calf roping, our final entrant of the day, Placid's own Matt Boyd."

Surely she hadn't heard right.

Rachel slid the box of popcorn and soda across the counter, told the woman, "It's on the house," and strode out of the concession tent without looking back. She stopped at the far end of the arena and verified that her ears hadn't failed her. There sat Matt on his old gelding Cody, waiting in the box. He wore a blue plaid shirt over a white T, a better pair of faded jeans and the tan felt hat she'd given him on his birthday the previous year.

After Matt nodded, the barrier dropped, releasing the calf from the chute. Matt took off in a flash, piggin' string in his mouth, rope whirling above his head. He'd barely traveled a few feet before he'd landed the calf, had the poor thing tied in a matter of seconds and raised his hands above his head. Rachel found herself holding her breath after Matt climbed back into the saddle and walked the gelding forward. The calf minimally struggled to break free of its constraints, but the knot stayed secured for the required six seconds. Only then could Rachel relax, as if she had a vested interest in his success.

"Ladies and gentlemen, we've saved the best for last! That cowboy is our winner, with a time of 6.9 seconds!"

That cowboy. Like so many women, she'd always been a sucker for the cowboy charisma, and Matt definitely still had it in spades. She thought back to all those times in high school when she'd followed him from town to town on the weekends, frequenting too many rodeos to count. He'd been more daring then, participating in bull riding as well as roping events. After a few cracked ribs and two concussions, she'd convinced him to give up the bull riding, much to her relief. At least now he knew his limitations, or so she'd thought. She wouldn't be a bit surprised if he entered every event, including climbing on the back of a raging bull, just to spite her.

How he chose to conduct himself shouldn't matter to her now, yet unfortunately it still did. Regardless of the fact that they would soon go their separate ways, she would never want to see any harm come to him. But she couldn't control his actions any more than she could control her continued attraction to him.

After Matt took off his hat and waved at the crowd to acknowledge their applause, Rachel headed back to man her station. She'd been there only a few moments before Mary Lou Tremaine, the fundraiser's chair, came flitting into the tent like a human hummingbird.

"Rachel, we need you," she said. "Come with me."

"Where?" Rachel asked.

"Matt's taking his win picture for the new website and you need to be in it."

That darned website had been her own father's doing, and possibly her undoing. She certainly didn't relish the thought of being immortalized on the internet with her soon-to-be ex-husband. "It's kind of busy here."

Mary Lou looked around at the empty tent and the two other volunteers standing near the ice machine, chatting. "Honey, it's about as slow as molasses right now. Besides, Nancy and Joe can cover for you."

Great. Just great. She searched her brain for another excuse, but if she protested too much, everyone would start to speculate, and she wasn't ready to face the rumors. "Okay, but I can only be gone for a few minutes in case it does get busy."

She followed Mary Lou out of the tent as the woman guided her past the arena and behind the small grandstand where seventy-something Harvey Gallagher, the town's only photographer, had set up shop. She glanced to her right to see Matt walking toward them, chatting with a cute, fresh-faced little blonde bearing a rodeo-queen sash and a smile that indicated she'd won the prize, namely Matt.

Her husband had always been an incurable flirt, and most of the time Rachel hadn't minded. After all, she'd trusted he'd be coming home with her. That was no longer the case. If jealousy were jet fuel, she could power an entire fleet of airplanes. Well, they weren't divorced yet, and she planned to make that quite clear to the cowgirl nymph.

As soon as Harvey directed Matt to stand in front of the makeshift wooden backdrop, Rachel walked to his side and inserted herself between him and the blonde. "Congratulations, sweetie. You surprised me with your agility. I didn't know you still had it in you at your age."

He looked more than a little surprised himself. "I didn't realize you were watching."

"Oh, yes. I wouldn't have missed it for the world."

"Where do you want me, Harvey?" Blondie asked.

In the next county, Rachel almost answered, but adopted a polite demeanor, even after Harvey directed the girl to stand on Matt's other side…and to move in closer.

When Rachel slid her arm around Matt's waist, she felt the dampness beneath his cotton shirt, the heat radiating from his body. She caught the trace scent of his aftershave and battled the urge to nuzzle her face in his neck. Heavens, she was tangled up in the throes of a pheromone attack when she should be keeping her distance. Worse still, it took Harvey forever to snap the picture.

After he dismissed them, Matt turned to the blonde. "Thanks, Tina."

"Thank you, Matt," she answered. "And let me know when you want to get together."

"I'll give you a call," he said. "Or you can call me at the number I gave you."

Rachel felt as if her head might explode off

her shoulders. She couldn't believe that her husband had so blatantly flaunted a rendez-vous with a young woman at least ten years his junior.

As soon as Tina left, Rachel dropped her arm and propped a hand on her hip. "Who was that?"

He had the gall to grin. "That's Jeb Henson's girl. Didn't you recognize her?"

"No, I did not. She's what, eighteen?"

"Twenty-one." He pointed to his right. "I've gotta go unsaddle Cody and take him home."

When Matt started away, Rachel froze for a few moments, cemented in place by her rage. She forced herself to go after him and order up an explanation, even if she didn't exactly warrant one. He was free to do as he pleased, with whomever he pleased. But she refused to become a joke in the eyes of the townsfolk because her husband had taken up with some hussy before the ink had dried on the divorce documents. He walked a few steps ahead as they crossed the gravel lot, while she intentionally stayed back. Granted, she should have her head examined, but she still appreciated his finer points, like the way he dangled his arms casually at his sides.

Strong, manly arms to match his very manly hands. And, well, his butt wasn't so bad either, and that was putting it mildly. Slim hips and great thighs encased in jeans that fit him well. She'd always been able to drive him crazy by tickling the backs of his knees with her fingertips before she'd work her way up....

She shook her head as if she could dislodge those pleasant memories. As if she could forget all those nights when she'd explored every blasted inch of his body.

Rachel waited a few yards back while Matt unsaddled the gelding and finished loading him into the aluminum trailer. Several times they'd made love in the sleeper compartment in that trailer when Matt had served as an on-call vet in various cities in the state. It hadn't bothered them a bit that the space had been limited. Matt had always had a way of making do, and he'd always done it well.

If she knew what was good for her— which she apparently didn't—she'd banish those memories immediately. He deserved a piece of her mind, not praise for a past she needed to forget.

As soon as Matt turned around from closing the double doors, Rachel moved forward and leveled her ire on him. "Do you mind telling me what you were thinking?"

He rounded the trailer and opened the driver-side door of the truck before facing her. "If you're referring to the roping, if I want to enter an event, I'm going to enter it."

"I don't mean only the roping," she said. "I meant your efforts to relive your youth like you're thirteen, not thirty-two."

Without regard to his surroundings, Matt undid his shirt cuffs then worked the buttons on the placket. "I've been roping cattle most of my life and I still do from time to time in the course of my job. That's not reliving my youth. That's my reality."

"Again, it's not just the roping. You were pretty cozy with the rodeo queen."

"What's it to you anyway?" He shrugged out of the shirt and pulled the white T-shirt over his head. "Are you jealous?"

Yes, and extremely distracted when Matt just stood there completely bare chested and not in any hurry to cover himself. Funny, she'd seen his chest thousands of times in their years together, knew every detail of his body by heart and by touch. The scar along his left rib cage, the scorpion tattoo circling his right biceps, the slight shading of hair above his sternum and the ridged muscle below that. Yet for some reason she gaped as if she'd never laid eyes—much less her hands—on him before. Since the moment they'd snapped the photo, she'd been acting as if he were some gorgeous, carefree cowboy she'd met only minutes ago. She shouldn't be so darned attracted to her husband after all this time, but she couldn't help it. And that attraction had only been enhanced with the knowledge he might be sharing his extremely remarkable attributes with another woman. Correction. Girl.

"Rachel?"

She looked up from studying his board-flat abdomen to meet his grin. "What?"

"You didn't answer my question."

Clearly most of her coherent thoughts had flown out of her brain the moment he'd flashed a little chest. "What question is that?"

"Are you jealous of Tina?"

Yes, not that she'd readily admit it. "Of course not, but I do care about what people think. I'd prefer not to become a laughing-stock just because you've decided to chase after some nubile, too-young blonde bomb-shell who also happens to be the constable's daughter."

After tossing his discarded clothes and hat into the truck, he retrieved a burgundy short-sleeved polo and slipped it on. "You have one hell of an imagination, sweetheart. But since you're worried, I'll be more than happy to set you straight. Tina's going to take your place in the office, not in my bed."

That should have given her some measure of comfort, but it didn't. "What does she know about running a busy veterinarian clinic? She probably barely knows long division."

He settled a baseball cap on his head. "She's got an associate's degree in business, plus she paid her way through college by working in a doctor's office. That makes her more than qualified. And since you're not taking care of my business anymore, I had to hire someone."

She had no doubt Tina was more than willing to take care of his business, and not the kind that involved accounts payable. "Don't act like I've totally abandoned you and the clinic. I've still been making deposits and paying the bills."

"But you've left the appointment scheduling to me, not to mention the supplies are getting low. I don't have time to see patients and run the office."

As usual, they were getting nowhere fast. "Fine. I hope it all works out with your new girl."

"I'll keep you posted."

"Spare me the favor."

He leaned a shoulder against the truck, looking much more relaxed than Rachel felt. "Speaking of favors, if you have some time to spare, I'd appreciate it if you stop by the clinic next week and show Tina the ropes. While you're there, we could talk about the assets."

Rachel had to think on that a minute, but only a minute. If she checked in on Matt's new hire, then she'd find out if more was going on than met the eye. She'd know if Tina had more on her mind than veterinary medicine. Question was, did she really want to know? "I could spend an hour or so Monday after lunch."

"Are you sure an hour's enough time to go over all the procedures with Tina and divide up our property?"

Yes, because she really didn't want anything from Matt, monetarily speaking. What she did want, he couldn't give her. "An hour will have to do. I don't want to spend all day babysitting the help."

"Suit yourself."

She planned to do just that for a change. After she turned to go, Matt called her name, forcing her to face him again. "What now?"

He favored her with the sexy smile that had always taken her by storm and spelled trouble. "Since you obviously liked what you saw a minute ago, you're welcome to polish my belt buckle at the dance tonight."

Like that was going to happen. "I'm going to be working at the dance, and that won't leave any time for polishing anything that belongs to you." But she would still have to see him, unless she faked a headache and shirked her volunteer duties so she could go home early. That wouldn't be fair to the fire department auxiliary ladies who were counting on her help with the final fundraiser.

He had the unmitigated nerve to wink. "Not even one turn on the dance floor for old times' sake?"

"Not on your life."

Before she caved and gave in to temptation, Rachel rushed away, the sound of Matt's laughter following her all the way back to the tent.

If she planned to get through this divorce, she had to avoid him at all costs, beginning tonight.

"She's definitely avoiding you."

Matt couldn't agree with Sam more. He looked toward the opposite end of the converted concession tent where Rachel had taken a seat, her back to the bar. Since the band had just begun to set up, the makeshift dance floor was deserted, allowing him a clear view of his wife. He'd caught her gaze a few minutes ago, but she'd steered clear of any eye contact past that point.

If she was bent on ignoring him for the time being, not a problem. Her attitude allowed him a nice long look at her body, from the tight blue, low-cut knit shirt to the curve-hugging jeans. If he didn't know better, he'd think she was on the prowl. Maybe she was—and that didn't set well with him at all.

She was still his wife, dammit. He'd find an opportunity to get her attention, whether she wanted to give it or not.

"Want a beer?" Sam asked.

Yeah, he did. Real bad. But he was bent on proving to Rachel he didn't have to rely on booze to have a good time. "Nah. I'm okay. But I'll be glad to get you one." A good excuse to make his presence known to his wife.

"Guess I better hold off, because here comes my kid."

Seven-year-old Jamie McBriar hurried across the tent as fast as her miniature cowboy boots would let her. She bypassed her dad, threw her arms around Matt's waist and smiled up at him, her grin as wide as the Mississippi. "Hi, Uncle Matt!"

She wasn't officially his niece, but she might as well be considering he'd known her since the moment she'd come into the world, kicking and screaming. "Hey, kiddo. When did you get here?"

Her face was smeared with pink sugar, compliments of the cotton-candy cone she had gripped in her hand. "It's my weekend with Daddy, so Mama dropped me off this morning," she said. "I saw you rope that calf and you won!"

At least someone appreciated his effort. "Yeah, I did."

She wrinkled her nose. "Did you ever ride a bull, Uncle Matt?"

Not since he'd learned to value his bones. "Yep, but I haven't done it in a while."

Her dark blue eyes went wide as wagon wheels. "Can you teach me how to rope a calf or ride a bull?"

"No bulls," Sam said. "I can teach you how to rope."

Jamie frowned. "Did you ever win a prize or ride a bull like Uncle Matt?"

"Yes, he did ride a bull." Savannah came to Sam's side and kissed his cheek. "I was there when he climbed on that beast. He was much younger back then and didn't have the sense of a goose."

Sam winked at his future wife. "Admit it. It turned you on."

She grinned. "Did I mention I didn't have the sense of a goose, either?"

Jamie tugged on Savannah's hand. "What did Daddy mean about turning you on?"

In order to save Sam from his kid's question, Matt swiped a chunk of Jamie's candy and stuck it into his mouth. The stuff was so sweet he had the urge to spit it out. "Both me and your dad can teach you how to rope. That way, if you need to rope a hurt calf to give it medicine, then you're ready to go."

"I'm sure Darlene's going to love that," Sam muttered. "Thanks for giving her a reason to limit my weekends with my daughter."

Matt had never known Sam's ex-wife to be anything but accommodating when it came to visitation. In fact, their relationship was so damn congenial, it was almost sickening. "I'll smooth it over with Darlene if you need me to."

"Mama isn't going to be mad," Jamie said. "She's too busy taking care of Brady."

The pang of regret took him by surprise. Jamie's half brother had been born two months before Caleb. A healthy baby boy. "So how do you like being a big sister?"

She looked as if she'd eaten a pickle, not candy. "Brady poops a lot and pulls my hair, but he's okay."

Matt laughed along with Sam and Savannah, even though he didn't feel like laughing. He felt more like punching a wall from frustration over his inability to ignore his guilt, even for one night.

"I'm going to take Jamie to your folks before it gets too wild around here," Savannah said. "Gracie said she can spend the night."

Sam gave Savannah a suggestive look that wasn't lost on Matt. "Good idea, and hurry back."

Jamie tugged on her dad's arm to get his

attention. "Are you gonna sleep over at Savannah's house?"

He couldn't resist ribbing his friend. "I was about to ask the same thing."

Sam sent Matt a sneer before he addressed his daughter. "No, but I will be home late and won't see you until breakfast. In the meantime, mind your grandparents."

Jamie rocked back and forth on her heels as if she couldn't stay still. "I wanna say hi to Rachel first."

"Okay," Savannah said. "But I'm not sure where she is right now."

Before Matt could reveal his wife's whereabouts, Jamie pointed across the way. "She's over there talking to that scary man. Who is he, Daddy?"

Matt turned to find some cowboy had taken the stool next to Rachel, but not just any cowboy. R. J. Harbin—a useless bronc rider with a badass reputation and a mouth to match. "What the hell is Harbin doing here?"

Sam peered across the room toward the offender. "He was supposed to ride today but didn't make it in time. Right now it looks like he's trolling for females. Anyone with a daughter over sixteen or a wife under sixty should lock 'em up."

Matt wasn't about to stand by and let some worthless, tail-chasing rodeo bum force himself on Rachel. But as soon as he started away, Sam grabbed his shoulder, halting his progress. "Hold up, Matt," he said. "If you go over there now, you're going to piss Rachel off."

She could join the club. He was already pissed off. Royally pissed off. "Don't you remember the rumors about him?"

"What rumors?" Savannah asked.

"Back when we were running the circuit in high school, some girl made a fairly serious accusation," Sam said. "But nothing ever came of it."

"That doesn't mean it didn't happen." And Matt wasn't going to take the chance that something might happen to Rachel at the hands of Harbin. "The least I can do is warn her."

Savannah touched his arm to gain his attention. "Sam's right about letting Rachel handle it. If all those technical fouls she got playing high-school basketball proved anything, she can hold her own. Besides, she's not going to go anywhere with him."

If it were anyone other than Harbin, he

might agree to let it go. "You're asking me to stand by while he makes a move on my wife."

"I know you're itchin' for a fight," Sam said. "But you'll only make matters worse if you interfere without cause."

Fine. He'd wait and watch for a reason to intervene. He watched while Harbin whispered something in Rachel's ear. He waited while she scooted her stool away from the jerk. But when Harbin moved his seat closer and landed a hand on her thigh, Matt was done with the waiting and watching. "I'm going to wipe that goatee off his freakin' face."

He was only mildly aware of Sam telling Savannah, "Get Jamie out of here," as he took off across the dirt dance floor.

Once he reached the bar, he inserted himself between the two, turning his back to the jackass to face his wife. "Are you okay?"

The look she gave him could have melted steel. "I'm fine."

"We were just having a little talk," Harbin said from behind him.

Matt glared at him over one shoulder. "Looked to me like you were doing most of the talking with your hands."

Rachel tugged on his shirtsleeve, regaining his attention. "Just chill, Matt. I told you I'm okay."

He couldn't chill when steam was about to pour out of his ears. "I'm not okay with him manhandling you."

"The lady didn't mind at all."

That sent Matt around to confront Harbin head-on, clinging to the last of his control, fists balled at his sides. "The *lady* happens to be my wife, and that sure as hell makes her off-limits to the likes of you."

Harbin rubbed his shabby chin. "If that's the case, why is she over here all by herself, while you're standing clear across the room? Did you two have a little lovers' spat?"

"That's none of your business, you son of a bitch."

Harbin slid off the stool and straightened to his full height, at least two inches shorter than Matt. "Maybe if you were taking care of business at home, she wouldn't come looking for me."

Rachel leaned around Matt and glared at Harbin. "I wasn't looking for you. In fact, I was trying to get away from you."

Harbin grinned at Rachel before turning his attention to Matt. "Well, now, Boyd. Looks like you got yourself a regular stuck-

up bitch dressed in slut's clothing. Congratulations."

The insult tripped a mental switch in Matt,
sparking his anger past the point of no return.
Without thinking, he drew back his left hand
and threw a punch square in Harbin's face,
knocking the bastard back against the bar.
He grabbed Harbin by the collar, unaware
anyone was behind him until someone jerked
him back, preventing him from going after
the ass again. And like the coward he was,
Harbin took advantage and delivered a right
hook to Matt's jaw, snapping his head back
from the impact.

"You're getting out of here, Matt, before I
have to arrest you."

Only then did he realize Chase was the
one holding him back. "I'm not done with
him yet."

Matt managed to yank away from the
hold, but Chase blocked his path before he
could get back into the fray. "Yeah, you are
done," he said as he pushed him toward the
exit where Sam now stood. "Make sure he
gets in his truck and leaves. I'll take care of
Harbin."

Matt didn't want or need an escort. He
took off across the gravel lot, heading for

his truck parked at the back beneath a halogen light. Once there, he noticed the copper taste of blood and examined the cut on the corner of his mouth in the side-view mirror. He checked to make sure his teeth were still intact and worked his jaw to rule out a break. Nothing he couldn't deal with, but the swollen knuckles on his left hand could be a problem when it came to work. He'd endured worse injuries before over the course of a lifetime, at least physically. The wounds inflicted by Rachel's departure and talk of divorce might never heal.

When he heard the sound of approaching footsteps, he braced both hands on the edge of the truck bed and lowered his head to study the ground. The posse had probably arrived, armed with a verbal arsenal that would likely include "I told you so" and "You've lost your mind." Chase might even make good on his arrest promise. If that happened to be the case, he could end up in a county jail cell. Not a good way to spend a Saturday night.

What the hell. If the deputy wanted to lock him up, not a problem. He could cope with a narrow bunk and a flat mattress for one night. His own home was pretty much a prison these days.

"Are you trying to recapture your glory days or have you totally lost all your common sense?"

Rachel. That was worse than confronting his friends.

He straightened, leaned back against the truck and came in contact with her scornful look. "Glory days?"

She folded her arms across her middle. "In the five years since this rodeo's inception, not once have you entered an event. Then I find you on the verge of hooking up with a girl who's way too young. And to top it off, you rush in with your macho guns blazing and break some worthless idiot's nose. If that's not trying to recapture your youth, I don't know what is."

He'd been trying to recapture her attention, even if he hadn't planned to do it by punching someone out. "I got a busted lip and bruised knuckles to save you from that bastard, and this is the thanks I get?"

She rolled her eyes. "You've got a bruised ego, and you certainly don't deserve any thanks. You didn't hit that guy to save me. You hit him because he insinuated you weren't taking care of me, and deep down you know he's right."

Maybe so, but there was a lot more to it than that. "R. J. Harbin's dangerous, Rachel. It's been rumored he's gotten rough with a few women on more than one occasion. You know as well as I do that I'm going to defend the people I care about whether you like it or not."

"I didn't need defending tonight," she said, not taking the bait. "I saw Chase standing outside the tent and I was going to go get him after that jerk said…" Her gaze drifted away with her words.

His imagination began to run wild as a prairie wind. "What did he say to you?"

"It doesn't matter now."

"It sure as hell matters to me."

"Give it a rest, Matt," she said. "The point is, at one time you knew when to keep your cool and walk away. That never made you any less of a man in my eyes—just the opposite. Now I'm not sure I know you at all."

If she really did know what he was feeling, she'd understand how much being away from her was killing him. "I'm the same man who's been in your life for almost twenty years, Rachel. You married me knowing I've got flaws, just like everyone else. So let's just forget this damn divorce and start over. If you'll come home, I promise I'll do better."

Even though his hand ached liked the devil, he reached for her, and she backed away. "If tonight proved anything, it convinced me I have to go through with the divorce," she said. "I don't believe you'll keep your promise and I don't trust you or the choices you're making. And I won't sit back and watch you destroy your life the way your father has destroyed his."

As Rachel walked away, one particular promise filtered into his mind.

I don't care what happens to me, Matt. Just promise you'll save our baby....

A promise he'd broken because he'd been forced to choose. That choice might have saved his wife, but it had ultimately cost his son's life.

CHAPTER FIVE

"WHAT ARE YOU still doing here?"

Rachel glanced up to see Chase Reed hovering above her, looking every bit the lawman in his khaki tailored shirt with the sheriff's department emblem embossed above the front pocket.

She'd questioned why she hadn't left hours ago, when the band had stopped playing and the crowd had thinned out to only a few people finishing drinks and conversations. Instead, she'd remained alone at the small corner table, nursing a cola and disappointment in her husband.

"I thought I might help clean up." The only logical excuse she could come up with at the moment.

Chase pulled out the opposing chair, sat and raked off his tan cowboy hat, which he set on the table, brim up. "All the equipment's going to be moved back to the community center by the fire department. The rental company's here to pick up the tables and chairs and take down the tent, and the fairground's crew has already cleaned up the trash and emptied the barrels. That means there's nothing left to do, unless you want to sweep the dirt."

Sweeping dirt beat going home by herself. "I guess you're right. I just don't have the energy to move at the moment."

"You look pretty worn-out."

More like stressed-out. "It's been an exhausting day."

"And the night didn't turn out too well, either."

"Thanks to Matt in the role of Mr. Macho."

"Can't say that I blame him," Chase said. "Harbin's a pretty seedy character and always has been. If the tables were turned and he'd been hitting on Jess, I might've done the same thing."

"I knew the moment he started talking he wasn't an upstanding citizen," she said. "That's why I was somewhat relieved when Matt showed up, even if I did resent the implication I can't take care of myself. Between him and my father, you'd think I was a totally helpless female."

"Matt just wanted to protect you," he said. "That's what we do around these parts."

She understood that, but she didn't always appreciate it, particularly when that protection came in the form of violence. "Where is this Harbin guy now?"

"In jail."

Jail? Rachel was admittedly relieved, but also worried over her husband's fate. "Did you arrest Matt, too?"

Chase settled his hat back on his head. "No, but it took some fancy stepping to avoid it. I had a hunch about Harbin and decided to run a check on him while he was in the E.R. As it turns out, he's got an outstanding warrant for assault in Nashville. I locked him up and we'll ship him off in the morning."

Rachel felt quite a bit better knowing R.J. wasn't on the streets, in case he should decide to hunt Matt down and exact some revenge. "I guess an assault charge should come as no surprise."

"Nope, and Matt knew what he was dealing with when he took it upon himself to run interference."

"He still could have been hurt if Harbin had been armed. But lately he's been so self-destructive, maybe he simply didn't care."

She paused to consider exactly who she was confiding in. "I'm sorry, Chase. Matt's one of your best friends and I shouldn't be criticizing him around you."

"Hey, you're my friend, too." Chase leaned forward and folded his hands on the table. "I might not entirely agree with Matt's recent behavior, but on some level I understand it."

She assumed Chase was referring to the confrontation he'd had with her brother that could easily have turned worse than it was. "You were justified in what you did to Dalton after what he did to Jess."

"I'm not talking about Dalton or Harbin," he said. "I'm talking about Matt's acting out to cover the grief and guilt. I'm an expert on grief and guilt."

"Because of your war experiences?"

"One experience in particular." He shifted slightly in the folding chair. "While I was over there, a child got caught in the cross fire, and I'm fairly sure the bullet that killed her was mine. The image of that little girl dying in my arms will never go away."

The sorrow in his voice and expression momentarily stole Rachel's breath. "Oh, Chase. I had no idea."

"Jess was the only one who knew about it

until now," he said. "I couldn't talk about it to anyone outside the military. Hell, I couldn't face it. The guilt nearly buried me on more than one occasion. Had it not been for reconnecting with Jess, I don't know where I might've ended up."

"But that wasn't your fault, Chase. Our son's death wasn't Matt's fault, either."

"True, but that didn't make me feel any less responsible. I imagine Matt feels responsible, too."

She agreed with Chase on one count. Her husband could be dealing with guilt, perhaps even more than grief. Guilt over never really wanting to be a father. "I have no idea what Matt's feeling, because he won't talk to me about it. And I've never seen him shed one tear, even at the funeral."

"Men are wired a whole lot different than women," Chase said. "We're not prone to discussing our feelings. Some of it's pride, some of it's fear we're going to be seen as cowardly if we admit how bad it hurts. My theory is Matt's venting that hurt by doing things normally out of character for him."

She was hurting, too. Badly. "I understand what you're saying, but I just can't handle it, especially the drinking. Who knows how much booze he had on board when he rushed in to rescue me?"

"Sam says he didn't even have a beer."

"That doesn't mean he didn't have a few before he came here. Regardless, the drinking's only one issue among so many more."

"We need your table, folks."

The booming voice nearly startled Rachel right out of her shoes. She glanced behind her to see a group of men gathered nearby, waiting for the two stragglers to finally leave.

She returned her attention to Chase to find he was already standing. "Time to call it a night," he said. "I'll walk you to your car."

Rachel knew better than to argue. All three men who comprised their circle of friends, including her husband, hadn't received the memo that chivalry was on life support. "I'd appreciate that."

After she came to her feet, Chase followed her outside to her car, which was parked near the entrance. She fished the keys from her pocket and tripped the lock before facing him again. "Thank you for listening to me, Chase. And tell Jess I'll call her soon."

"Not a problem. Just one more thing I need to say."

One more thing might be more than she

could handle, but she did appreciate having a male perspective on Matt's problems. "Sure."

He looked much too serious for Rachel's comfort. "Before you make this split permanent, I hope you exhaust all your options first. The two of you owe each other that much."

Rachel felt as if the option bank was quickly running out of funds. "I will."

He hooked a thumb over his shoulder. "I better get home to my wife. She gave me strict orders to be there before midnight, since Danny's at a sleepover. I'm already five minutes late and that means I could have hell to pay."

"If she's not already out like a light. When I was pregnant, I could barely keep my eyes open past sundown."

He grinned. "Not Jess. She's about to wear me out."

Rachel returned his smile in spite of that same old twinge of envy. "Have a good night, and thanks for listening."

"Anytime."

After Rachel gave Chase a brief hug, she slid inside her car and tipped her head back against the seat. The urge to see Matt tonight, to talk things out, almost overwhelmed her. But she was feeling too vulnerable, too lonely, to take that risk.

She'd have to wait until Monday afternoon for the next spousal showdown…if she decided to show up.

SHE WASN'T GOING TO SHOW.

Or that's what Matt thought when two o'clock rolled around and no Rachel. Then the clinic's door chimed, followed by the recognizable voice speaking to Tina. He should probably go into the reception area to greet her, but he opted to wait until she came to him—unless things got tense between his wife and the new office manager, forcing him to mediate to avoid a catfight. So far he hadn't heard any raised voices or angry words, only polite conversation and even an occasional laugh. At least he'd avoided a confrontation. One down, one left to go.

After ten or so minutes, a succession of raps sounded, followed by Rachel opening the door and peeking inside. "May I come in?"

"Yeah." He didn't mean to sound so irritable, but he wasn't too pleased with her formality or her tardiness.

She stepped inside the room, briefcase in

hand and a self-conscious look on her face. "Hope I'm not disturbing anything."

He was disturbed, all right, but not in the way she might think. Her slim-fit black skirt, purple sleeveless silk blouse and deadly high heels nearly did him in. The full face of makeup and her dark hair curling around her shoulders only added to his misery.

Under normal circumstances, he'd stand and give her a kiss, but the way he felt right now, he'd be better off if he remained seated. And chances were she didn't want a kiss from him anyway. She sure as hell wouldn't appreciate his obvious below-the-belt reaction to her appearance. He thought back to a time when she would round the desk, stand behind him and drape her arms around his neck before kissing his cheek. He also recalled going about his business without really acknowledging the gesture. What he wouldn't give to take it all back, to relive those times. That hindsight being twenty-twenty thing kept coming back to bite him.

After Rachel moved into the room, he gestured toward the chair across from him. "Sit."

"Okay." She took a seat, clutching the briefcase to her chest as if she thought it might take off without her. Or maybe she'd caught him looking and was trying to conceal the hint of cleavage.

"Where've you been all dressed up?" he asked.

"At the bank's weekly staff meeting."

"Since when do you attend that?"

"Since my father decided to extend his vacation and asked me to stand in for him."

That could mean old Edwin still didn't know his daughter had left her husband. "I'm bettin' you were the best-looking woman at the conference table."

"I was the only woman there." She momentarily looked away before meeting his gaze again. "Tina seems to have everything under control, so it appears she won't need my help. What an asset for you, an office manager who's both pretty and smart."

Her tone lacked any sincerity—not that he was surprised. "Yeah, she's pretty sharp. But her coffee sucks."

She smiled but it faded fast. "Perhaps you should learn to make your own coffee."

"*Perhaps* I will."

She looked around the room as if she'd never seen it before. "How's your hand?"

He flexed his fingers. "Still bruised and fairly stiff, but it'll heal in a week or two. It does kind of make it hard to work in certain situations."

She brought her attention back to him. "If you're looking for sympathy, I'm all out."

He didn't want or need her sympathy. He did want her to understand why he'd done what he'd done—to protect her. "I guess you heard Harbin wound up in jail."

"I know. Some sort of assault charge."

"*Sexual* assault."

From the shock in her expression, it was pretty obvious she'd been kept in the dark. "Chase didn't mention that."

"Probably because he didn't want you to know exactly how much danger you were in. And if I hadn't come along, I'd hate to think what Harbin might've done to you."

She rolled her eyes. "It's not as if I'd actually go anywhere with him."

Hardheaded woman. "And it's not like he couldn't have waited till later and followed you to the car."

"Okay, fine. You rode in on your horse and saved the day. Is that what you want to hear?"

"*Thank you* would be sufficient."

"Thank you. Now, could we please get started on the reason why I'm here?" She retrieved a lined tablet from the briefcase and set it on the desk. "I've drawn two columns beneath our names, indicating what I feel is an equitable division."

In an effort to shake her up, Matt stood, walked around the desk and peered over her shoulder. "You have the house under my name."

"Yes. I'm not interested in keeping it."

He leaned forward a little more and caught a whiff of her perfume. She smelled so damn good he wanted to bury his face in her neck. "I'll buy out your half of the equity. Same goes for the clinic."

She glanced back at him before returning to the tablet. "I don't want either. It's all yours."

"Whatever floats your boat." He had no intention of going through with this nonsense anyway, even if he had no idea how to convince her to stop the process. Then he noticed one asset that he hadn't considered before. She'd handed him an opening and he planned to stroll right through it.

"Any reason why you have the cabin under your name?" he asked.

"If you recall, I used my trust fund to buy it," she said. "And since I've given you the house, it's only fair."

None of this was fair as far as he was concerned. "The key word is *us*. It's in both our names."

She sent him a champion frown over one shoulder. "You're not going to make this easy on me, are you? And would you please go back to your chair? You're making me nervous."

That gave him a small measure of satisfaction, he realized as he reclaimed his seat. "If you want easy, then agree to give me the cabin. Or we could continue to own it jointly and rent it out."

"Or we could sell it and split the proceeds."

He wasn't particularly fond of that option, but it did lead to an idea. A good idea that could present a great opportunity. "I don't have a problem with selling it, but that means we'll need to take a weekend trip and clean out the contents together."

Her frown told him she didn't welcome his idea. "I'd prefer if you box everything up and bring it back here to sort through."

Obviously she couldn't stand the thought of spending time alone with him. Or maybe something else was bugging her. "Are you worried you might not be able to resist me if we spend a few days cooped up in a cabin together?"

The slight flush on her cheeks spoke volumes. "Why on earth would you think that?"

He couldn't quite control his smile. "Oh, I don't know. Something about a hot tub and winding up with my jeans around my ankles a couple of weeks ago."

"I haven't given that *mistake* a second thought. But now that you mention it, I don't trust that you wouldn't pull that stunt again."

"Stunt? You're the one who started it by climbing out of the tub buck naked and taking your good sweet time drying off. And I sure as hell don't remember you putting up a fight. In fact, you didn't fight me at all. You did do quite a bit of moaning, though."

She held up a hand to silence him. "Let's just drop it, okay? I'll split the cost of gas with you if you'll just bring the cabin stuff back here."

Matt scraped his brain for some argument that might sway her to his side. "Fine, but I'm going to toss some of it while I'm packing up. I'm thinking your souvenir napkin collection could be in jeopardy."

Her dark eyes went about as round as a

basketball. "You wouldn't dare throw that out!"

"Maybe not intentionally, but when you've got a lot of paper lying around, anything's possible."

"We'll compromise. I'll go up one weekend and pick up my things. You can go the next."

She'd just trampled the last of his patience. "That's a waste of gas and time. The place has two bedrooms and two bathrooms, so you don't have to come anywhere near me if you don't want to. And I figure since my hand's still not a hundred percent, this weekend would work. I'll close the office from Friday until Tuesday and have Riley take emergency calls for me."

She blew out a frustrated sigh. "If I agree to do this, which I'm not saying I am, I have no idea if I could even go this weekend until I check the date."

"Friday's the twenty-seventh."

She looked almost alarmed. "Are you sure?"

Matt turned the desktop calendar around and pushed it toward her. "It's right there in black and white. It's the last weekend in April."

She stared at the calendar for a few seconds before her gaze shot to his. "I just remembered something I need to do."

"This weekend?"

She shoved the tablet back into the briefcase and shot to her feet. "No. I meant now."

Before he could get another word in, she took off out of the office. He caught up with her in the parking lot as she fumbled with her keys. "What about this weekend, Rachel?"

"I'm not sure." She tripped the lock and opened the door. "I'll call you and let you know."

With that, she slid inside the sedan and backed out as if she was going to put out a pasture fire.

Matt mulled over her strange behavior and tried to remember something significant about the date. Something that would upset her. He couldn't think of a thing.

Now he'd just have to wait for her to call and give him her answer. But even if she turned him down this time, he wasn't going to give up. Taking her back to their honeymoon cabin could only help his cause. They'd be surrounded by good memories of their life together, and maybe, just maybe, she'd finally realize what they stood to lose if they lost each other.

RACHEL DRUMMED HER fingertips atop the table at the back booth in Stan's Diner, both from impatience and stifling anxiety. If her friend didn't get there soon, she'd be forced to call again. Of course, she could have postponed the meeting until tonight at the guesthouse, after the maid had finished cleaning. Or waited until tomorrow, for that matter. But the delay would have been unbearable. Intolerable. Excruciating. She'd already spent one sleepless night worrying over the possibility.

The moment Rachel reached into her purse to dig out her cell phone, the screen door opened and thankfully in walked Jess. And right behind her, Savannah.

Great. As much as she appreciated both her friends' support, she truly didn't want the woman handling the divorce to know what she was up to. Not that she couldn't trust Savannah to be discreet. She was simply worried the entire process could come to a screeching halt.

As soon as Jess slid into the booth with Savannah taking her place beside her, Rachel leaned forward and lowered her voice. "Do you have it?"

"I brought three." Jess rifled through her oversize zebra-print bag and pulled out a brown paper sack. But before she handed it off to Rachel, she surveyed the room like a practiced spy.

"For heaven's sake, Jess," Savannah said. "It's pregnancy tests, not contraband. Just give them to her."

Rachel and Jess shushed her simultaneously.

"Sorry," Savannah muttered. "But there's not a soul in this place who's paying attention to us at the moment. In fact, there's no one here aside from the teenager behind the counter, and she's too busy texting to care."

"You're right," Rachel admitted. "But I can't afford for this to get back to Matt. That's why I had Jess buy the tests. Which reminds me. What do I owe you?"

Jess slid the bag across the table. "An explanation. Why do you need these?"

Going into detail was the last thing she cared to do. "Because I was extremely stupid one night and had unprotected sex, that's why."

"I understand that, but with whom did you have unprotected sex?"

Savannah winked at Rachel. "With an appliance repairman. He came to make sure her oven was heating correctly and he ended up lighting her fire."

Jess elbowed Savannah in the side. "Very funny, Savannah Leigh."

"It was Matt," Rachel interjected before the assumptions got out of hand. "The same evening we all met down at the pond."

Now Jess looked insulted. "And you didn't say anything to us about it?"

"She told me," Savannah said. "But that was during a meeting about the divorce."

"You're not going through with the divorce now, right?" Jess asked.

"I don't know what I'm going to do." And she honestly didn't. She did regret being so utterly foolish and wondered if perhaps she'd subconsciously wanted to become pregnant again.

"How late are you?" Savannah asked.

"At least a week. Maybe two. I haven't paid much attention to my periods in the last few months." She'd had little reason to pay attention.

Jess and Savannah exchanged a look before Jess said, "It could just be stress. But you won't know until you take the test, so go do it."

That had to be the most ludicrous suggestion her friend had ever made. "I'm not going to go into a public restroom and pee on a stick. I'll wait until I get back to the guesthouse."

"That's up to you," Savannah said. "But you have to let us know as soon as you know. And that brings me to one important question. With your previous problems, will you be considered high risk if you are pregnant?"

She had thought about that several times over the past twenty-four hours. Worried about it, even. "My doctor told me that there's a chance the eclampsia could return in the next pregnancy. I'd definitely see a specialist so I could be prepared, in case it happens again."

"And that leads us to another issue," Jess added. "If the test turns out to be positive, when are you going to tell Matt?"

She hadn't gotten that far in her planning. "I have no idea when I'd tell him or if I even should."

"He has a right to know," Savannah said.

"You can't go through this alone. Besides, I'm sure he'll be over the moon if you are."

If only she could believe that. "He doesn't want children, and I realize now he never really has."

"Did he say that?" Jess asked.

"Not in so many words, but it's been implied through his actions. I just chose to ignore it."

Savannah reached across the table and laid her hand on hers. "He might surprise you this time, Rachel."

He might also break her heart again if he refused to accept responsibility for their child. "I truly don't know what I'm going to do right now. And I may not have to do anything at all if the test is negative."

"I hope it's positive," Jess added. "I'm going against popular opinion, but I think another baby could make a huge difference in healing your marriage."

If only Matt had even hinted at wanting another child, she might actually believe he'd come around. She wouldn't allow herself to get her hopes up. "The way things stand now, it would make it worse between us. Matt still hasn't come to terms with losing Caleb, or that's what I feel is going on with him. It's hard to know, when he won't open up to me."

"He's still not talking about it?" Savannah asked.

"No. He won't provide any details about what happened after I gave birth, and he knows I was too out of it to remember much of anything except that brief glance of Caleb. I suspect he may have left the hospital and our son died in the presence of strangers."

Jess sent her a sympathetic look. "I can't imagine Matt would do that, Rachel."

At one time she would never have considered it, either. "If he won't talk to me, then I'm inclined to assume the worst."

Jess sighed. "It's really a shame the two of you can't find some common ground. What if you went away together for a weekend?"

"Funny you should mention that," Rachel said. "When I met with Matt yesterday, we decided to sell the cabin and split the proceeds. He then insisted we go together this weekend and divvy up the belongings before we put it on the market."

Jess's expression turned as bright as the overhead fluorescent light. "That's great. You'll have some time together to see if you want to go through with the divorce."

"And time to tell him about the baby," Savannah interjected. "Of course, that depends if you're pregnant or not."

Rachel knew only one thing for certain—spending a weekend with her husband could turn out badly. "I haven't agreed to go with him yet."

"What's holding you back?" Savannah asked.

Many things, the least of which was fear. "I'm just worried about being in such close quarters with him. He has this way of making me forget all our problems."

"You mean he's really good at wooing you with sex," Jess said in a simple statement of fact. "Look at it this way—getting pregnant won't be an issue if that happens."

"Provided I'm pregnant." Rachel sincerely wished her friend would get off the baby topic. "I still feel so vulnerable around him. I want to be stronger, but all he has to do is look at me a certain way, and all my strength flies out the window."

Savannah squeezed her hand. "You have an opportunity to find out if you can work through your issues with Matt. Go with an open mind and heart, and you might be surprised."

Maybe her friends were right. Maybe she could put Matt to the test and get him to open up to her. The cabin had always been the one place where they'd connected on a much deeper, emotional level. But still… "I'll think about it tonight and decide tomorrow."

"Don't think about it," Jess said. "Just do it. Take out your cell and call him right now before you have time to change your mind."

She couldn't fight them both. Besides, they could be right. "Okay. I'll do it."

Jess and Savannah looked on expectantly while Rachel withdrew her phone from her bag and hit the speed dial for Matt's cell.

After four rings, Rachel considered hanging up. And when she heard "Matt Boyd" in the familiar deep, masculine voice, she almost wished she had. She hesitated a few moments before she made a decision that could affect the course of her marriage—for better or for worse.

"Hi, Matt, it's me. About the weekend trip to the cabin. I've decided to go."

CHAPTER SIX

MATT COULDN'T BELIEVE she'd agreed to go. He'd spent the entire day moving through the motions at work, waiting for another call to say she'd changed her mind. Luckily, that call hadn't come. At least not yet.

In order to get an early start in the morning, he'd already packed a bag, gassed up the truck and made all the necessary arrangements at the clinic. Only one last task to handle. A task that wasn't unexpected, just poorly timed and highly resented. Exactly why Matt found himself running an errand at 11:00 p.m. on a ten-mile drive he didn't care to make. But after he'd been summoned a few minutes ago, like always, he'd dropped everything for the weekly parental rescue.

Anyone who didn't know the back roads might miss the flat-roofed structure with peeling white paint and a sign that read Scruffy Mo's Bar that hung at an angle above the red door. But he'd been there so many times, he could practically find his way to the place blindfolded. Unfortunately, so could his father.

After parking the truck near the entrance, he made his way into the dive, greeted by the suffocating smell of stale smoke and beer. Even if the place hadn't been deserted, he wouldn't have had a problem locating his dad. Ben Boyd had always been a barfly, and that's where he sat, his head lowered on crossed arms.

The fortysomething mountain-of-a-man proprietor stood on the far side of the room, sweeping the floor as if a passed-out patron was a common occurrence. Probably because it was.

Barely clinging to his last scrap of composure, Matt approached Mo Bailey and hooked a thumb over his shoulder. "How long has he been this way?"

Mo leaned the broom against the paneled wall, picked up a chair with one overly tattooed arm and turned it upside down on a table. "About an hour."

"Why the hell didn't you cut him off?"

He slicked a hand through his greasy blond

hair. "He only had a couple of beers. My guess is he was drinking before he got here."

Like that wasn't a given. "From now on, if you even think he's already had a few, don't serve him."

Mo puffed up like a rooster. "Hey, I'm not his keeper. You're lucky I didn't call the law."

Yeah. Real lucky. "Help me get him up and out of here." He walked to the bar and shook his father's shoulder. "Wake up, Dad."

Ben lifted his head and stared at him before recognition finally dawned. "Hi, son. You come to have a drink with your old man?"

"No. I'm here to take my old man home."

"No fun at all," he muttered as he slid off the stool and stumbled to one side.

Matt righted him and gripped his left arm, while Mo did the same with the right. Together they practically dragged Ben to the truck and hoisted him inside the cab.

After reluctantly thanking Mo for the help, he slid into the driver's side and started the truck. He glanced at his dad to discover he was out cold again, the side of his head resting against the passenger window. He continued to sleep—and snore—all the way back to the house where Matt had spent his youth. The house that had once been a home but now served as his father's self-imposed prison.

He managed to get his dad out of the truck with less effort than it had taken to get him in. But they'd both been there before. Many times. As always, Ben came to long enough for Matt to get him inside and into the bedroom. He helped him undress down to his boxers and undershirt and get into the bed. And the final step of their routine, a wasted father's empty apology. "Sorry, son. Been a bad day."

When wasn't it a bad day? "Go to sleep."

Ben flipped a hand toward the bedside table. "Set the alarm. Don't want to be late to work."

"You retired two years ago."

"Oh, yeah."

Matt stared down at the wilted white flower on the pillow that used to belong to his mother. He wondered for the millionth time how it had come to this. How his father had been so consumed by his grief that he could barely function without his wife. Then again, he could relate a little better now that Rachel was gone. But he hadn't given up completely. "When are you going to stop this, Dad? When you drink yourself into an early grave?"

On cue, the tears began to form in his father's weary, bloodshot blue eyes. "I miss her, Mattie."

He hated being called by his childhood name. Hated that he'd assumed the role of his father's parent during his childhood and it still continued to this day. "I miss her, too, Dad. But she wouldn't want you doing this to yourself. Not when she fought so hard to live."

His words fell on deaf ears, he realized when Ben rolled to his side, facing the opposite wall, one arm thrown across the empty space beside him, the sound of his steady breathing echoing in the silent room.

On his way to the bedroom door, Matt paused to survey the shrine set out on the dresser. The whole room could be mired in dust, but not the photographs lined neatly in a row along the marred wooden surface. His mother's bridal portrait, alongside pictures of their wedding day. Photos of him as a baby in his mother's arms, before she'd been too weak to hold him. Photos of her during holidays and birthdays and those taken for no reason at all. Harsh reminders that she'd once

been able to smile, before the pain had taken
her joy away.

After turning off the light and closing the
door behind him, Matt made his way into the
kitchen to straighten up. He washed the few
dishes in the sink, bagged up all the trash and
put the plastic sack on the porch to carry off
when he left. He tossed in a load of laundry
and made a mental note to buy some groceries first thing in the morning, before he set
out for Tennessee.

Hell, he might as well stay there and sleep
on the sofa, if he could even sleep at all. Not
only was he anxious about taking the trip
with his wife, everything about his surroundings served as a solid reminder of his childhood. The same old woven rugs still covered
the hardwood floors. The same rose wallpa-
per still hung in the outdated kitchen. A few
years back, Rachel had offered to help fix
up the place, but his dad would have none of
that. He liked things the way they were, so
nothing had changed. Nothing ever would.

Before he settled in for the night, Matt
had one last remaining task to undertake.
He opened the top cupboard above the refrigerator and took down the half-full bottle of cheap vodka. Apparently his dad had

given up rotgut whiskey for something a little less obvious. Like anyone would be fooled enough not to know he'd been drinking.

He uncapped the bottle and started to pour it down the drain, but reconsidered. Vodka, straight up, the night before a seven-hour drive, might not be a banner idea, but he needed something to take off the edge. Something to calm him enough to get some rest. After tonight, no more booze, at least for the next few days. He had to convince Rachel he wasn't heading down his father's path.

He filled an oversize plastic cup to the brim, set the bottle aside and headed for the living room. After he kicked back on the blue striped sofa, he took a solid swig of the booze. It burned as it slid down his throat, but not as badly as the sudden onslaught of memories when he centered his attention on his mother's favorite chair. He recalled her constant struggles with multiple sclerosis. Remembered how she'd never complained, even when the pain had been so unbearable, sometimes she hadn't gotten out of bed for days.

At times he'd wanted to hang out with his friends, but he'd never begrudged helping her when she hadn't been able to help herself. He'd done all the household chores when she'd been too weak and too tired. He'd served as her legs when she'd become wheelchair-bound for good. He'd been her eyes when her double vision had been so bad, she couldn't read her favorite poetry.

She'd called him her "tough little guy," and he'd tried to live up to that. Still, for nights on end he'd buried his face in his pillow and cried. The crying stopped the day of her funeral. In the eighteen years since, he hadn't shed a tear, not even when he'd lost his son. And his wife still hated him for that.

With his mind racing, Matt set the cup on the coffee table, pulled off his boots, stretched out on the couch and hoped he could get to sleep without having more to drink. But when he closed his eyes, he could see only Rachel. The familiar ache and overwhelming urge to talk to her sent him upright and reaching for the phone on the end table.

On afterthought, he checked the clock hanging on the opposite wall. Half past midnight. Most likely she was already asleep. Then again, she was inclined to be a night owl, especially when it came to her habit of reading in bed. But she might have turned in early because of the trip. Or she could still be awake, worrying about the trip. If he made the call, three things could happen. She'd ignore him, she'd talk to him or she'd hang up on him. Regardless, he wouldn't get any rest if he didn't at least try to get in touch with her.

He drew in a deep breath and let it out slowly as he dialed her cell. After only one ring, Rachel answered with a breathless "Hello," as if she'd either been jogging or waiting for his call. Or a call from someone else. That prospect conjured up all sorts of possibilities he didn't care to consider.

"You're still up." Nothing like stating the obvious.

"Yes. I was actually thinking about calling you."

He suspected that might not be a good thing. "You've changed your mind about going."

"Not at all. In fact, I just finished packing. What are you doing at your dad's house?"

Damn caller ID. If he told her the entire truth, she might decide to unpack. "Just taking care of a few things for him before we leave tomorrow. What did you need from me?" He could think of one need he'd gladly tend to regardless of the time. Wishful thinking at its best.

"You go first."

He didn't know if it was the effect of the booze or the high from hearing her voice, but he couldn't resist playing with her a little. Too bad it wasn't literal playing. "What are you wearing?"

"We're not going there, Matthew."

He smiled over her taking the bait. "Get your mind out of the gutter. I was inquiring about your attire for the trip."

"I don't know. Probably jeans and a T-shirt. Why?"

"Guess that means I should probably nix wearing a tux."

"Look, if you called simply to tease me, let's end this conversation now and go to bed."

She'd strolled right into that snake pit. "My bed or yours?"

"If you don't behave, I'm hanging up."

That was the last thing he wanted. "Okay. I called to tell you I might be there to pick you up an hour or so later than planned. I have to grab a few groceries for Dad before we take off."

"He can't do it himself?"

"He could, but he won't."

She released a frustrated sigh. "When are you going to stop enabling him, Matt?"

His internal defense mechanism kicked into gear. "When you stop making excuses for your father after he puts someone out of their home because they're late on a loan."

"That's different. At least my father doesn't rely on me for every move he makes."

His anger began to brew. "Do you really think I enjoy this? I've been parenting him since I was thirteen, and frankly, I'm damn sick of it. For once I'd like to wake up in the morning knowing I'm only responsible for myself."

The sudden silence told him he'd dug himself a deep hole and fallen into it, mouth-first. "I'm not talking about you, Rachel."

"I'm a big girl, Matt. You're not responsible for me."

"You know what I mean."

"Yes, I'm afraid I do."

This wasn't the way he'd planned to begin their time together, with more animosity hanging over them. "Sorry. I'm just tired and spouting off. You still haven't said why you were calling me."

"It's really not important."

"At this late hour, it had to be important."

"It can wait. I'll see you in the morning."

She hung up without saying goodbye, but at least she hadn't backed out on him. Not yet.

He placed the cordless phone on the receiver and eyed the drink. If he finished off the vodka, he'd probably be drunk. If he didn't, he probably wouldn't sleep worth a damn. What the heck. If he couldn't have his wife beside him tonight, he'd have to settle for demon liquor as his companion.

He'd picked up the cup and brought it halfway to his mouth when one thought hit him full force. If he kept going, he'd be no better than his father. He risked becoming his father.

On that thought, he went to the kitchen and dumped the vodka from the cup and the bottle down the drain. A sleepless night was preferable to traveling down the road to hell with no way out and no wife at all.

POSITIVE.

Rachel had repeated the word to herself several times since she'd taken the tests last night—all three of them—at the urging of the Pregnancy Patrol in the form of Jess and

Savannah. Even after seeing confirmation in triplicate, she was still consumed with disbelief, caught somewhere between absolute elation and abject terror.

All her fears had come home to roost. Fear of losing another baby. Fear of raising a baby alone. Those fears had led her to the decision to call Matt and tell him. But after he'd voiced his desire to shirk responsibility for everyone but himself, she'd reconsidered. On one hand, she understood his frustration. On the other, she recognized that his admission could be the driving force behind his reluctance to be a father.

At least he'd been open with her about his feelings, not that she felt any better for it. And that presented a huge dilemma—exactly when she would tell him about the baby. Of course, he would need to know eventually, but she didn't have to decide right now when to make the revelation. She did have to get through the weekend without blurting the truth at the wrong time. She just hoped he didn't make it his goal to push her buttons.

When she heard the truck and trailer coming up the road, Rachel grabbed her bag and hurried out to meet Matt before he asked to come inside. She didn't quite understand the strong sense of anticipation, even excitement, when he exited the cab and approached her, his clear blue eyes fixed on hers. He certainly didn't look to be at his best. His hair was still shower damp, his jaw shaded with whiskers, and the faded navy T-shirt, scuffed boots and jeans had seen better days. But he wore dishevelment as a king wore a crown, more than worthy of female worship.

How in the world would she be able to ignore him while cooped up in a cabin for three days? She couldn't, but she didn't have to subject herself to his charms on the drive. "I've decided to take my car," she announced the minute he reached the porch.

He scowled. "We've already discussed this. No need to waste fuel, not to mention I'm not up to driving, so you're going to have to do it."

He tossed her the keys, which she barely caught with one hand. "Excuse me if I'm wrong, but you've never allowed me to drive your precious truck with the trailer attached."

"You can handle it, as long as you don't have to back up any distance."

True, she did suck when it came to maneuvering the trailer in Reverse. "Do you mind telling me why the change of heart?"

He swept a palm over his jaw. "Because I might fall asleep at the wheel before we reach the Tennessee state line."

As if she'd had all that much sleep the night before. "I was up as late as you were." Then something occurred to her, a logical assumption if past history prevailed. "Are you hungover?"

"I slept on a sofa that's about as comfortable as landing in a briar patch," he said in a defensive tone. "Then I ran into Pearl Allworth at the store and had to endure a ten-minute conversation about her inability to housebreak Buttons, her poodle. Can you top that?"

Oh, yes. She'd learned she was going to have a baby, a discovery she chose to withhold for the time being. "Fine. Since you had to tolerate Pearl's ramblings, I'll drive." Besides, if he snoozed the whole way, she wouldn't have to worry he'd try to lay on the he-man act and distract her.

"If you get too sleepy, we can always pull over and take a nap," he said. "Or whatever."

The suggestion sufficiently served to resurrect one particular memory involving a rest stop and the backseat of the extended-cab pickup. "Let's get one thing straight, Matthew. There will be no *whatever*."

Clearly he wasn't too tired to grin. "Whatever."

Rachel picked up her bag, tossed it to him and strode to the truck without looking back. After she slid onto the seat and closed the door, she waited for Matt to settle in on the passenger side. For some bizarre reason, her gaze landed right below the seat belt he'd just secured and lingered there for a few seconds. She looked up in time to catch his knowing smile and immediately turned her attention back to the ignition. But before she could start the truck, Matt unsnapped the belt and leaned over her to rummage around in the driver's door side pocket.

She froze like a human ice sculpture against the leather seat. He radiated heat at every point his body touched hers, and heavens, he smelled so good, like the clean cotton scent of his preferred soap. "What are you doing?" Aside from making her entirely too hot and bothered.

"Just making sure I have the new proof-of-insurance card, and here it is." He finally straightened, giving her some breathing room, but not before the damage to her resolve had been done.

She shot him a dirty look. "It didn't occur to you to ask me to look for it instead of climbing all over me?"

He put the card in the glove box and worked the seat belt closed again. "Sweetheart, I have a feeling you'd like for me to climb all over you."

She made two attempts before she finally had the truck started. "You're imagining things."

"I wasn't imagining you checking out my fly a minute ago and most likely fondly remembering what's behind it. And by the way, do you remember how to work my gearshift?"

If she had half a mind, which she obviously didn't, she'd get out and go back inside. "If you value your gearshift, you'll stay on your side of the truck."

He released a low, grainy laugh. "You're kind of scary when you're sleep deprived."

And he was entirely too sexy for this earth. "Go to sleep, Matthew."

He reclined the seat, tipped his head back, closed his eyes and folded his arms across his broad chest. "Wake me up if you want me to take over in a few hours."

She had no intention of doing that, but they would have to make a couple of fuel stops and bathroom breaks. "Don't worry. I'll get us there in one piece."

She depressed the clutch, put the truck in gear, then lurched forward, stalling the diesel engine. She prepared for a patent Matt Boyd snide remark, but she glanced to her right to find he was already asleep.

Good. Now, if he only stayed that way. But if her reaction to his blatant innuendo was any indication, she didn't stand a chance when he was fully awake. And he'd have to wake up eventually.

She drove down the driveway without incident, feeling much more secure in her ability to maneuver the truck and trailer. After she went through the automatic gate, she had to stop at the main road and wait for a slow four-tractor parade. That allowed a few moments for her to study Matt while he slept. His lashes fanned below his closed eyes, and his gorgeous mouth twitched slightly, as if he might smile. He looked so innocent, she saw in him the boy she'd loved for so long, submerged beneath the man with the wicked grin and the wounded soul.

People had always told them they'd make pretty babies, and that thought prompted Rachel to touch her belly. She decided right then and there that she'd do what she could to salvage her marriage this weekend. She wasn't naive enough to believe they could solve all their problems in a matter of two days. It would require stripping away her resentment, total honesty and Matt's cooperation. But it could be a start. A new start. They owed it to their unborn child.

Granted, things could get worse before they got better. She only hoped better won out. If not, she'd have to continue with her plans, even if that meant raising her child alone.

"BETTER WAKE UP, sleepyhead. We're here."

Matt opened his eyes to a canopy of tall trees overhead, the rustic cabin looming before the truck and Rachel staring at him from the driver's side. He powered the seat up from the reclining position, every muscle in his body protesting his lack of activity for the past few hours. "I thought you were going to let me take over after we stopped for fuel the last time."

She pulled the keys from the ignition and handed them to him. "I was, until you crawled back into the truck and immediately fell asleep again."

Man, his fatigue had really caught up with him. "I'm wide-awake now, so let's go."

Keys gripped in his left hand, Matt reached back with his right and grabbed both their bags from the backseat. He stepped out onto the gravel drive, thankful to finally stretch his legs and to be back in a place that had been a cornerstone of their marriage from the beginning. Rachel followed him up the steps and lagged behind as he unlocked and opened the door.

He moved aside to let her enter first, but she hung back and surveyed the area. "What are you waiting for?"

"I want to take it all in for a second, in case this might be our last visit here."

Not if he could help it. But at least she'd said "might." That gave him some cause to hope. "Fine. I'll see you inside."

He walked into the cabin and did a little looking around, too. Everything seemed in order, just as he'd requested that morning before they'd set out on the journey. The shutters surrounding the partially open windows had been pulled back throughout the den, allowing a good view of the woodlands that sloped down into the valley. But the best view could be found on the balcony at the back of the house, accessed by the kitchen and the bedrooms. A person could see for miles from that vantage point, and he'd taken in the scenery more than once with his wife. They'd done some major fooling around on the double outdoor chaise a time or two, as well. Too bad he couldn't count on that happening during this trip.

With that in mind he set the bags on the sofa, since he wasn't sure how the sleeping arrangements would go. If he had his way, they'd spend the next three nights in the same heavy pine, four-poster king bed where they'd made love the very first time. But he couldn't afford to pressure Rachel. Subtly encourage her, yes. Push her, no way. Not unless he wanted to find himself locked out of his own vacation home.

After he heard the screen door open, he turned to see Rachel standing there, frowning. "Did we forget to put the dust covers on the furniture the last time we were here?" she asked.

"Nope. Helen took them off. I called her this morning and let her know we'd be in today. She opened the place up for us."

"That was so nice of her," Rachel said. "And thoughtful of you."

Damn. She'd actually thrown him a bone. "Helen's a great lady." And the wife of Judge Jack, the man who'd officiated at their wedding. He could only imagine how disappointed the couple would be if they knew the current state of his and Rachel's marriage.

"It looks like she left us a note." Rachel strode into the kitchen, removed the paper attached to the refrigerator by a magnet, turned and began to read. "'Dear Rachel and Matt. Welcome back. I put fresh sheets on the bed, and I also brought you a few staples in case you can't get to the market for supplies until morning. I'd love to see you both soon. Hugs, Helen.'"

When she took on a seriously concerned look, Matt worried she'd left something out of the note. "What else does it say?"

She folded the paper and set it on the black granite countertop. "That's it."

"Then why do you look like you just got bad news?"

"Because she said *I'd* love to see you, not *we*. Do you think something's happened to the judge?"

His wife had a habit of finding trouble where trouble didn't exist. "He's fine. I heard him in the background when I talked to her this morning. I'm sure he's still overseeing the weddings of at least half the couples of eastern Tennessee."

"I'm sure you're right." She opened the refrigerator and peered inside. "Looks like she left us some milk and eggs and cheese. And a few drinks."

He walked up behind her and looked over her shoulder—not because he was all that interested in the fridge's contents. He just wanted an excuse to be close to her. "Are you hungry?"

"I could eat." She began to close the door, forcing him to take a step back.

"So could I," he said as she faced him. "Those cheese crackers wore off about three hours ago."

She took a quick check of her watch. "Since the café's about to close, I guess we'll have to make do with what's here. I'll scramble some eggs."

When she bent and opened a cabinet, Matt realized he had the means to impress her. Every little bit helped. "I'll make us omelets."

She glanced back over one shoulder. "You're kidding, right?"

"Nope."

She straightened, pan in hand and genuine surprise in her expression. "Since when do you know how to make an omelet?"

"Since I was ten years old." He instinctively wanted to leave it at that, clam up, avoid the truth. But she'd complained that he'd never shared enough of his past with her. This would be a start, but the emotional cost could be high. "My mother taught me to cook quite a few things."

"Really?"

"Really." He took the pan from her grip, put it on the stove and gestured toward the island. "Take a seat."

Still looking a little shell-shocked, Rachel washed and dried her hands, rounded the island and pulled up a bar stool. After he washed up as well, Matt turned his back to her and retrieved what he needed from the refrigerator. Then he went to work cracking eggs into a bowl, adding milk along with salt and pepper, and whipping the mixture probably a little more than necessary. He turned on the burner beneath the nonstick pan and waited for it to heat to the correct temperature, all the while wondering what his wife was thinking.

"What else can you cook?" she asked.

"Good old Southern fare." He poured the eggs into the pan and opened the package of grated cheddar. "Fried chicken and gravy, corn bread from scratch, shepherd's pie. And collard greens, but I can't stand them."

"How is it after all these years you never told me this?"

Explaining could take all night, so he settled for the abbreviated version. "Cooking is tied to a lot of memories of her."

"Good or bad?"

"Both, but mostly good, I guess." He took a plate from the cabinet, slid the omelet onto it and turned to Rachel.

She supported her cheek on a palm, questions in her eyes. "It seems to me if you have good memories of cooking with her, you'd want to relive them."

He set the plate, napkins and utensils in front of her. "That depends. Sometimes the good memories are just as painful as the bad if they remind you of what you've lost."

She reached across the bar and touched his hand. "I'm sorry."

Most people would welcome the comforting gesture, but not him. His inability to accept any kind of sympathy caused him to pull away. The return trip to the refrigerator had as much to do with avoidance as forgetting to give her something to drink. "Do you want water? Or there's a bottle of your favorite wine in here." Along with a six-pack of his favorite beer. It took all his strength not to grab a can and guzzle it.

"No wine, but I'll take some milk."

Apparently she'd decided to surprise him, too. He poured her a glass and took it to her. "I've never known you to turn down chardonnay for milk."

She smiled in that angelic way that he'd missed a lot over the past few months. "Maybe we still have a lot to learn about each other after all."

"Maybe so."

And maybe those discoveries—and a few rediscoveries—would make a difference in their marriage. Maybe by the time the weekend was over, everything would be settled, once and for all.

CHAPTER SEVEN

SHE NEEDED A BATH and a bed, but more than that, she needed answers.

Yet she realized if she pressed Matt too hard, he could very well withdraw again. But he'd definitely had a breakthrough when he'd spoken about his mother, and she hoped to find out more.

While Matt cleaned up the kitchen, at his insistence, Rachel wandered into the den and surveyed the built-in shelves that flanked the stone fireplace. The mementos served as a chronology of their marriage, from souvenir glasses to fossils they'd found on their frequent hikes. She immediately went for the photo album on the middle shelf and brought it to the sofa. She settled onto the black leather cushions and opened it to the first plastic-protected page. Front and center in the album, the snapshot featuring the bride and groom and handsome, silver-haired Judge

Jack that Helen had taken on their wedding day. She couldn't help but smile over how young Matt looked, but then so did she. Perhaps because they were young. Maybe too young.

"Do you want me to get the empty boxes out of the trailer?"

Rachel looked back to find Matt standing behind the sofa. "Not tonight. I'm too tired to pack anything." Hopefully by Sunday evening, there would be no need to pack. That depended solely on Matt's cooperation and his reaction to the baby news, once she gathered the courage to tell him.

When he sat down beside her, she rested one half of the album in her lap and the other half in his. "We were such babies back then."

He smiled. "Yeah, we were. Hard to believe it's been almost fourteen years. Seems like only yesterday I was carrying you over the threshold of this very cabin."

She pointed to one photo in the corner of the second page. "Here I am, the blushing bride on her honeymoon. That pink flannel robe was so sexy."

He draped his right arm over the back of the sofa and inched closer. "It was sexier lying on the floor. But I have to tell you, I almost expected you to be wearing footed pajamas underneath."

Rachel laughed. "I wasn't quite that hopeless. Maybe it wasn't the most revealing white gown, but it was still a gown." White and lacy and, yes, long.

He tucked her hair behind her ear and studied her eyes. "You were beautiful. You still are."

It would be much too easy to fall into old patterns—Matt looking at her with undisguised desire in his incredible blue eyes, her offering herself up like the foolish female she could be in his presence.

In order to avoid old habits, she turned the page to the next set of pictures and focused on that. "Oh, my gosh. I'd almost forgotten the time we went tubing in Townsend."

Matt chuckled. "I've never forgotten it. You flipped your tube and lost your bikini top."

Heat started at the base of her throat and spread to her cheeks. "That was your fault. If you hadn't been harassing me, I wouldn't have reached for you and fallen off. Thank heavens there weren't any children nearby."

"And if I hadn't loaned you my T-shirt, you would still be in that river." He rubbed his shadowed jaw. "I don't know what I appreciated more, you being topless for a few seconds, or you in a wet T-shirt on the drive home. It's a toss-up."

"If my memory serves me correctly, you couldn't wait to get your T-shirt back the minute we walked into this cabin."

"And best I recall, I took it off, right here on this very couch. We never made it to the bedroom."

Rachel's heart beat a little faster when she remembered how unrestrained they'd been. How totally hot they'd been for each other. She flipped to another page, another photograph. Something a little safer to discuss. "And here's the picture of the gang down at the dance hall." Gang as in their local friends, most retirement age or better. They'd always been the youngest couple in the unincorporated town of Wayhurst.

Matt pointed to one fortysomething couple in the photograph. "What were their names?"

"Josie and Brad something. They owned the cabin closest to the chapel. Helen told me they sold it because they divorced."

"Too bad. They were a nice couple."

She and Matt had always had that reputation, as well. And look at them now. "I know. It's sad, really. They seemed so happy."

"I'm sure we seem that way to most folks around here, too."

Rachel dreaded telling their friends, especially Helen and Judge Jack. Hopefully, she wouldn't have to. She tried not to be too optimistic, but she felt as if she and Matt had reached a turning point. A place where they could talk and reminisce without all the recent relationship garbage getting in the way.

She closed the book to their past and mentally searched for a transition into his. "You really should bring some photos from your dad's house and let me put together an album for you."

He frowned. "What for?"

If for no other reason, for the sake of his unborn child. "You said you have some good memories of your mother. Why not put those in a memory book where you can actually see them?"

"I don't need any visual reminders. Every moment I spent with her is branded in my brain, good and bad."

She refused to let the slight edge of anger in his tone deter her. "You mentioned the bad memories earlier. It might help to talk about those. Then you could begin to focus on the good."

He sat forward and swiped both hands over his face. "I don't care to talk about her tonight."

The next suggestion was risky and would probably lead to another conversation dead end. "Okay, then let's talk about what happened the day Caleb was born."

"Drop it, Rachel."

Definitely a dead end. Matt's mastery of shutting down emotionally wasn't anything new for her, but she still found it bothersome and exasperating. Maybe she was simply expecting too much from him. Maybe she'd done exactly what she'd vowed not to do— put too much pressure on him. But if they couldn't come together on the issue of his secrecy, they had no hope for reconciliation.

Part of her wanted to gently pursue the issue further, but fatigue had begun to set in. As badly as she hated to give up, she needed sleep. She'd try again tomorrow. "Okay, I'll drop it. For now."

When she pushed off the sofa, Matt caught her wrist. "You don't know what you're asking when you want me to go back there."

She knew exactly what she was asking—

for him to be the husband she needed him to be. "I'm only asking you to share all your life with me, past and present, like spouses are supposed to do. You originally said you didn't want a divorce, yet for months you haven't been willing to make the changes that could help repair our relationship. I need you to try to be more open with me. I want to be the person you lean on for a change, not the other way around."

He let her arm go and sighed. "I wish I could be like you, Rachel, willing and able to discuss my feelings with anyone who'll listen, but that's never been me. It never will be."

Rachel felt totally deflated and borderline defeated. "Then I think we're done here." If not done for good. "I need to shower and go to bed."

"As far as the bed thing's concerned, we should—"

"Don't say it, Matt."

"Don't say what?"

"That we should sleep together."

A hint of anger flashed in his eyes. "Don't worry, sweetheart. You've made it real clear where you stand on that issue. Before you jumped to conclusions, I was going to suggest you sleep in the master bedroom because you'll be more comfortable there. Excuse me for trying to be accommodating."

She experienced a tiny bite of guilt over her assumption, but considering his usual behavior, her suspicions were justified. Then again, he hadn't made any suggestive overtures, and that should tell her something. What, she wasn't sure. "I'm sorry I misunderstood. I'm just really, really tired." And really, really disappointed.

He came to his feet and gathered their bags. "Your thinking the worst of me is a little hard to take, but I guess on some level it's deserved."

Rachel was taken aback by the admission. "You were just trying to be considerate, and I overreacted."

"Exhaustion will do that to you."

So would frustration. "I honestly don't mind sleeping in the guest room on the daybed. Since you need more room than I do, you should take the king."

"I insist you take it."

She didn't have the energy for an all-out debate. "Okay, if you insist." She held out her hand. "Hand me my stuff. I can take it from here."

He played keep-away with her bag. "I'm sure you can, but I'm going to do the gentlemanly thing and walk you to the room. If you're worried I'm going to force my way in, don't. I won't invade your personal space without your permission, darlin'."

She'd obviously angered him more than she'd originally thought. "Fine. Lead the way."

Rachel followed behind Matt as they walked down the corridor in total silence. Once they reached the master bedroom, he held open the door and stepped aside for her to enter first. Everything was in its place, from the bed to the bureau and the small forest-green club chair in the corner. And right beside that…the maple cradle that had been Matt's when he was a baby, carefully crafted by his father. She'd completely forgotten they'd brought it with them last summer, during the only trip to the cabin they'd taken the previous year.

"Do you want me to get rid of it?"

An unexpected surge of resentment spun Rachel around to face him. "Like you did with the nursery furniture before I left the hospital?"

"So we're back to that, huh?"

She yanked the duffel from his grasp. "We've never resolved it, Matt. Please explain to me why you believe that by taking away any reminders, I'll suddenly forget about our son."

She expected to see absolute fury in his expression, but he only looked resigned. "I didn't expect you to forget. I thought I was making things easier on you."

"You thought wrong."

"You've made that fairly clear the last four months. And just so you know, whatever decisions I've made to this point, I've always had your well-being in mind. Maybe they weren't the best choices, and maybe they were wrong, but I made them because I loved you."

Matt left, closing the door behind him, while Rachel stood in the middle of the room, clutching the bag to her chest, tears streaming down her face. Of all the words he'd said, one weighted her heart like a sack of stones.

Loved. Past tense.

The thought that Matt might not love her was almost too much to bear. That might actually help her make a clean break, but the only break right now was happening in her heart. As much as she wanted to know—

needed to know—if they could resolve their problems, she worried she'd waited too long to try to mend their marriage.

W̲HEN HE SAW the shadowy figure move in front of the French doors, Matt sat up on the edge of the daybed. His wife obviously couldn't sleep and neither could he. But he couldn't imagine why she was having a problem settling down in their top-grade bed, while he'd been assigned to a too-short, too-narrow mattress that was about as comfortable as a cement slab. His excuse for not being able to sleep. One of them.

For well over an hour he'd been replaying their last conversation in his mind, and he'd come to recognize that Rachel hadn't asked that much of him. She only wanted honesty and answers that he'd been hard-pressed to give. Providing those answers meant tearing open old wounds, and that wasn't something he readily embraced. Maybe doing so might even lessen some of the burden he'd been carrying around for years. He owed it to her to try.

The trees afforded enough privacy that he could walk outside in his birthday suit, even with the half-moon hanging overhead. He'd done it before. Many times. But he didn't want to offend Rachel's delicate sensibilities, so he climbed out of bed, rummaged through his bag and pulled out a pair of pajama bottoms and a T-shirt. After he dressed, he opened the double doors to find her standing at the balcony, her long hair falling down her back in soft waves, which told him she'd gone to bed with it wet. She wore the crazy nightshirt with the caricature horse print he'd given her two Christmases ago, along with a pair of thick socks. Funny, he'd never seen anyone look so sexy in flannel.

In order not to startle her, he cleared his throat before he stepped onto the wooden deck. She sent him only a brief glance before staring off into space again.

He moved beside her, keeping enough distance so he didn't crowd her. "Trouble sleeping?"

"Yes."

"Me, too. I slept too much on the drive here. It's also kind of hard to close your eyes when you can't turn off your brain."

"True."

Her one-word answers told him he was getting nowhere fast. He could give up and go back to bed, or he could just dive in with the revelations from the distant past. Time to take the plunge and hope he didn't drown in the memories. "My mother was cold-natured, just like you. She used to turn on the heater when it was sixty degrees outside."

"That sounds familiar." She surprised him with a smile. "What was she like, aside from being cold-natured?"

The time had come to see how far he could go with the disclosures without falling apart. He might be willing to bleed, but he'd be damned if he'd suffer a breakdown in front of his wife. "She wanted to be a dancer," he began. "She also liked to sing."

"Was she good at it?" she asked.

"Not really, but she was loud. She said singing helped her cope with the pain." The memories came back, sharp as a switchblade, immobilizing him for a few moments. He drew in a breath and let it out slowly before continuing. "She loved flowers. Her favorite was the snowdrop because it symbolized hope. She said she wanted to hold hope in her hands for as long as she could. My dad used to leave one on her pillow every now and then. He still does."

She sighed. "I can't imagine being loved that much."

If that was the case, then he'd failed her more than he'd realized. "Everyone loved her. She was just that kind of person."

She faced him and leaned a hip against the railing. "I wish I'd known her better. I only remember seeing her a few times when she picked you up from school."

"She pretty much stopped leaving the house when she had to rely on the wheelchair to get around. Aside from her immobility, you'd never know she was sick, because she didn't let that stop her. And she never complained. She just kept right on going until the MS wouldn't let her go any longer. That's when I had to step in and help her when my dad was at work."

"I'm sure she appreciated having you around."

His wife, always looking for the sunny side of a cloudy situation. But if he continued, he was in for some stormy weather. He had to keep going to prove to Rachel he could share his past with her, even the ugly parts. "I wasn't around when it counted the most. I wasn't there when she died."

She sent him a sympathetic look. "It's not your fault you weren't there. You were at baseball camp that summer."

For years he'd tried to convince himself of that, but it hadn't worked. "I could've been there. I had a choice—go or stay home. I chose to go, and I did because I wanted to get away from all of it. I wanted to be a kid and hang out with my friends, and I'll regret it for as long as I live."

"You *were* a kid, Matt."

"A kid who knew his mother was going die and he left her anyway."

"How could you have known that's what would happen?"

Now came the toughest part, the admission that would cost him almost as much as the other one he couldn't yet make. "The day before I left, she told me to take care of Dad because he was going to need me. Looks like I didn't do such a hot job reading the signs or the taking-care-of-Dad thing."

She laid a hand on his arm. "You were barely thirteen. You shouldn't have had to take responsibility for your father. And whether you stayed or went wouldn't have changed your mother's outcome."

It might have erased his guilt. "If she'd asked, I swear I would've stayed."

"I know you would have, because that's the kind of person you are. But did you ever consider that she wanted your last memories of her to be good ones?"

He smiled at the recollection in spite of his own pain. "They were good memories. Right before I left, we worked together on a jigsaw puzzle all day long. A big puzzle of New York. We talked about all the things I just told you, and we finally finished it at midnight. I kept telling her we could go back to it when I came home from camp, but she wanted to keep going until we were done. She said she wanted to see the New York City skyline again."

"Again?"

"Yeah. One summer my dad served as a woodworking apprentice in upstate New York, and that's where they met. She even drove him into the city to see a couple of Broadway musicals."

"It's hard for me to imagine your dad getting all dressed up and going to a theater," she said.

"Me, too, but I figure he did it for her. She told me she'd always wanted to be a dancer. But then they got married at the end of the summer and came back to Mississippi."

"Wow. Married after a three-month courtship. It must have been love at first sight, huh?"

He was way too cynical to believe in that. "More like a youthful lack of common sense."

"You could say the same thing about us."

He probably could, but he wouldn't. "We were different. We knew each other longer than three months. And neither of us asked the other to give up our dreams when we got married."

She dropped her hand from his arm. "Maybe she didn't see it that way. Sometimes you simply make sacrifices for those you love."

Matt wondered if his goals had overshadowed hers. "Have you ever felt like you've sacrificed too much for the sake of my career?"

She shook her head. "I wanted the clinic to succeed as much as you did. I've always been proud of the life we've built together."

Yet she'd been willing to throw it all away. He didn't want to get into that now. He only wanted to prolong the conversation, spend as much time with her as he could before they returned to separate beds, even if it required more gut spilling.

He straightened and shifted to face her. "My mom had plans to open a dance studio in Placid, but she decided to wait until after I was born. When I was less than a year old, she was diagnosed with MS. Pretty ironic, huh? An aspiring dance teacher who couldn't walk, much less dance. Sometimes life is damn unfair."

Instead of offering a response, Rachel did something that caught him completely off guard. She slid her arms around his waist and laid her cheek against his chest. Having her so close, holding her again, was worth every gut-wrenching memory he'd unearthed. He rested his chin atop her head and enjoyed the moments, for however long they might last.

She pulled back but didn't pull away. "Thank you for finally sharing your mother's story with me. You have no idea how much it means to me."

And she had no idea how much she meant to him. How much he wanted to make everything right between them. How badly he wanted to carry her to bed and make love to her. But he'd promised to give her space, and that was a promise he had to keep. He'd already broken one too many.

He brushed a kiss across her cheek, and

although it killed him to do so, he let her go. "Guess it's back to the bad box springs and shoddy mattress."

"You poor baby," she said. "You should have grabbed the big bed while I was feeling generous."

"I'll manage." He doubted he'd sleep much anyway knowing she was in the next room, only a few feet away. "Sweet dreams."

"Good night." She walked to the door leading to the master bedroom, then suddenly turned. "I can't do this to you. I'll sleep in the guest room."

"The bed sucks, Rachel. You need to be comfortable in your current condition."

"Excuse me?"

He could've sworn he'd heard a little panic in her voice, but he was probably imagining things. "You drove all day, so you've got to have a stiff back. Like I said, I'll get by."

She stood there for a few minutes without making a move to go inside the room. "This is ridiculous. We've slept in the same bed for most of our adult life. I don't see any reason why we can't do that tonight."

"Deal."

He was at the door in a flash, but she halted his progress by pressing a palm against his chest. "Can you honestly do this, Matt? Can you sleep in the same bed with me and not expect more than sleep?"

Why did he feel as if this was some kind of a test? "I promise you won't even know I'm there."

But he'd know she was there, close but not quite close enough. That was okay. For weeks he'd wanted nothing more than to have her beside him again. He'd gladly take whatever she was willing to give under any condition. Maybe now he might actually get some decent sleep.

When Rachel opened the door, Matt followed her into the room and took his place on his usual side of the bed, closest to the door. She quickly climbed under the covers while he stripped off his shirt. But as he started to untie the pajama drawstring, she said, "Leave those on."

As if not being able to touch her wasn't bad enough, now she was asking him to veer away from his normal habit of sleeping in the buff. "You know I don't like to wear clothes to bed."

"Sorry, but I'd prefer you keep your weapon concealed."

"Weapon?"

"Your heat-seeking missile."

She could've gone all year without drawing attention to that. "Am I sensing a little missile envy?"

That earned him a grin. "You know what I mean."

Oh, yeah, he did. She meant to torture him. "I guarantee you'll be safe from me and my artillery." He couldn't guarantee he wouldn't salute if she came anywhere near him during the night.

Matt threw back the comforter and stretched out on top of the sheets on his back, while Rachel covered up to her neck.

After a few seconds, she lifted her head and stared at him. "Are you going to get the light?"

Some things never changed. "Sure. While I'm up, do you want me to make you a snack or maybe do a few magic tricks?"

"No. Just the light."

He got out of bed, snapped off the switch near the door and returned to assume his position on his back. When she shifted slightly, he caught a whiff of her shampoo. The scent reminded him of all the times they'd showered together, and that led to some pretty dirty thoughts.

He continued to lie there, stiff as a pine plank. All of him. Unable to get comfortable, he punched his pillow and turned onto his side to face the wall.

A few moments later, he felt a light touch on his shoulder. "Matt?"

Could he be lucky enough that she'd reconsidered the hands-off policy? Highly unlikely. "Yeah."

"I'm cold."

He sure as hell wished he could say the same for himself, especially when he rolled over to face her and found she'd moved closer. "Do you want me to turn on the heat, or would you prefer I go out and chop some wood to start a fire?" Either way, the pants were coming off, missile or no missile.

"You could just hold me."

Definitely torture, and the ultimate test. He could do this. He could show her he could be trusted to keep her warm without trying to make her hot. But not before he gave her a hard time. "Did you shave your legs?"

"Hush up."

"I'm just saying—"

"Are you going to do it or are we going to discuss it?"

He'd always preferred action over talking. "Come here."

When she scooted toward him then turned her back, he took his cue and wrapped his arms around her. She wiggled around for a few seconds, like a squirrel burrowing into the nest for the winter. Hell, didn't she realize it was spring and that her cute little butt was way too close to the armory?

Finally she stopped moving and her breathing settled into a steady rhythm. At least she was relaxed and able to sleep. On the other hand, he couldn't seem to shut off the thought faucet.

But this was good, having her in his arms. He couldn't remember the last time he'd held her like this. Yeah, he did. Last December, about a week before she'd given birth. He'd been rubbing her lower back, which had been bothering her, and she'd fallen asleep during the process. He'd held her close, his hand on her swollen belly so he could feel their baby kick against his palm.

That night, he'd let himself imagine what it would be like to raise a son. He'd let himself believe that he could be a good father. That he had the power to protect him, which he hadn't. He'd hadn't been able to save his child, just as he hadn't been able to save his mother. He'd failed Rachel on many levels and continued to fail his father.

Maybe wanting to stay in this marriage wasn't fair to Rachel, because he didn't have the heart or the guts to go through it all again. But he couldn't stand the thought of losing her for good. He'd take that out and examine it later. Right now he just wanted to hang on to her for as long as he could.

CHAPTER EIGHT

AT SOME POINT during the night, he'd let her go. Rachel felt almost bereft when she woke without his arms around her. Funny, she'd been going to bed for months without Matt— before and after she'd left him. She should be used to it by now.

When she felt the mattress bend, she turned her head to see he hadn't actually gone anywhere. He'd simply changed positions and flipped onto his back. He'd also stripped off his pajamas, she realized when she noticed a gap where the sheet, loosely draped over his hips, revealed his bare leg from waist to foot. No real surprise there. He'd walk around naked all day if he could.

His left hand rested low on his abdomen and his right arm, the one closest to her, lay at his side. His sleep-tousled hair and unshaven face were patently appealing. Too appealing for her to remain close to him, at least physically. She did feel more emotion-ally connected to him after their most recent conversation. Yet she didn't quite trust that she'd completely broken through the internal fortress he'd built throughout his lifetime. They still had a lot of ground to cover and a short time to cover it.

She climbed out of bed, gathered her clothes and went into the bathroom to com-plete her morning ritual. When she returned to the bedroom, Matt hadn't moved an inch, but he had managed to turn over—without the sheet. Great. Nothing like beginning the day with an anatomy lesson. But she'd seen his bottom before, many times, and ignoring it wouldn't be a problem. After all, it was just a nicely toned, gently curved male butt like any other male butt.

Who was she kidding? If she didn't leave soon, she'd be tempted to explore the ter-rain as if she'd been given a brand-new boy toy. She chalked up her insane desire to hor-mones and took the corner chair to put on her sneakers. Yet the cradle captured her atten-tion, a solid reminder of the secret she still held close to the vest. A secret she should reveal to her husband soon. But she wasn't ready to make that revelation. Not until she knew for sure where he stood on having another baby. One step at time, she reminded herself. First, she needed to get out of there before Matt woke and delayed her departure.

"Where you going, sweetheart?"

Oh, that low, rough morning voice she'd come to know so well. That familiar, endearing and extremely sensual tone that could be very persuasive. Her gaze snapped from the shoelaces she'd been tying to the owner of that voice, who'd managed to flip onto his back without her noticing. She definitely noticed him now. His aversion to sheets was showing and so was everything else in all its glory. Anatomy lesson, part two.

"Could you please cover up?" Her tone sounded tentative, as if she wasn't sure that's what she wanted.

He folded his arms behind his head, clearly demonstrating he had no intention of honoring her request. "Nothing you haven't seen before."

Very true, but she didn't want to see it now. Correction. She didn't *need* to see it now. To avoid staring, she went back to tying her shoes. "I'm going to the grocery store in a few minutes."

"First, could I interest you in—"

"No, you couldn't." Actually, yes, he could, and that's why she had to leave.

"Dammit, Rachel, would you stop anticipating what I'm going to say before I say it?"

She came to her feet, thankful to discover the sheet now strategically covered him. "I'm sorry, but when you start a sentence with 'Could I interest you' and you have…" She gestured toward the cotton tent. "That."

"*That's* what's known as an erection. Been having one in the morning for as long as I can remember."

His use of the anatomically correct term was surprising and, for some odd reason, absurdly sexy. "How well I know. And because you've always been very good at persuading me to take care of *that,* what did you expect me to think you were going to say?"

"Oh, I don't know. Maybe something like could I interest you in having breakfast down at the café? You've been second-guessing me for years and it drives me crazy."

"You're exaggerating."

"No, I'm not. You have a bad habit of not letting me finish sentences."

If that happened to be true, and she wasn't certain it was, she should probably feel remorseful. "I only finish your suspect sentences."

"Then that means almost every word coming out of my mouth is suspect in your eyes."

Maybe she had been guilty of making too many assumptions. "Okay. From now on, I'll give you the benefit of the doubt and stop running over your words. But I'll pass on the breakfast offer. I want to stop by and see Helen and Jack after I buy a few supplies. Feel free to go to the café without me."

He released a rough sigh. "You're taking my only means of transportation."

She pushed out of the chair and strolled to the mirrored dresser to brush her hair. "It's less than half a mile, so you can walk. Maybe if you jog you might work off a little steam."

"Or I could take a shower."

She regarded him in the mirror's reflection as she pulled her hair into a high ponytail and secured it. "Didn't you already have one last night?"

He sat up and stretched his arms above his head. "Yeah, but unless you want to come over here and take care of my *problem,* I'm going to need a cold one."

She turned and pointed at him. "That is exactly why I won't let you talk."

He had the gall to grin. "You're just afraid if you hear it, you'll want to do it, so you cut me off at the pass."

Oh, yes, she definitely wanted to do it. She wanted to kick off her shoes, pull off her sweatshirt and jeans, toss away her underwear and have at it with her husband. She couldn't, wouldn't play into his hands, even knowing that those hands could play her like a baby grand piano.

Before she did something totally stupid, she had to get away. "I'll be back in a while."

"Drive carefully," he called out as she started down the hallway to the front door.

She needed to be careful. Very, very careful. She was bordering on throwing caution to the wind with a lot still left to resolve. Yet she felt as if they were moving in a positive direction. She had high hopes for the rest of the day.

SO FAR THE DAY HAD STARTED out great. The sun was out, not a cloud in the sky, and he'd had a nice breakfast down at the greasy spoon. Most important, he'd spent the previous night with his wife in his arms. Yeah, a great day. And if he had his way, it would only get better.

He hammered the last nail into the loose board on the porch, straightened and surveyed his handiwork. Nothing like a little manual labor to work off some nervous energy. As soon as Rachel returned, he'd suggest they go for a hike down one of the trails they hadn't explored. He'd work his way into asking her to go to the rec hall this evening for a little dancing to set the mood. And when they came home tonight…well, anything was possible.

When his cell rang, he set the hammer down on the railing and pulled the phone from his pocket. He'd expected Rachel might be calling, only to discover that wasn't the case. But he did recognize the number, and this particular caller could mean his good day could very well go south. "Hey, Chase."

"Hey. Sorry to bother you, but this couldn't wait."

"Is this official business or personal?"

"A little of both."

As crazy as it seemed, Matt hoped someone had vandalized the clinic or broken into the house. Insurance would cover that. But he had a feeling none of the above applied. "What's up?"

"It's Ben."

Exactly what he'd feared. "What did he do this time?"

"Dad arrested him last night on a drunk-and-disorderly charge."

"Was he back at Scruffy's?" If Mo had gone against Matt's wishes, the bartender would have hell to pay.

"No. He wasn't in a bar at all. Buck found him wandering around downtown, drunk as a skunk."

That was a first. "I'm guessing he's still locked up, since I'm the only fool who'll bail him out."

"Yeah, he's locked up and he's still not sober. He really tied one on."

So much for having some quality time with Rachel. "It's going to take me seven hours to get back there."

"Maybe you should just leave him here for a few days instead of bailing him out."

Matt had considered that before, but he'd never had the guts to do it. "I could, but he's going to start drying out, and that could be dangerous if he gets the DTs."

"We have a protocol we follow in this situation. I'll have the staff nurse monitor him on a regular basis, and if he's in any danger at all, we can send him to the hospital."

"I didn't plan to be back until Monday, so that means he'll be without the booze for three nights, counting last night."

"And he should be clean by then. When you get back, maybe you can finally convince him to get the help he needs."

Another choice he didn't want to make. "If anything happened to him, I'd feel responsible. I'm sure Rachel would understand if I head back."

"Would she, Matt? You're already skatin' on thin ice with her. And don't you think it's way past time to let Ben sink or swim? He's going to have to hit rock bottom before he makes that upward climb."

He was caught between saving his dad and saving his marriage. In reality, the first had influenced the second, and not in a good way. For years he'd asked his wife to tolerate his father's antics, and she'd done so at the expense of their relationship. It had taken a possible divorce to force him to see that, among other things.

Once again, he chose Rachel. And this was one choice that should make her happy. "You'll call me if something goes wrong?"

"You bet. Normally we'd have to leave him unsupervised for short periods of time, but

I'll make sure someone's checking on him all the time, even if I have to do it myself."

"Then keep him there. I'll deal with it Tuesday morning."

"You've made the right decision, Matt."

Probably, but that didn't make it any easier. As Rachel had pointed out, he'd been enabling his dad for years, and the time had come to stop. "Thanks, bud. I owe you one."

"You can pay me back by fixing your marriage," Chase said. "Jess has worried nonstop over it, and that worries me. By the way, how's it going with Rachel?"

"Good. Better than I expected." And he hoped like hell he hadn't just jinxed it.

"And I expect you to come back, ready to ditch the divorce. And who knows? Rachel might even be pregnant again."

That was the last thing they needed.

"RACHEL BOYD, I haven't seen you in ages!"

The high-pitched voice echoing across the parking lot grated on Rachel like a fork against a metal pan. She could throw the groceries into the truck, climb into the cab and pretend she hadn't heard a thing. Or she could get the inevitable inquest over with.

After setting the bags on the floorboard

of the front seat, she turned to see pint-size Rita Kendrick coming toward her as fast as her short, stocky legs would allow, a massive aqua faux-suede bag hanging from one shoulder of the purple scrubs she always wore, not an ultrateased strand of bottle-black hair out of place. The nurse was to Wayhurst what Pearl Allworth was to Placid—queen of the busybodies.

Rachel closed the truck door and tried on a fake smile. "Hello, Rita."

"Sugar, you look so good! It took me over a year to get my figure back after I gave birth to Lila. Actually, I never really did." She barked out a laugh, then leaned around Rachel and stared into the truck. "Does that handsome husband of yours have the baby with him?"

"Well, no—"

"That's okay if you left it at home. Couples need their time alone together. Was it a boy or girl? What did you name it? I bet it's a pretty thing, whatever—"

"The baby died," Rachel blurted out in order to end the woman's diatribe.

Rita laid a plump hand over her equally plump breasts. "Oh, no! What happened?"

She did not want to get into a lengthy explanation of everything that had gone wrong during Caleb's birth. "He was premature."

"That is such a shame, sugar. But you know, sometimes nature has a way of taking care of these things. A blessing in disguise, really."

The spurt of anger took Rachel by surprise. She tamped it down through sheer willpower alone. "I'm so sorry, Rita, but Matt's waiting on me. It was good to see you." Not.

Rita hugged her so hard, she feared for her rib cage. "Chin up, sugar. I'm sure the next baby will be perfectly fine. Say hello to Matt and I hope I see you again real soon."

"Same here." If a sudden storm blew in, she'd surely suffer a lightning strike right there on the asphalt.

Rachel couldn't get into the truck fast enough. Although Rita had meant well, Rachel never understood how anyone could believe losing a baby was a blessing and be so thoughtless as to actually voice that opinion.

She could definitely use a sympathetic ear, a leaning shoulder, and she knew exactly where she could find one. With that in mind, she continued down the road a bit and pulled into the familiar drive. The white-and-yellow cottage-style house was a direct contrast to the rough-hewn cabins dotting the mountainside community. But Rachel had always found the place to be absolutely charming and completely fitting for a Southern gentlewoman like Helen Van Alsteen.

Before she could ring the bell, the door opened to a smiling woman, her silver hair streaked with copper highlights and her green eyes still as vibrant as they'd been almost fourteen years ago. She stepped onto the porch and opened her arms wide. "Rachel Boyd, it does my soul good to see you!"

She accepted Helen's hug and returned her smile. "It's great to see you, too. I'm sorry I didn't call first, so if you're too busy—"

"I'm never too busy for you. Come in and sit a spell."

Rachel followed Helen into the parlor filled with pristine antique furniture and knick-knacks galore. She joined her on the pink floral settee where they'd had many a conversation. "First of all, thank you so much for getting the cabin ready and for the food you left in the fridge. You saved our lives last night."

Helen laid a careworn hand on her throat. "Oh, heavens, child. I doubt that. I would have brought you a casserole, but that might have cost you your life, since I'm such a terrible cook."

How could she put this gently? "You're not that bad, Helen."

"And you're too kind, dear. Jack will attest to that, poor man. It's a good thing he's never objected to dining out."

Rachel centered her gaze on the weathered brown recliner, Jack Van Alsteen's favorite place to sit. "Speaking of the judge, where is he?"

Helen looked strangely uneasy over the question. "He's napping."

"Is he feeling okay?"

"He's fine, dear. Would you like some coffee and a muffin?"

She almost declined until she realized she hadn't had breakfast. "That would be great, if it's not too much trouble. Do you have decaf?"

Helen rose from the small sofa. "That's all I drink these days, and it's no trouble at all. The muffins are store-bought, which is a good thing. Two sugars and cream, right?"

"Right."

"I'll be back in a sec."

Rachel thought back to Helen's note and worried she wasn't being forthcoming about

Jack's health. She'd never known the retired judge to be idle during the day, much less take a nap in the morning. Then again, he was in his late seventies, so she could be reading too much into it.

After a few minutes, Helen returned with a tray that she set on the coffee table. She handed Rachel one delicate gold-rimmed cup and gestured toward the plateful of muffins. "Help yourself."

"I'll have one in a minute," Rachel said when she realized they were poppy seed, one of her least favorite.

Helen picked up her cup and took a sip before setting it back on the tray. "Now, tell me how you've been holding up since you lost your little angel," she said, both her tone and expression reflecting sincere sympathy.

She hadn't spoken to Helen since Caleb's birth, which left only one possible scenario. "Did Rita call you?"

Helen looked as if she'd just consumed a bottle of brine. "Heavens, no, honey. I avoid that woman like the plague."

"I wish I could have avoided her. She way-laid me in the parking lot, then proceeded to tell me that losing Caleb was some sort of blessing in disguise."

Helen looked thoroughly disgusted. "Rita's mouth travels at the speed of light, while her brain runs at a snail's pace. I'm sorry you had to endure that."

Now that Rita had been ruled out, Rachel could think of only one other person who might have delivered the information. "Did Matt tell you about the baby?"

"Yes, when he called me yesterday to say you were coming in for the weekend. And, honey, I'm so very, very sorry. I know from personal experience how difficult it is to go through that."

Rachel was totally taken aback by the admission. "You do?"

Helen took another sip of coffee and dabbed at her mouth with a napkin. "Yes, I had a miscarriage a year before J.W. was born. I was only three months along and it was devastating. I can't begin to imagine how difficult it would be to lose a baby so late in the pregnancy."

"It's been the most difficult thing I've had to deal with." Aside from her estrangement from Matt. "How did you cope?"

"One day at a time," she said. "But even after forty-six years, I still find myself wondering about that child. In my mind the baby was a girl. I would have named her Hannah, after my grandmother, and I've always imagined she would have grown up to be an attorney, like her father. Of course, she would've had it all—marriage, career and children. Silly in some ways, I suppose, but that's how I've kept her alive in my heart without having the grief consume my life."

Rachel set her coffee down without taking a drink. "I haven't really let myself think about Caleb in that way. If I did, I'm afraid I would never get over losing him."

Helen patted her cheek. "Give yourself time, honey. The pain will lessen eventually, even if it never entirely goes away. But you're a strong woman, and there will be other babies."

In about eight months, she wanted to say but chose to withhold the information. She didn't feel right telling anyone else before she told Matt—the reason she hadn't called Jess and Savannah to confirm the pregnancy.

A subject change was definitely in order. She could use some marital advice. Who better to ask than a woman who'd been blissfully married to the same man for fifty years? "Things haven't been good between Matt and me. In fact, we've been separated for over a month."

"Oh, dear. That breaks my heart."

The disappointment in Helen's voice broke Rachel's heart, too. "I never wanted this to happen, but our problems seem insurmountable at times."

Helen's expression brightened. "Well, you're here together now, so I assume that means all hope is not lost. And if you still love each other, no problem is too big to overcome."

"I do still love him, Helen. But everything just fell apart between us after Caleb died."

"Sadly, in some instances a tragedy highlights troubles in a marriage that we tend to ignore during the good times. Even insignificant issues are magnified by grief. It's also human nature to want to blame someone, even ourselves."

She questioned whether Helen had hit on something she hadn't considered before. Maybe Matt did blame himself or perhaps her. "Matt seems to want to avoid any conflict altogether by burying himself in work." And a bottle, a fact she preferred not to reveal.

Helen sighed. "Honey, I've learned a thing

or two about men through the years. Most are simple creatures with simple needs. Give them a full belly, cable TV, a wife who's an angel during the day and a—pardon my crudeness—whore in bed, and they're happy. They don't like to talk about feelings unless you ask them how they feel about their favorite football team's chances at a championship."

She laughed in spite of her shock. "You're so right about that."

"They also have short memories," Helen added. "The things that drive us batty are lost on our spouses because, well, frankly, they can also be completely oblivious unless you draw them a picture. It's important to bring those things to light and be done with them. You'll feel much better and your husband will be enlightened. He can't change if he doesn't know what's wrong."

She wasn't certain she agreed with that plan. "Won't that only create more friction between us?"

Helen took Rachel's hands into hers. "Problems are like blisters. They continue to fester until they're ready to burst. It's better to let them burst rather than become infected with resentment. It's the only way to heal your relationship."

That did make some sense. "Okay, let's just say I lay everything out in the open and tell Matt all the aspects of our marriage that I'm not happy with. What if he doesn't reciprocate?"

"That's possible, but you can't force him. And he just might surprise you. Men can also be very unpredictable."

She leaned over and gave Helen a hug. "I knew I could count on you for good advice. You truly are the mother I never had."

Helen looked as though Rachel had handed her the key to paradise. "I'm honored you would say that, sweetie. That makes you the daughter I never had."

Rachel grinned. "Does that mean I can borrow your nice wool jacket?"

"Why, of course. As long as I can borrow those four-inch black heels and some bunion pads to go with them."

They shared in a laugh and another hug and a little lighter catch-up conversation before Rachel glanced at her watch. "I really need to go. I'm sure Matt's wondering where I am." She was more than ready to follow

Helen's advice and commence with the blister bursting.

Helen gestured toward the tray. "But you didn't have a muffin."

"I'll take one to go," she said in an effort to be polite. "And give Jack my love when he's through napping."

Helen wrapped a muffin in a napkin and handed it to Rachel. "You can tell him yourself down at the community center tonight. It's Saturday and all the old fogies will be there, including us. We could use your youth to liven up the place."

The impending conversation with her husband would determine whether they attended the customary event. "We'll be there if we can."

Helen's expression went suddenly somber. "Before you go, I have one more piece of marital advice."

"I'd welcome any help you can give me." And she truly would.

"When you wake in the morning," she began, "imagine what life would be like if that space beside you became permanently empty. It makes you appreciate what you have in Matthew and what you stand to lose."

In all the years she'd known Helen, she'd

never seen anything but joy in her eyes. The tears that began to form told her something was very, very wrong. "Helen, is there something wrong with Jack?"

"Yes, I'm afraid there is."

Exactly what she'd suspected. "What is it?" she asked, even though she dreaded the answer.

"He has Alzheimer's."

CHAPTER NINE

WHEN THE TRUCK CAME into view, Matt stopped what he was doing in order to greet his wife. He thought about telling her about his dad's current situation, but he decided to hold off on that for now. He wanted to avoid any extra conflict at all costs, particularly since they'd begun to bridge the gap between them.

Rachel shut off the truck and got out, two canvas bags clutched in her arms. "Need any help?" he called to her as she started up the stone walkway.

"No." She glanced at the porch plank he'd just secured. "It's about time you fixed that."

"Nice to see you, too," he muttered as she brushed past him and went inside.

Matt tossed the hammer into the toolbox and walked into the house to find Rachel putting away groceries with a vengeance. She was definitely in a foul mood and he wondered what he'd done now. He figured he'd find out soon enough.

When she continued to ignore him, he took a seat on the bar stool at the island and braced for a probable tongue-lashing. "What's wrong, Rachel?"

"Why don't we own a dog?" she asked as she shoved a box of microwave popcorn into the pantry.

That was the strangest question he'd heard coming out of her mouth in a long time. Now to come up with an answer that suited her. Or a nonanswer. "Beg your pardon?"

She slammed the pantry door and leaned back against it. "You're a vet, Matt. You're supposed to like pets. After Buddy died, you never even suggested we get another dog. It's been three years."

She'd resented that he'd put the Lab mix down, but she hadn't seemed that fond of the dog. "Best I recall, you never mentioned you wanted another one. I do remember you complained a lot about Buddy's chewing habit."

She glared at him. "No, I didn't like his chewing, but I loved him. I cried for days after you *put him out of his misery*. I think that's what you called it."

Here we go again. "He was suffering, Rachel. His joints were shot and he could barely walk. Not to mention his kidneys were starting to fail."

She took a head of lettuce and a tomato out of the bag and set them on the counter. "If my joints were shot, would you put me out of my misery?"

He wished she'd put him out of his misery and tell him what was bugging her. "That's a pretty weird question."

She nailed him with a glare. "So now I'm weird?"

"You're acting weird."

"So sorry I don't act the way you think I should act." She yanked open the refrigerator, pulled the crisper drawer out and tossed the produce inside.

He'd hate to be that head of lettuce about now. "Did something happen while you were gone that ticked you off?"

She turned around and began folding one of the bags with precise creases. "I'm just tired of festering."

She made no sense whatsoever. "Festering?"

She put the folded sack aside and grabbed the other, which she clutched in both hands as if she wanted to rip it in half. "Yes, festering. I've been holding in all the little things that have been bothering me for years. I feel the need to do some soul cleansing."

If he ever needed a beer, now would be the time. But that would be like adding kerosene to the campfire. He'd just have to suck it up and let her have her say. "Go ahead and cleanse. I'm not going anywhere."

She tossed the sack aside, picked up a can and slammed it into one cabinet before facing him again. "First, I don't appreciate the fact you won't wear a wedding band."

No surprise she'd bring that one up. "We've been through this before, Rachel. I can't wear a ring while I work."

"And for some reason, you can't wear one when you're not working."

He recognized a battle he couldn't win when he saw it. "Fine. I'll buy one and wear it, if that makes you happy."

She propped a hand on her hip. "Do you know what would really make me happy? If you finally accepted that you can't fix anything with bandage sex."

Okay, he'd bite. "Bandage sex?"

"Yes. For some reason you believe that sex is the answer to everything that's wrong with us. If I even try to be serious, you bring out that whole 'come here, baby, take off your clothes and let me take you to paradise' thing."

Never in his life had he ever used the word *paradise* in that context. "Hell, if I really sound like that, no wonder you won't come near me."

She started terrorizing the groceries again, this time targeting a white paper-wrapped package that she tossed into the freezer. "Oh, and let's not forget your need to put away my shoes. It drives me absolutely insane."

This whole conversation was driving him insane. Certifiably. "Excuse me for trying to help out."

"I don't see it that way. In fact, the day I moved out, I hadn't even considered leaving you until I went into the bathroom to get my slippers and you'd stuck them in the closet."

The second strangest thing to leave her mouth. Or was it the third? "You left me because of your shoes?"

She looked at him as if he could use a padded room. "That wasn't the only reason, just the last straw. I should be able to put my shoes anywhere I please, even if it's on the roof."

"Even if I almost break my neck tripping over them?"

"Again, you exaggerate."

Not by much. "Okay. I promise never to touch your shoes again."

"Fine. And in case you're interested, which you're probably not, I did give up a dream for you."

That really threw him for a loop. "You said last night—"

"I know what I said, but I didn't want to admit exactly how much I gave up for you. I wanted to go back to school and get an MBA."

She was just full of surprises. "Then go back to school. No one's stopping you, least of all me. I'll support you in whatever you do."

She frowned as if she expected an argument from him. "I don't want to go back to school, at least not in the immediate future."

Of course she didn't. "Whatever you want."

"I want you to answer another question."

"Shoot." He prepared for the impact.

"Why didn't you touch me after we lost the baby?"

This was a lot deeper than discarded

dreams and shoes and deceased dogs. "I swear I wanted to touch you, Rachel, but you acted like you didn't want me near you. I was damned if I did, damned if I didn't."

"But you didn't even try."

She had him on that one. "Maybe I was afraid I'd hurt you or that you'd take it the wrong way."

Tears began to pool in her dark eyes. "Did it ever occur to you that I just needed you to hold me? Did you ever consider that maybe I blamed myself for Caleb's death?"

He wanted to hold her now, but worried she'd turn him away again. This time, the need to comfort her overshadowed his fear of rejection. He rounded the island and pulled her into his arms, and amazingly she didn't pull away. She just laid her cheek against his chest, her tears dampening the front of his shirt. "I'd never blame you, sweetheart. Like the doctor told us, the preeclampsia is sometimes undetectable until the problems set in. You had no way of knowing what was going on."

She raised her tearstained faced, sheer sorrow in her eyes. "Life is so unfair sometimes. One moment everything's fine, then in the next, babies are born too soon and good people come down with incurable diseases. I don't understand it at all."

He had a feeling she wasn't referring to only losing their son and that her anger only partially had to do with their problems. Determined to get to the bottom of her meltdown, he took her by the hand, led her to the sofa and brought her down beside him. "What's really going on here, Rachel?"

She leaned over, pulled a tissue from the holder on the end table and wiped her eyes. "It's Judge Jack. Helen told me he's been diagnosed with early-stage Alzheimer's."

That explained a lot, and it also made him sick inside. "How long have they known this?"

"Since last November. He started to forget names when he performed weddings. That's when Helen became suspicious, and rightfully so. The judge never forgets a name or face, especially when it comes to the couples he marries."

He pulled her closer. "You're right. It's not fair at all. Jack doesn't deserve this and neither does Helen."

She leaned her head against his shoulder. "And you didn't deserve my outburst. I'm sorry."

Her up-and-down attitude was akin to a nonstop roller-coaster ride. One minute, she hated the sight of him. The next, she was apologizing. She'd had her moody moments in the past, particularly when she'd been pregnant, but nothing like this. "No apology necessary. I probably did deserve it."

"I handled it poorly. I really did want to get all of those issues out in the open, but in a much more civil and logical manner. I was just feeling so bad about Jack, and I was so angry over the circumstance."

"I'm glad you told me what's been bothering you. Especially the part about going back to school. I think it's a great idea."

She tensed. "I can't even consider that now."

"What's stopping you? We have the money and now I have someone to manage the office. Seems to me it's the perfect time for you to go for it."

"I'll think about it." She straightened and shifted to face him. "Look, I've just told you what's been bothering me. Now it's your turn. Don't hold back."

He could add one more of his faults to the list—he'd been keeping something important from her for months. But that couldn't be handled in a simple conversation or with a catalog of his shortcomings.

First, he wanted to let her know how much she meant to him, rebuild the marriage foundation. Win her back before he begged her forgiveness. "Let me think. I hate it when you come into the office and smile at me, because I can't concentrate at work. And I really hate it when you feel like you have to wear makeup, because you're beautiful without it. And let's not forget your habit of putting down the seat when I forget and you never complain about it. That really drives me nuts."

She smiled. "Are you making fun of me?"

He pushed aside a strand of hair from her cheek. "I'm trying to say that I don't expect you to be perfect. When I married you for better or worse, I meant it."

"You've definitely seen me at my worst."

"Your worst is better than most people's best."

"Now I feel really awful for giving you grief."

He brought her back against his side and wrapped an arm around her shoulder. "Don't feel bad. You said what needed to be said. At least now I know if I put your shoes up, you might cut off my hands or something else."

"I promise I won't do that 'something else' part. That would clearly be a waste."

"Glad you think so, ma'am."

She yawned and stretched her arms above her head. "I don't know why I'm so tired. I slept better last night than I have in a long time."

So had he. Better than he'd slept in a year. "It was fairly late when we got to bed, and we did get up early."

"You're right. I could use a nap."

"So could I." When she opened her mouth as if she might protest, he added, "Before you start questioning my motives, I mean a nap as in sleep. In fact, we can sleep right here on this old sofa like we used to." Not the best alternative to the other naps they took in the bed, minus the nap. But it would have to do.

"That sounds like a good plan," she said as she stood. "I'll be right back."

After Rachel left the den, Matt opened the windows flanking the fireplace to let in some cool mountain air and then fed Rachel's favorite classical CD into the player. Normally he'd turn on the TV to watch a baseball game or opt for country music, but he wanted this entire trip to be about her and for her.

He sat on the edge of the sofa to pull off his boots before stretching out on his back. A few minutes later, Rachel returned wearing a pair of ragged sweats that rode low enough to reveal her navel and a thin white tank top with no bra.

She had him at an unfair advantage, but he was bent on proving to her that he could maintain control—unless she made the first move. Then all bets were off.

To make room for her, he scooted over as far as he could. She settled beside him, her head tucked between his jaw and shoulder, one arm loosely draped across his belly.

"Comfortable?" he asked.

"Very. Are you?

Not exactly. "I'm okay, although I'm thinking we should trade in this couch for one of those suede sectionals. We'd have more room that way."

When she didn't respond, he realized he'd offered up a future plan when their future in this cabin, and together, was still in jeopardy. But she hadn't even mentioned packing, so he took that as a hopeful sign. Or maybe he was just fooling himself.

"Matt?"

"Yeah?"

"I know you're avoiding all the things about me that bug you, but I need to know in order to correct them. It's only fair."

He could think of a few things, none of them all that significant. "When you're not always right, but never in doubt or you make us late because you can't choose an outfit, I always consider one thing. Putting up with your habits wouldn't be nearly as bad as waking up every morning without you beside me."

She framed his jaw with her palm and kissed him softly. "Thank you."

"For what?"

She laid her cheek back on his chest. "For being you. And for being such a fabulous diplomat."

Diplomacy had nothing to do with it. He'd told her the absolute truth this time. He really didn't know how he would survive if she was gone for good. He didn't want to find out.

RACHEL AWOKE TO find Matt gone. She sat up on the sofa and waited for the haze to clear so she could regain her bearings. The ribbons of light streaming into one window were dimmer now, indicating sunset was approaching. How long had she slept? When had she fallen asleep? She remembered Matt's wonderful words followed by silence, the soothing strokes of his fingertips against her bare arm and then closing her eyes. He'd always been good at lulling her into a state of oblivion, with or without lovemaking.

Her favorite Rachmaninoff concerto played softly from the overhead speakers. Clearly he had thought of everything to please her, right down to saying all the right things. Or had he only said what he thought she'd wanted to hear?

Her mind was cluttered with confusion and the occasional glimmer of hope. But she couldn't let herself believe all would be right until he accepted the news about the baby. And speaking of that, she realized she hadn't eaten anything since she'd choked down the muffin Helen had given her.

On her way to the kitchen, the sound of hammering sent her straight to the front window. She peered outside to find her missing husband repairing a section of fence that bordered the drive. She should have known he wouldn't stay still for long. He'd always been the kind of man who couldn't remain idle. He liked using his hands, and he could use them very well, particularly on her. Only one more thing she loved about him.

She prepared a plate with apples and cheese, plus a few crackers. Not the most substantial snack, but it would have to do until dinner. And with Matt playing carpenter, who knew when that would be?

After she finished eating, Rachel noticed the hammering had stopped, prompting her to look out the window again to see if Matt might be coming inside. Instead, she found him leaning against the porch's railing talking on his cell. His serious expression told her something was up, and it might not be good.

Without regard to her bare feet, she padded onto the front porch and waited for him to finish the call.

"Okay, just let me know," he said. "And thanks."

After he pocketed the phone, she approached him cautiously, half expecting him to tune her out. "Problems?"

He rubbed the back of his neck with his palm. "Yeah, you could say that. It's my dad."

"What's wrong with him?" Aside from his obvious alcoholism.

He pushed off the railing. "If you want to take a walk with me, I'll explain."

Miracle of miracles, he wasn't closing her out. "Sure. I'll be right back."

Rachel hurried inside, re-dressed in her sweatshirt and sneakers and practically sprinted out the door and down the porch steps. She met Matt at the top of the drive where a break in the fence led to a familiar path that snaked through the woods. A path they'd explored many times before. She was extremely pleased when he took her hand as they started forward, reminiscent of better days and better times.

Surrounded by the scent of pine and sheltered by a canopy of trees, they traveled several yards until they reached the clearing containing two ancient fallen logs. They'd deemed it their magical place because they'd made plenty of magic there, lying on a blanket beneath the stars, making love sometimes until dawn.

Matt guided her to the makeshift bench, where they sat side by side. The temptation to prod him for answers nearly overwhelmed her, yet she opted to wait for him to talk.

He leaned forward, arms resting on his knees, hands laced together. "Chase called this morning while you were gone. My dad's in jail on a drunk-and-disorderly charge."

She was stunned he hadn't insisted they return immediately to Placid. "Why didn't you tell me sooner?"

"Because I didn't want to bother you with his problems. You've had to deal with that too much as it is."

"I know, but he's still my father-in-law and I worry about him, too." She could also see a premature end to their time together. "Do we need to head back?"

He shook his head. "No. I'm not bailing him out this time."

Another shocking piece of news. Countless times she'd asked him to consider that, and each time he'd refused. "Are you sure you're okay with that?"

He sent her a sideways glance before returning his gaze to the ground. "I wasn't at first because the drying-out process can be dicey. But Chase assures me he's under medical supervision. He called a minute ago to report it's been pretty tough on the old man, but he's hanging in there."

She touched his arm. "You know, it's a good thing you have broad shoulders. You've had to carry a lot of weight in your lifetime with your mom and your dad and, of course, me."

He gave her a meaningful look. "Not you. If anything, you've carried me quite a bit during our marriage."

She'd always thought of Matt as the strong one. The cornerstone of the marriage. "I've never felt as if I have."

"Believe me, you have," he said. "You pushed me to get my bachelor's in three years."

"We pushed each other," she reminded him.

"Yeah, but I couldn't have made it through the entrance exam without you."

"And I couldn't have made it through those awful science courses without you."

"Don't forget I took you away from your dad and dragged you all the way out here for four years while I finished vet school."

She hooked her arm through his. "But those were good times. Hard, but good. Besides, you had it much worse than I did with the hour commute every day into Knoxville. I only had a thirty-minute drive into Gatlinburg."

"Where you had to work in that damn ski

shop for that jerk Grimsly so we could make ends meet."

She'd almost forgotten about that lecher. "I suppose that makes us even. But we did end up with the cabin as our reward. I've always believed fate had a hand in you choosing this place for our honeymoon and then to have it available for rent during those four years. That was a godsend."

"If you hadn't been so persistent with Harvey Minor, we might never have had the opportunity to buy it. You underestimate your powers of persuasion."

That had been the first and only time he'd let her use her trust fund for a major purchase. "I just couldn't stomach the thought of letting the place go after you finished school." The thought of doing that now made her heart ache. The thought of letting Matt go was even more painful.

When he fell silent again, Rachel suspected his thoughts had returned to the present. "Are you sure you don't want to go check on Ben? We could always come back some other weekend." Now she sounded as if she might be buying time.

He straightened and took her hand again.

"I came here to be with you at least until to-morrow, and that's what I intend to do."

He'd slipped up and clearly didn't realize it. But she couldn't judge him, considering she'd actually planned the same thing. "I thought we came to the cabin to pack up our belongings."

"I was prepared to do that," he said. "But only if I had to. I've been hoping we might not need to."

Rachel wasn't sure how to answer. "Well, we obviously haven't done any packing, but I'm not sure we can rule it out yet. I'd say we'll know for sure by tomorrow evening."

He sent her a half smile. "Then I might've brought that pile of boxes for no reason?"

"Could be."

His grin arrived full force. "That's the best news I've heard in a long time."

She hoped he was as enthusiastic over the other news she needed to tell him. Had it not been for his father's current predicament, she might have decided to make the disclosure now. "Thank you for choosing to stay here with me."

His expression went suddenly somber. "I chose you to be my life partner, so why stop choosing you now? I'll always choose you."

One of the sweetest things he'd ever said to her. Little by little she'd begun to believe he did still love her. Perhaps she'd been wrong to ever doubt him. Wrong to doubt they could move past the tragedy that had threatened to tear them apart.

She leaned over and kissed him for the second time today, with every intention of keeping it light. Then Matt kissed her back. *Really* kissed her the way he used to do when they were so wrapped up in each other. Before kisses became simple shows of affection, a predictable habit or a prelude to lovemaking. A kiss for the sake of kissing.

Rachel acknowledged this could lead to more if she didn't put a stop to it. She didn't want to stop, even when Matt slid his hand beneath the back of her sweatshirt and caressed her bare flesh with his calloused hand. Even when he pressed her closer until they were completely flush against each other.

Matt broke away first and tipped his forehead against hers. "We should probably head back to the house before this gets out of hand."

Truth was, she didn't care if it got out of hand. She still wanted him. Needed him, even. But what would the return to intimacy cost her with so much still left unsaid? She leaned back and tugged at the shirt's hem. "It's almost dinnertime. I bought steaks, and after we eat, we can talk some more."

"I have a better idea," he said. "We can grab a bite at the diner, then go to the rec hall to see our old friends. Maybe even do a little dancing."

How easy it would be to say yes, but their time together was limited. "We still have a lot to cover before Monday morning."

He released a rugged sigh. "Can't we take one night to forget all our troubles and just be together?"

Their troubles were too severe to disregard, but she was sorely tempted to agree. One carefree night spent with her husband certainly couldn't hurt. They both deserved that much.

CHAPTER TEN

THE MINUTE RACHEL WALKED into the Wayhurst Community Center with Matt, she noticed the place was a little less crowded than normal. But prime tourist season was still a month away, when the transient population nabbed the rental cabins. Most of the regulars were there, the seniors who'd chosen Smoky Mountain retreats over Miami beachfront condos. By their standards, she and Matt were equivalent to teenagers. Sometimes she wished they still were. Life had been much simpler back then.

She surveyed the room and glanced to her right to find Helen waving them over. And next to the judge's wife, one silver-haired, debonair man dressed in his usual classic golf attire. No one would guess that a man of such an intimidating stature would have such a soft spot for young couples in love.

She tugged on Matt's sleeve to gain his attention. "I see them. Corner table."

Matt raised his hand in acknowledgment. "I don't know what I expected, but the judge looks as fit as a fiddle."

But beneath that healthy veneer a horrendous disease was attacking his brilliant mind. "Helen said it's important to treat him normally."

"I can do that," he said as he clasped her hand.

Together they waded through the handful of couples dancing to classic tunes delivered by A.W., the eightysomething DJ. As they approached, Rachel noticed Helen whispering something in Jack's ear.

At first the judge looked a little confused before recognition dawned in his expression. Then he stood and grinned. "If it's not my favorite twosome."

While Helen and Rachel hugged, Matt stuck out his hand to Jack for a shake. "Hey, Judge. You're looking mighty prosperous these days. Is that a new watch?"

"It is," Helen said when Jack hesitated. "I gave it to him for our fiftieth anniversary two months ago."

Matt pulled out a chair for Rachel, and as

soon as they were seated, Jack removed his glasses and folded his hands on the table. "Now, how long has it been since I married the two of you?"

"Fourteen years in August," Rachel answered. "It's hard to believe it's been that long."

"Seems like yesterday the two of you showed up at the chapel," Jack said. "You were flat broke and nervous as caged cats. But I knew the minute I laid eyes on you both that I didn't need to give you the special treatment."

Rachel frowned. "Special treatment?"

"A form of counseling," Helen said. "He used to…" She turned to the judge. "Why don't you explain it?"

He assumed his sophisticated demeanor. "Gladly, missus. You never tell it right anyway."

"Oh, hush and get to it, Jackson."

"I will, woman. Just give me some time."

Rachel exchanged a smile with Matt over the banter that was as familiar and welcome as hot chocolate in winter. She'd never known two people so suited for each other, and that almost made her sad. At one time she'd felt the same about her and Matt.

"Usually the bride and groom plan the wedding well in advance," Jack continued. "When they'd come in to discuss the ceremony, I'd tell them four things. Don't blow your parents' savings on a wedding that lasts fifteen minutes. Divorce costs more than the wedding, so don't take the nuptials lightly unless you're prepared to pay. Don't cheat each other or on each other. And…" He looked a little forlorn. "I can't remember that damn fourth point."

"Expect a lot of crap through the years and learn how to deal with it because nobody's perfect," Helen said before regarding her and Matt. "The day you two walked into the chapel, so young and obviously in love, he told me, 'Helen, those two kids—'"

"Are going to make it," Jack finished. "I was right."

As Rachel swallowed around the knot forming in her throat, Matt squeezed her hand. "You're a good judge of character, Judge," he said.

Helen took Jack's hand into hers. "Yes, he is. Amazingly, all but six couples he's married over the past twenty years are still together."

"And the six that aren't?" Rachel asked.

"Five divorces and sadly one death," Helen said. "It's illogical to assume that all of them would make it."

"What's your secret?" Rachel asked.

Jack chuckled. "Crap-management skills. If we fight before bed, we call a truce and duke it out in the morning when we've had some sleep. We have two different TVs and we do our own laundry. She lets me play golf and I let her have her poker club. We've got it down to a science, don't we, sugar?"

"We certainly do, dear heart."

So touched by their unmistakable love for each other, Rachel still felt as if she might cry. Her emotions kept spiraling out of control, either from hormones or the monumental task of trying to save her marriage.

"Would anyone like a snack or a drink?" Helen asked.

Rachel shook her head. "Not now, but I might want some cheese fries in a little bit."

"After that plateful of food you just ate?" Matt looked and sounded incredulous.

She shrugged. "I'd only had the muffin Helen gave me. And I'm eating extra because..." *I'm eating for two.* Thankfully she pulled the words away before they jumped out of her mouth.

"It's the mountain air," Helen offered. "It makes for a hearty appetite."

So did a lack of sex, another point she would keep to herself. "You're right. I'm always hungrier when I'm here."

"And I'm personally tired of sitting." Matt pushed back from the table, stood and regarded Jack. "How about a game of pool, Judge?"

Looking as eager as a pup, Jack came to his feet. "Sounds like a fine idea, J.W."

"It's Matt, dear heart," Helen corrected. "But come to think of it, he does look a little like Jackson Wayne."

Jack scowled at his wife. "I know who he is, Helen."

"Of course you do, honey," Helen said. "It's just an honest mistake. That's all."

Matt walked to the judge's side, thankfully interrupting the awkward moment. "Come on, Jack. I've got a five-dollar bill with your name on it if you beat me. Ten if you let me win at least one. In the meantime, you ladies have a nice chat."

Jack elbowed him in the ribs. "Hope you aren't too attached to that five spot, boy. I might be an old goat, but I can still whip you nine ways to Sunday at the table."

After Matt gave her a wink and walked away with the judge, Rachel turned back to Helen. "Guess we won't be seeing those two for the rest of the evening."

"It's worth it to know Jack will be enjoying something he loves so much," Helen said. "Matthew's such a good, considerate man, Rachel."

"Yes, he is." A good man and, at one time, a good husband. If only he could be that man again. If only he realized he could also be a great father. A strong sense of melancholy settled over her and came out on a sigh.

"Honey, are you okay?"

The question brought Rachel out of her momentary funk. "I'm fine. Just a little tired, that's all."

"You look tired," Helen said. "But very pretty, too."

"Thanks." Helen's diplomacy skills were second only to Matt's. The pair of faded jeans and black knit shirt she wore wouldn't be considered fashion forward. But she hadn't packed for an outing because she hadn't planned to leave the cabin. She hadn't planned to be dealing with so many conflicting feelings, either. Tell Matt about the baby tonight; wait until tomorrow before they headed home.

Helen scooted her chair back and stood. "I'm going to get a beer. Do you want your usual wine or would you prefer something stronger?"

Oh, that she could have a glass of wine to relax. Unfortunately out of the question. "No thanks on either. I could use some water."

"Water it is. I'll be right back."

Rachel rested her bent elbow on the table and supported her chin with her palm. She watched several couples twirling around the floor to a country-music waltz and found herself longing to be where they were in forty years. She wanted to still be with Matt, still in love. Still holding on to each other as they had for so long. Growing old and gray together with kids and grandkids to carry on after they were gone. Her fantasy, not his.

Helen returned with a mug of amber draft and a bottle of water that she set before Rachel. "I remembered you mentioned cheese fries, but unfortunately they're all out tonight."

Her appetite had all but disappeared. "Don't worry about it. If I eat anything else, I'll have to unbutton these jeans."

Helen looked toward the pool tables before retaking her seat. "Looks like the boys are having fun."

Rachel glanced over her shoulder to find the judge slapping Matt on the back, both of them laughing as if they didn't have a care in the world. "Jack looks good. You'd never know anything's wrong."

"Except for the memory lapses," she said. "The new medicine has been helping with that, although he still has mood swings now and then. At times he acts as if he despises me."

Rachel couldn't fathom Jack despising anyone, let alone his wife. "He doesn't despise you, Helen. He adores you."

"I used to think so, but lately he's been snapping my head off. Sometimes he gets downright belligerent over the smallest things. I realize that part of it's the disease and part of it's boredom. I know he misses performing weddings even though he swears he doesn't."

"When was the last time he officiated?"

"Last fall. After he was diagnosed, I closed the doors to the chapel. But I can't stand the thought of letting it go."

Rachel could relate. She felt the same way

about the cabin. "Is there anyone who could possibly perform the weddings with Jack assisting for as long as he's able?"

"That would be the best option, and I've actually made a few calls to some folks in Gatlinburg. So far I haven't found a soul who'd be willing to drive all the way out here to perform even weekend weddings."

An idea suddenly occurred to Rachel. A great idea. "What about J.W.? Since he's an attorney, I'd think he'd be authorized to do weddings."

Helen sighed. "I did consider that, but our son is very busy with the family. Our grandson graduates high school this year, and our granddaughter's a freshman. There's a lot going on when you have children that age."

"Would he agree to two weekends a month?"

Helen shook her head. "I doubt it. Apart from his schedule, he's never really approved of our decision to open the chapel."

She couldn't comprehend why anyone would object to that. "Why not?"

"Because he believes that a former esteemed district judge and an economics professor should retire in sunny Florida, play golf and have parties, not dump their resources in a less-than-lucrative wedding chapel."

Rachel couldn't imagine Helen and Jack being anywhere that didn't include mountains. "I'd think he'd be grateful you remained close to home instead of several states away."

"You'd think that, but again, he's never understood why we decided to buy it."

She'd always been curious about that, as well. "Why did you?"

"To be together. When I was still teaching and Jack was still on the bench, we rarely saw each other. This was our dream, to work side by side in an endeavor we both enjoy. It's made our marriage stronger."

That made perfect sense to Rachel. Many people had thought that she and Matt would tire of each other, since they worked together. That had never been a problem before now. "Doesn't J.W. understand the importance of respecting his father's choices under the circumstances?"

Helen twisted her wedding ring around and around her finger. "He doesn't know about the Alzheimer's."

Rachel was stunned. "You haven't told him?"

"Jack asked me not to say anything until it was absolutely necessary. And even if we decided to tell J.W, who knows when we'd have the opportunity to do it face-to-face? I could break the news over the phone, but that's unacceptable as far as I'm concerned."

Rachel felt Helen's despair as keenly as if it were her own. "When did you see them last?"

"It's been months. I invited the family for Easter dinner, but they had a cruise planned for the kids' break. Last Christmas they took a ski trip to Vermont. As far as the weekends go, their calendar is full."

She'd met the Van Alsteens' son only once, and he'd seemed decent enough. A little reserved, but polite and relatively nice. Clearly first impressions weren't always accurate. "That's horrible, Helen. He only lives a little over an hour away."

"It's not that J.W. doesn't care about us, because he does. He phones most Saturdays and he never forgets our birthdays. It's simply an unfortunate fact that children move away and move on with their lives. That's why I cherish what Jack and I have together. It makes our son's absence a little more tolerable because we still have each other."

All the more reason why she was glad

she'd stayed close to her father. All the more reason why she didn't want to raise this baby alone. Making it work with Matt meant more now than ever. "I really do wish you could keep the chapel open. It's always been such an integral part of this community."

"Even if I could find someone to take over the officiating duties, the chapel needs work. The roof needs a few repairs and the whole place needs painting, inside and out. Oh, and the plumbing is a mess."

"Surely you can hire someone around here to take care of all that."

"Jack's as tight as a guy wire when it comes to money," she said. "He always insisted on doing everything himself to save a few dollars. The fees we charge go into the chapel's upkeep, and what's left goes into a college fund for the grandchildren. He's determined to make certain Luke and Mindy have all the money they need for school that he didn't have growing up. Never mind they have a father who does quite well financially."

Jack and Matt were cut from the same cloth. "I'm so sorry, Helen. I just wish I could do something."

"There is something," she said, a thoughtful look on her face. "Tell me when your baby's due."

Rachel was shocked senseless. "How did you know? I haven't even told Matt yet."

"Actually, I only suspected you might be pregnant. You've never been a big eater, so that was the first clue. You also haven't had your usual glass of wine. And the most telling, you kept touching your belly earlier today, and you've been doing it tonight."

She hadn't even been aware of that, and she wondered if perhaps Matt had noticed, too. If he suspected anything, he would have asked. Then again, maybe he didn't want to know. "I'm not sure of the exact due date. I just confirmed it right before we left to come here. I haven't even been to the doctor."

Helen studied her with concern. "You said Matt doesn't know. Is there a reason why you're waiting to tell him?"

So many reasons she could spend the rest of the night reciting. "I'm not sure how well he's going to take it. And the weekend's been going so good so far, I don't want to spoil it with news that might ruin our progress."

"He'll be thrilled, Rachel. What man wouldn't?"

The man she'd married. "I just feel I need

to wait until the right time." When that right time might be still remained to be seen. "Were you worried when you became pregnant so soon after you miscarried?"

"Of course, but not only because I feared losing another baby. I worried that I could be trying to replace my other child. But don't believe that for a minute. Life does go on, and your next child could never be a replacement for the first. That precious little one will take its place in your heart, right beside the son you lost."

"Thank you for putting it in perspective." Rachel summoned all her willpower to keep from giving in to the emotional meltdown that had been threatening all night. Instead, she put on a shaky smile that she hoped didn't look forced. "Since it doesn't appear our boys are coming back anytime soon, what do you say to joining them?"

"I say let's do. I wouldn't mind shooting a game or two and showing them up. Between the two of us, surely we can take them."

"We surely can try."

Before Rachel could get out of her chair, Helen laid a hand on her arm. "Honey, I want you to do me a favor."

"All you have to do is ask."

"Take tonight and find a quiet place in your soul," Helen said. "Forget about all the regrets and should-haves and, above all, the anger. Try to recapture what you once had with your dear husband. Just love Matthew like you'll never have the chance again."

"ARE YOU OKAY TO DRIVE?"

Not at all surprised by the question, Matt stuck the keys into the ignition and turned on the truck. "Did you see me have a beer?"

"No, I didn't. I'm sorry."

He hadn't expected an apology, only her usual doubt. He was mighty pleased she hadn't belabored the point. "Tell you what. If you're worried, you can give me a Breath-alyzer test."

She snapped her fingers. "Darn. I didn't bring one."

"Not a problem. We'll improvise."

Before she had a chance to protest, he leaned over and kissed her thoroughly. Kissed her until he almost asked if they could take this little test into the backseat. But he didn't want to push his luck.

"Are you satisfied I'm okay to drive?" he asked after he pulled back.

She cleared her throat. "I'm convinced. I

was about to ask you to turn on the heater, but I'm not sure that's necessary."

He grinned. "Just think of me as your own personal heater."

He was about to kiss her again when his cell started ringing. He took the phone out of his pocket and offered it to Rachel. "See who it is. If it's Chase, I'll take it."

She looked at it for a second and frowned. "It's Helen."

He almost took the cell back in case it was bad news, but he didn't want to borrow trouble. "Go ahead and talk to her."

"Hi, Helen." After a few seconds, she said, "We had a great time, too." Another bout of silence passed before Rachel laughed like she'd heard a good joke. "I'll tell him. Have a nice night and I'll stop by before we leave on Monday."

He didn't like being reminded they had to go home in a day's time. "What's so funny?"

Rachel handed him the phone back. "Helen said she wants a rematch because she's sure you and Jack cheated. She also said Jack was happier tonight than she's seen him in a long time and to thank you for that."

He pocketed the phone and shrugged. "I

didn't do anything out of the ordinary. I always play pool with the judge."

"That's the point. You didn't treat him any differently and Helen appreciates that. So do I."

"Not a problem." Finally he'd done something right without even trying. "What did you two talk about while we were playing pool?"

"Just general stuff. She did tell me that J.W. doesn't know about Jack's illness."

He found that weird. "Why not?"

"Jack doesn't want him to know yet. And worse, Helen says he hasn't visited in months. She tried to defend him by saying they're busy with the kids, but I frankly don't buy that excuse. Jack and Helen are getting up there in years. He should come around more often while he has the chance."

"I agree, but people tend to get wrapped up in their own lives and overlook the important things." He'd been guilty of that. "I'm sure once J.W. knows, he'll make the time."

"True, but each moment with Jack is precious, and according to Helen, he's been depressed since he had to stop officiating weddings. Apparently Helen can't find anyone to take over for him, not to mention the chapel's in a state of disrepair. I can't imagine the place being closed down for good after all these years."

Neither could Matt. Not the place where it had all begun for the two of them. That would signify an end of an era, and he couldn't accept that it might somehow be an omen of the future of their marriage. "You know, I have an idea. Why don't we go to the chapel tomorrow and see what we can do to clean the place up?" Not only would they be helping friends, he'd be buying some more time with his wife. Maybe even an extra day.

"It's not just cleanup, Matt," she said. "It's going to require some painting and plumbing repair and who knows what else."

"Then we'll call a few people to help. This community has always banded together and they'll be more than happy to do it for Helen and Jack."

Rachel sat quietly for a few moments as if digesting his words. "You're right. If we make a few calls, we can have a whole slew of people at the chapel after lunch. Maybe not a slew, but enough to make a dent in the repairs. As soon as we get back to the cabin, I can call a few women to make some potluck dishes and you can call the men to bring paint and tools."

That wasn't what he had in mind to do when he got back to the cabin. "You're forgetting it's almost midnight and too late to start organizing tonight."

She screwed up her face into a frown. "Most of the people I'll be calling were in the rec hall tonight."

"Yeah, and most of those people left hours ago. If you recall, we closed the place down. Harry and Barb Sanders were the only people left, and they were waiting on us so they could lock up."

"You're right. We can start calling first thing in the morning and catch people before they leave for church." She grinned. "You're brilliant, Matthew Benjamin."

"And you're cold," he said when he noticed she was chafing her arms. Another brilliant idea hit him. He flipped up the console separating the split-bench seats and patted the space beside him. "Why don't you slide over here and sit next to me?"

She looked at him as if he'd grown a second nose. "Are you serious?"

"Yeah, I am. You used to do it without thinking."

"Yes, when I was still in my teens. In fact, I can't even remember the last time I sat beside you."

Too long, as far as he was concerned. "I'm pretty sure there's no rule that states two people in their thirties can't sit side by side, so we won't be breaking any laws. Now, if I told you to get naked and get over here, that would be cause for our arrest, although it would be mighty fun." And that last comment could be cause for her to climb out of the truck and hoof it back to the cabin.

"Okay."

Just like that, without further argument or even a minor objection to his "naked" talk, she slid right next to him and secured the seat belt. He shoved the gearshift into First, inadvertently brushing the side of her leg. With three more gears to go, he figured she'd probably move so it wouldn't happen again. Oddly, she didn't, and that gave him enough courage to rest his right hand on her thigh as they hit the main road to home.

When Rachel circled her arms around his arm and leaned her head against his shoulder, he couldn't have been more pleased. And halfway back to the cabin, when she brushed a kiss across his neck, he couldn't have been more turned on. He rubbed his thumb along the inside of her leg in a slow, rhythmic motion. She shifted a little, leading him to believe she wasn't completely unaffected by his touch.

Damn if he didn't feel like a kid again. A jacked-up teenager who wanted to pull off onto a back road and engage in some heavy petting. But they had less than a mile to go and a cabin complete with a big bed at their disposal. If his luck held out, maybe they'd use that bed for something other than sleeping.

As soon as he pulled into the drive and shut down the truck, he got out of the cab, Rachel sliding out after him. After he closed the door, she immediately walked straight into his arms, where they kissed some more. He really wanted to pick her up and carry her into the bedroom, but he remembered her accusation that he used sex to smooth over their problems. That led him to consider another plan, one that involved some romance. A plan that would prove he wasn't a totally oversexed Neanderthal, although throwing her over his shoulder wasn't totally out of the question.

Stick to the plan, he told himself as they

walked arm in arm toward the house. When they reached the porch, he let her go. "Wait here."

"Matt, I'm freezing."

She wouldn't be for long. "Hang on. I'll be right back."

He walked inside and grabbed a sweater from the hook hanging on the wall. Then he turned and tossed it to her through the open door. "Put this on and don't move."

She opened her mouth, but he didn't hang around to hear what she had to say. Instead, he strode to the entertainment center, located the appropriate CD and slid it into the player. It took a little longer to adjust the surround sound to play through the outdoor speakers, but he was banking on her considering it worth the wait.

He arrived on the porch to find Rachel leaning against the railing, hugging her arms close to her body. He wouldn't be surprised if her teeth started chattering. Nothing he couldn't remedy with the plan.

He unfolded her arms, took her hands and tugged her close. "Since we didn't dance tonight, I thought we might as well do it now."

She wrapped her arms around his waist

and smiled up at him. "Are you trying to seduce me?"

Well, yeah. "I'm trying to be romantic.
Any objections?"

"Not as long as you keep me warm."

"I can do that." He'd gladly keep her warm
and safe and well loved, if she let him.

They swayed to one of her favorite songs,
a country-music ballad that talked about closing out the world because the only thing that
mattered was being with someone you loved.
He'd never paid much attention to the lyrics
before that moment, but then, he'd been at
fault for not paying enough attention to her
and what she needed. That ended right here,
right now. He vowed to do better by her every
day and night from this point forward…as
long as she gave him another chance.

She laid her head against his chest while
he pressed his palms against her back. And
when she lifted her face, he angled his head
and kissed her again. They stood that way for
a long while, kissing as if they had traveled
back to a time when that had been enough. It
might have to be enough. It could be all she
was willing to give him tonight.

She pulled back and stared at him, a

dreamy kind of look in her eyes that he knew all too well. "Let's go to bed."

He also knew better than to presume anything. "To sleep?"

"No."

Hot damn. "Then I don't have to toss a coin to see who gets what bed?"

"You only have to get me to our bed, unless you want to have your extremely wicked way with me right here on the porch."

"Not a bad idea, except for the possibility of splinters. We'll try that some other time." As much as he wanted to grab her hand and head toward the bedroom at a dead run, he had an important question to pose. "If we do this, no regrets in the morning?"

She sighed. "Helen said something to me tonight that made sense. She told me sometimes it's best to forget all the garbage and make love like there's no tomorrow, at least for one night."

She might not be proposing "bandage" sex, but he wondered if this could be goodbye sex. Even if it turned out it wasn't the last time they made love, he planned to love her like it was. "Helen's a wise woman."

"Yes, she is."

Without another word, he took her by the

hand and led her inside, releasing her only long enough to lock the door. He wasn't going to rush this—the reason he took his time getting to their destination, stopping before they reached the hall to give her another kiss and then another before they entered the bedroom.

When he paused by the bed and tugged her into his arms, she wrested herself away and took a step back. "Don't go anywhere."

The only place he'd be heading was crazy from need. "Where are you going?"

She failed to answer him as she walked to the bureau, opened the drawer and took out something she concealed in her arms. He could only tell it was black, and that sent his imagination straight into overdrive. When she passed him, he tried to catch her arm to satisfy his curiosity. She managed to evade him and backed into the bathroom. "Have a little patience, Matthew. You won't be sorry."

But he might be dead from a lack of oxygen in his primary brain, since all the blood had pooled below his belt. After she closed the door, he tugged off his boots and socks and set them on the floor at the end of the bed. He tackled the buttons on his shirt and practically ripped them off when they didn't want to cooperate. He managed to strip out of his jeans and underwear in record time and made a three-pointer when he hurled his clothes into the corner chair.

Now, to cover up or not to cover up. He picked not. After raking back the comforter and sheets, he sat on the edge of the mattress and waited. And waited.

What in the hell was she doing? Maybe that black thing she'd pulled out of the drawer happened to be a full-body wet suit. Getting that off her could be a challenge, but he was a resourceful kind of guy. And he was obviously losing his ever-lovin' mind. A wet suit?

Not even close to a wet suit was his first thought when Rachel came out of the bathroom wearing a short, lacy gown that barely covered her birthday suit. His second thought—what had he done right in his life to deserve a beautiful woman like her?

She turned in a circle and smiled. "Tell me what you think."

His voice momentarily went the way of the wind with his mind. "Did you bring that with you?"

"You don't remember giving me this two years ago for our anniversary? Unfortunately, you were so impatient that night, I never had a chance to put it on. It's been in the drawer ever since."

Oh, yeah. He remembered that night. He'd been in such an all-fired hurry they'd never made it to the bedroom. Another sofa night.

He caught both her hands and brought her between his parted knees. "I'm going to be real patient. I'm going to let you leave that on so I can enjoy the sight. For a few more minutes anyway."

He made good on that promise as he brought her down onto the bed in his arms, not bothering to turn down the light. That was okay. He wanted her to be able to see every detail when they made love. On that thought, he grabbed both pillows and propped them beneath her head, allowing her a clear field of vision.

He started with a light kiss on her lips, then lowered the straps and kissed her shoulders. He kept going, taking the barely-there scrap of lace with him as he worked his way down, lingering a little while at her breasts. After he pulled the gown to her waist, he rested his chin on her sternum and looked up at her. "Do you remember the first time I did this?"

She drew in a ragged breath. "Yes. The

second night of our honeymoon. I was scared to death."

"You were shaking, like you are now." He moved lower and traced a line from her throat to her navel with a fingertip. "Believe it or not, I was scared, too."

"Really?"

"I was scared I might hurt you." He had the means to hurt her now with the truth she'd been seeking for months. He refused to think about that.

"You definitely didn't hurt me," she said, sounding winded. "I'd never felt that way before."

"I'm still surprised you let me that first time."

"I trusted you, Matt."

"Do you still trust me?"

She hesitated a little longer than he would have liked before she said, "Yes."

That was all he needed to hear. He slipped the gown completely away and tossed it aside, then lifted her leg and brushed a kiss on the inside of her thigh. They'd learned a lot about each other through the years, initially by reading the signals until they'd finally become comfortable enough to talk about it.

No words passed between them tonight. No words were necessary. He knew what she liked. He'd learned how to use his touch, his mouth, to give her the kind of pleasure that came with this ultimate intimacy. He knew when to up the ante until she shifted restlessly against the impending climax, as she was doing now. He knew when to let up and wait while she rode every wave.

He kissed his way back up her body, her skin damp beneath his. Before they went any further, he still felt the need to ask the question that he'd forgotten to ask the last time they'd made love. The question that had set her off like a firecracker. "Do we need to worry about—"

"Pregnancy? Trust me, that's not an issue."

Fortunately she didn't sound angry. And he did trust her. A good thing, because he wasn't sure he could stop now, even if he wanted to. He didn't want to.

He twined her fingers with his and lifted her arms above her head. Then he eased inside her and watched her satisfied smile come into view. Take it slowly, he kept telling himself. Easy does it. He called on all his endurance to make it last. He was winning the battle until Rachel let go of his hands, planted her palms on his back and rolled, taking him with her. She rose above him and claimed complete control, leaving him happily defenseless. And from the victorious look on her face, she damn well knew it, too.

Her power play was such a turn-on, he wasn't sure how much longer he could hang on. And with one wicked twist of her hips, he let go as he'd never let go before.

After a time, she stretched out and rested her head against his pounding heart that refused to immediately return to a normal rhythm. They remained that way for several minutes, holding each other in the silent room.

When his body calmed and his thoughts came back into focus, he brought his lips to her ear to say the words he needed to say. Words he hadn't said often enough. "I love you, baby."

He held his breath and waited, worried she might not return the favor. More worried she no longer felt the same.

Then she opened her dark eyes and gave him the prettiest smile. "I love you, too."

CHAPTER ELEVEN

As Matt steered the truck up the steep drive, Rachel felt as if the years had done an about-face. Not only were they approaching the place where their life as a married couple had begun, she believed they were close to establishing a new beginning. Last night had been incredible and in some ways miraculous. Her husband still loved her, and he'd told her so, and she'd told him. He'd also shown her how much he cared about her in ways that would make a statue blush. Thinking back on those moments gave her a sense of euphoria, made her want to stay at the cabin indefinitely, where their world seemed to right itself. Yet that wasn't reality. Eventually they would have to return home, hopefully with their marriage intact.

Matt shoved the truck into Park and turned off the ignition. "It might take more than a day to fix this place," Matt said.

When Rachel brought her attention to the picturesque chapel bathed in early-morning light and saw the peeling paint on the facade and overgrown flower beds crowded with weeds, she had to agree. "Nothing a little yard cleanup and fresh paint won't cure."

"But that's just the outside," he said. "No telling what we'll find inside."

True, but if the phone call she'd made that morning worked, they should have a few people to assist them. "Did Brody say what time he was meeting us to let us in?"

"He left the key under the mat by the front door."

Not her idea of adequate security, but then Wayhurst wasn't known for a high crime rate. Basically, it wasn't known at all outside Tennessee. That made the small community all the more appealing.

"Let's get this show on the road." She grabbed the handle to open the door, yet Matt failed to move. He continued to stare out the windshield, his brows drawn down in concentration. "Matt, are you coming?"

He seemed startled by the question. "What?"

"I thought we should get a head start, since I don't expect any volunteers until after lunch."

"Okay."

His lack of enthusiasm flabbergasted her. Something was out of kilter. "What's wrong?"

He draped an arm over the wheel and sighed. "Chase called about Dad around 4:00 a.m."

She feared the worst might have happened. If so, he'd never forgive himself. "I didn't even hear your phone ring."

"You were pretty out of it."

Thanks to their unbelievable lovemaking. "What did he say?"

"He told me they took Ben to the hospital for treatment last night, but he's okay and back at the jail. I had Chase put him on the phone, just to be sure."

"And you felt reassured after you spoke with him?"

"Yeah, I did. He sounded more coherent than he has in years. I thought he was going to be mad, but he wasn't. He actually thanked me, and then he apologized and told me things would be different from now on."

Good news, as far as Rachel was concerned. "That should make you very happy."

"He's said the same thing before, and he's

fallen off the wagon more times than I can count. I hope he follows through this time."

His justifiable concern for his father had put a damper on the day. "Matt, if you feel like you need to be with him, we can leave now."

"He's where he needs to be." He reached over and took her hand. "And so am I."

He sounded sad and not quite convincing. "But you hate it."

"I hate what he's done to his life," he said. "I hate it had to come to this before he gets the help he needs. *If* he gets the help. And I really hate that he stopped being a good father after my mom died. I've missed the dad who used to take me fishing and taught me how to throw a curveball more than he'll ever know."

She scooted over and kissed his cheek. "He can be that father again, Matt. I know it's hard to hope, but don't give up on him yet."

"I'll try." He patted her thigh. "Are you ready to do some painting?"

She planned to avoid painting at all costs due to the fumes. "I'm going to leave that to you and whoever else wants to tackle it. I'm like a race-car driver with a paintbrush."

"But you painted those horses on the walls

in the…" His gaze briefly faltered. "At the house."

He still couldn't say *nursery,* a reminder of what they still had to discuss. "I used stencils and craft paint." Nontoxic paint because she'd been pregnant. "That's a lot different from taking on an entire wall. I'm going to polish the pews and floors and clean whatever needs cleaning."

"Guess we won't know that until we get inside. Let's do this."

Shades of the past echoed in Matt's words. And when she walked into that small chapel, that past landed on Rachel's heart. Everything looked much the same as the day they'd entered to join together for life, only a little more aged. The red runner, now slightly faded, pointed the way to the arch where Jack had stood. And to the right was the piano that Helen always played to announce the bride's entrance.

She immediately walked to that piano, took a seat at the bench and raised the cover to expose the keys. She hadn't played in ages, yet she couldn't resist trying. Pachelbel's Canon immediately came to mind, a fitting piece for a wedding chapel. The same music Helen had played that long-ago day. She started and stopped twice, yet it didn't take long for it all to come back to her as she filled the silence with meaningful music that brought back so many good memories.

"Sounds good."

She hadn't noticed Matt had come in. She glanced up to see him standing in the doorway, a bucket full of cleaning supplies in one hand and a toolbox in the other.

When he came up behind her and peered over her shoulder, she lost all concentration and gave up. "Keep going," he said.

"I can't do it with you staring at me." She lowered the cover and turned around on the bench to face him. "Besides, I'm really rusty."

He set the bucket down at her feet. "You could've fooled me. You should play more often."

"I don't have a piano readily available, unless you want to buy me one for my birthday next month."

"I had something else in mind for your birthday, but I'm not opposed to reconsidering. Where do you want me to have it delivered?"

She realized he was baiting her into saying she was coming home, a step she wasn't quite ready to take. "Never mind. If I want to play, I can always do that on my old piano at Dad's."

"Guess that's more convenient anyway." He didn't try to disguise the disappointment in his expression and voice.

She hopped up from the bench and put on a cheerful face. "Time to get to work if we want to be finished in time to surprise Jack and Helen today. I'll start with the pews."

"I'll check out the plumbing."

Matt looked so dejected, Rachel felt the need to throw him a lifeline. "I think a piano would look nice in the corner of the great room, in that empty space by the picture window."

She expected a happier look on his face, but that wasn't the case. "Guess we should hold off on where to put the piano until you decide if you still have a place there."

She chalked up his mood to his dad's problems and being in an atmosphere with so many reminders of what they'd once had. Not to mention the realization they still had a lot of relationship territory to cover. They couldn't do that until they finished this particular project.

The sound of a truck rattling up the drive drew Rachel to one of the small windows cut in the wooden door. And behind that truck a lengthy procession of vehicles, from sedans to SUVs. "Matt, come here."

He joined her a few seconds later and looked out the second window. "I'll be damned. Someone called out the guard."

"I called Rita and she called out the guard."

She walked outside at the same time Brody Engle emerged from the truck and retrieved a ladder from the bed. Then came Rita carrying two casserole dishes, followed by her husband, LeRoy, lugging a folding table. She had her beehive bound in a floral cotton scarf and wore a baggy paint-spattered shirt that contrasted with the heavy bejeweled chains draped around her neck and the gaudy earrings hanging from her lobes. "LeRoy, put that table inside the foyer," she barked out as she walked right up to Rachel. "Happy morning to you, sugar."

Rachel looked behind her at the stream of citizens, both older and younger, walking toward the chapel carrying food and supplies. "Wow! I had no idea you'd find this many people to help."

She handed Rachel a casserole. "Promise the folks a good meal and a good cause, they'll show up."

"But I wasn't expecting anyone until after church."

Rita frowned. "Sugar, you can't be a Good Samaritan sitting in a sanctuary."

A valid point. "Thank you, Rita. Helen and Jack are going to appreciate your generosity."

"Jack maybe, but not Helen. She still hasn't forgiven me for that little incident five years ago."

She couldn't deny her curiosity, but she didn't have time for Rita's inevitable lengthy explanation. "Let's go put these in the kitchen and decide where we need to start first."

After handing off the other casserole to a passerby, Rita spun around and let go an ear-piercing whistle. "Right this way, troops!"

Rachel couldn't help but laugh over the woman's antics. You didn't need a megaphone when you had Rita. She experienced a sudden bout of giddiness, a sheer sense of joy. She had a feeling this was going to be a good day. A great day. Maybe the best day she'd had in months.

MATT HAD JUST SECURED the final shingle when he heard, "Hey, sexy guy on the roof. Do you want some lemonade?"

He looked down to see Rachel standing at the corner of the chapel, holding a red plastic glass. Stray strands of hair had escaped her messy ponytail, framing her face that was dotted with smudges of dirt. Her light pink T-shirt didn't look much better, yet she still looked as good as if she'd been wearing pearls and a prom dress. But then, she'd always worn dishevelment well.

He backed down the ladder and joined her at the side of the chapel, away from the people planting flowers in the beds. "Thanks," he said as he took the drink and downed it. "Is everything finished?"

"Aside from what's left of the landscaping, yes. I've been helping out with that most of the day."

"That's fairly obvious," he said as he pulled a piece of grass from her hair.

"You should take a look inside. Everything's beautiful."

So was his wife. He couldn't recall the last time he'd seen that kind of excitement in her dark eyes. Come to think of it, he could. Around 6:00 a.m. this morning when they'd made love for the third time. "It's a good thing, since we're running out of daylight."

"I still can't believe we got it all done," she said. "Everything's fresh and painted, including the kitchen and reception area in the back. I was just sure they wouldn't get that finished. The floors are polished, and oh, the man who owns the hardware store in Townsend, I think his name is Frank, brought all new plumbing fixtures and new toilets."

"I know," he said. "I helped install them before I started on the roof patching."

"Anyway," she continued, "Frank knows someone named Buster who brought a crew to retile the kitchen counters and add a backsplash. And Buster knows an appliance guy who replaced the stove. It's not new, but it's bigger and better than the old one and—"

He cut off her words with a kiss. A thorough kiss that didn't last nearly long enough before Rachel put a halt to it. "What was that for?"

"Just trying to shut you up so you could catch a breath."

"Sorry, but you didn't exactly aid my respiration." She wrapped her arms around his waist. "I'm veritably panting."

"And I'm feeling a little bit dirty at the moment." In more ways than one.

"Could I interest you in a—"

"Shower when we get home?"

She gave him a sour look. "Now look who's making assumptions."

He'd probably blown the deal because he couldn't keep his enthusiastic libido in check. "I'm just saying since we both could use one, we might as well do it together."

She draped her arms around his neck. "Before you so rudely interrupted me, I was about to suggest we take a bath together in that whirlpool tub we rarely use."

"I'm not normally a bath kind of guy, but I could make a few concessions. Should I bring my rubber ducky?"

She grinned. "It wouldn't be a party without it."

This time she kissed him as if she meant it, right there where anyone could come upon them acting as though they'd taken leave of their senses.

"You two stop swapping gum and get up to the front. The Van Alsteens are on their way."

The high-pitched voice was about as irritating as hot pavement on the soles of your feet. It motivated Rachel to practically bolt from his arms and move back. "We'll be right there, Rita," she said.

Matt aimed a stern look at Rita that sent the infuriating woman scrambling around the corner before turning back to his wife. "We'll finish this later."

"Yes, we will."

With their arms around each other, they strolled to the front of the chapel to take their place in one of the lines formed on either side of the walkway. Matt chose a spot closest to the parking lot so he could get a good view of the road.

"Do you think they'll be surprised?" Rachel asked.

He winked. "Am I the world's greatest lover?"

"I'm serious, Matt. What if someone tipped them off?"

He knew of only one person who'd do that, and he'd sworn him to secrecy. "Relax. They won't know a thing until they get here."

And that was about to happen, Matt realized when he saw the black SUV pull into the drive. Dusk had settled in, but Helen, who exited first, made up for the dim light with a sun-bright expression. Jack climbed out next, followed by a younger version of the judge, only with brown hair, as well as an attractive blonde and a teenage boy and girl.

Rachel looked at Matt with awe. "That's J.W. and his family."

"Yeah, I know."

"But how did they know?"

"I called him this morning when you were in the shower. I told J.W. what we were planning, and I asked him to keep Jack and Helen occupied."

"You did a good thing, Matthew Boyd." She suddenly looked a little worried. "Did you tell him about—"

"The Alzheimer's? No. It wasn't my place."

"So he came on his own?"

"Yep, he came on his own—after he mentioned his golf game and I told him I thought his parents might be a little more important than honing his swing."

Rachel gave him a squeeze. "Good. He needs to understand the importance of spending time with his folks."

As Helen approached, she held out her arms to Rachel. "What have you done, my darling girl?"

Rachel hugged her hard. "Matt and I decided the place needed a little fixing up. I called Rita this morning, and she called everyone in eastern Tennessee. The crew's been at it all day, and I think you'll be pleased with the results."

Helen doled out a quick hug to Matt. "The two of you are gems. I can't tell you how much this means to us. And I take it you summoned my son, too?"

"Matt did," Rachel said. "J.W. was more than willing to help us out with the secret."

"And a fine secret it is," Helen added. "Let me pry Jack away from Brody and gather the kids for the tour. I can't wait to see what you've done inside."

"You won't believe it," Rachel said as she walked away with Helen.

Matt waited outside with a few stragglers while the rest of the masses filed in behind the honorary couple and their offspring. He'd been happy to help out with the renovations, but the chapel reminded him that his marriage also needed a major restoration.

A few minutes later, when Jack emerged through the double doors, Rita began clapping her hands. And when she couldn't get anyone's attention, she let go that godawful whistle. "Listen up, people!" she shouted, even though the crowd had begun to quiet down. Then again, she might have shattered their eardrums. "Jack has a few things to say."

Rachel returned to Matt's side and took his hand. "I hope he makes it through this okay."

"He'll do well. I can feel it in my gut."

With the outdoor lights as his backdrop, Jack looked every bit the stately judge as he surveyed the crowd, his family gathered around him. "First of all, Helen and I would like to thank you all for this remarkable surprise. However, Helen will now expect you to come do the same to our hall bathroom."

He waited for the chuckles to subside before he began again. "Seriously, this sense of community is the reason why we've enjoyed living in Wayhurst for these last twenty or so years. We truly appreciate your support, and we will need that support in the days to come."

He glanced at Helen, who hooked her arm in his. After a time, he cleared his throat and streaked a hand through his silver hair. "I spent my entire career seeking the truth, only to conceal my own out of fear and probably a little pride. I started to realize that no matter how bad that truth might be, the people who care about you deserve to know."

Rachel tightened her grip on Matt's hand

when Jack paused to draw in a deep breath. "A few months ago I went to the doctor because I was suffering from what we like to call Old-Timer's disease. Unfortunately, it's the real deal." When a collective gasp rose from the crowd, he raised his hand to silence them. "As bad as having this Alzheimer's might seem, I can think of worse things, like never having the honor of knowing all of you. Or never having the opportunity to help young people start their lives together." He looked down at Helen. "Definitely never having known the love of a woman who's just this side of sainthood."

Helen elbowed him and smiled. "That's me all over. Saint Helen."

Jack kissed her cheek before returning his attention to the volunteers. "So if you happen to see me on the street and I forget your name, just remember it's the disease. Or it could be that I borrowed your power tools and forgot where I put them."

Again, more laughter, but Matt noticed it was quieter this time.

"And in closing," he continued, "the road ahead will be much tougher on my Helen than it will be on me, so I humbly ask of you to look after her when I'm not able. She's the best thing that's ever happened to me."

He leaned over and gave Helen another kiss, this time a light one on the lips, before he straightened and smiled. "Now let's eat."

Matt's respect for the judge rose even higher, if that was possible. More important, his words about telling the truth had really hit home. But the truth he still concealed could obliterate the bond he and Rachel had begun to build over the past two days.

He glanced at his wife to find tears trickling down her cheeks. "It's okay," he told her. "They have a strong marriage and they'll get through this together." He wished he could say the same for his own marriage.

Rachel swiped the moisture from her face with her fingertips. "It just makes me so sad to think he won't be the same the next time we see him."

Question was, would there be a next time? Matt had every intention of finding out.

THEY RODE HOME in silence, and it continued even after they entered the cabin. Rachel understood why Matt didn't feel like talking. She wasn't much in the mood for conversation, either. As satisfying as the day had been, it had inadvertently ended with the realization that life's burdens were beyond control, and time was a treasured commodity.

She followed Matt into the bedroom, hoping to douse the sadness with the promised soak in the tub. But when he dropped onto the edge of the mattress and lowered his head, she began to doubt that both would happen anytime soon.

Rachel sat beside him and laid a hand on his back. "Tough end to a good day, huh?"

"I've had worse endings. The day you walked out comes to mind."

Both his words and his acid tone stung. "Did I do something else today to upset you?"

He forked both hands through his already ruffled hair. "I just need to know what comes next. Do we start packing up our stuff or leave it? And when we go back to Placid, do we return to the way things were, with you at your dad's place and me in the house we built together?"

"I honestly don't know how I feel about anything right now." And she didn't, aside from the fact she wanted desperately to mend their marriage. She couldn't do that if he didn't cooperate.

He leveled his gaze on hers. "What about

last night? Did you make love with me because you wanted me, or was it only because I happened to be available to scratch your itch?"

That hurt more than he could ever know. "I told you I love you, and I meant it. But that doesn't make it all better."

"No kidding."

She hated his sarcasm, the abject pain in his blue eyes. "I was foolish to believe we could settle everything in a weekend."

"I don't care if it takes all damn night. Let's settle it now. Tell me what you want, Rachel. Tell me what I have to do to make it better. I swear to God I'll try."

She considered several requests, but chose the easiest one first. "You can go with me to the grief-counseling sessions."

His scowl told her she'd already lost round one. "I'm going to have my hands full trying to convince my dad to go to AA meetings. I might even have to drag him there, kicking and screaming."

"I understand the importance of that, but isn't your own mental well-being just as important? If you don't come to terms with your own grief, you might end up needing those AA meetings, too."

His expression went cold, unforgiving. "I don't need to drink to deal with a damn thing. I haven't had a drop the whole time we've been here, in case you haven't noticed. And, lady, if I've ever had cause to tip a few back, this state of limbo you've been keeping me in is a mighty good reason."

His continued denial worried her almost as much as his response to her next appeal. "Okay, if you want to know what I really need, it's another baby. Are you on board with that?"

"A lot of couples decide not to have kids and they do fine."

That was the first time he'd brought up that argument against procreating. "Why are you so afraid of being a father? You definitely have the skills to succeed. I remember the day Sam was trying to learn how to put a diaper on Jamie. You told him it wasn't rocket science and had it accomplished in seconds. You're great with all our friends' kids."

"The operative words are *friends' kids*," he said. "I don't have complete responsibility for their well-being."

"Look, I know you had that responsibility growing up when you had to parent your father. But it would be different with our own children."

"I'd probably screw that up, too."

Now they were getting to the crux of the matter. "You didn't screw up your dad. He did that all by himself."

He studied her for a long moment, questions in his eyes. "Aren't you even the least bit afraid of the risk you might be taking with another pregnancy?"

"Only a slight risk, according to my doctor. And yes, it's still scary, but not scary enough give up on trying again. I refuse to let fear paralyze me and prevent me from living."

He pushed himself off the bed and began to pace, hands laced together behind his neck. "You don't understand what it was like for me the morning you gave birth, Rachel. If you did, you wouldn't ask me to go through it again."

"How can I understand when you won't talk to me about it?"

He stopped at the French doors and kept his back to her. "Believe me, you don't want to know what really happened. If you did, you'd hate me."

Alarms rang out in her head, while her heart told her to let it be. But she couldn't do that. "I want to know, Matt. I *have* to know. You owe me that much."

He turned toward her, looking resigned. "Fine. I'll tell you the whole truth. I'll despise every minute of it, but I'll lay it all out on the line."

She wanted to ask him to sit beside her again, to hold her in case the truth was too much to handle. Yet something in his demeanor and tone told her she might not want him near her when all was said and done. "I'm ready."

He dropped into the chair and leaned back to stare at the ceiling. "Do you remember when I told you the medevac helicopter had been delayed?"

"Vaguely. That's why they decided to deliver the baby at County, because he was in trouble."

He finally met her gaze. "You were in more trouble. That's why they asked me to decide what came next. Either deliver the baby at County immediately to prevent the eclampsia from worsening or wait at least twenty more minutes to transfer you both to Jackson where they were better equipped to handle a premature infant."

Her head began to spin as she tried to sort

through the admission. "What are you saying, Matt?"

"I'm saying I chose to save you."

CHAPTER TWELVE

"YOU BASTARD."

He wasn't surprised by the venom in her voice, but he hadn't prepared for the unmistakable loathing in her eyes. "I know you're furious, but—"

"Can you blame me? You promised me, Matt. You promised you'd save our son no matter what."

He wasn't getting through to her, and worse, he wasn't sure he ever would. "I did the only thing I could do, Rachel. I had only a matter of minutes to decide." Both the longest and shortest minutes of his life.

She fisted her hand against her chest as tears streamed down her cheeks. "Oh, God. If you'd only waited for the helicopter, waited twenty more minutes, my baby might still be alive."

"But you might not be, and I couldn't take

that chance. I couldn't stand the thought of losing you." He'd probably lost her anyway.

When her face went pale and she began to sway, he rushed to her side to take her arm, only to have her yank out of his grasp. "Don't...touch...me."

He held his hands up, palms forward, and backed away. "Fine. Just sit down and let me get you some water."

"I don't want any water." She claimed a place on the edge of the bed, her shoulders slumped as if all the energy had seeped out of her. "I want to know how you could have gone all these months without telling me the truth. I want to know what gave you the right to decide the fate of our child without consulting me."

She evidently had no recollection of how sick she'd been. "You were sedated and couldn't give consent. The responsibility fell on me."

Her laugh was caustic, cutting. "And we both know how much you adore responsibility. Now that I think about it, the decision was probably easy for you. You never really wanted a baby in the first place."

She might as well have punched him in the gut. He'd like to think her anger was doing the talking. That she really didn't believe he would be that coldhearted. "Easy? It was the worst thing I've ever been through in my life. If you only knew…" He just couldn't go there right now. If he did, he might lose it.

"Knew what, Matthew?"

"Since that day, I've been second-guessing myself for months. Should I have taken you to Jackson myself when we first thought you were in labor? Should I have prayed harder? Should I have been a better husband? A better son? A better person? I began to realize that no matter what I did or didn't do, time wasn't on our side that day."

"And it's time for you to go." She grabbed his duffel from the bureau and hurled it at him. "I can't deal with this right now. I can't even look at you. I just want you to leave me alone."

He'd give her space tonight and hope that she'd calm down enough to talk about it again tomorrow. Maybe she'd find some way to understand, even if she couldn't forgive him. "Fine. I'll see you in the morning."

"I want you gone first thing in the morning."

"I'm not leaving you here without the means to get back to Placid."

"I'll find my way home."

But not her way back to him. He came to his feet, bag in hand, his hope in shambles. "You have to give me another chance, baby."

She raised her chin and sent him a determined look. "I don't have to do anything, Matthew. You've already told me all I need to know."

And just as he'd predicted, she hated him for it.

As he turned to go, Rachel called him back. He faced her to discover she was removing her wedding band with shaking fingers. Then she walked over and handed him the ring she'd worn for almost fourteen years. "I don't want this anymore."

Meaning she didn't want him. Meaning that everything they'd accomplished this weekend, every word they'd said, every moment they'd made love, had been for naught.

Without another word, he left the master bedroom and bypassed the guest room on his way to the den, a crushing weight in his chest. He couldn't stay in this cabin one more minute now that the good memories had been tainted by the bad. Before he left, he found a pen and paper on the kitchen island and jotted down a few parting thoughts to his wife.

Then he twisted the front-door key off his key ring, laid it on the note and said a silent send-off to their shared past one last time. If Rachel didn't come around, he'd be forced to say goodbye to their future, once and for all.

AFTER A VIRTUALLY sleepless night, Rachel had awoken that morning to find Matt gone. Aside from the key and note he'd left behind, it was as if he'd never been there and all the moments they'd spent together had only been an illusion. Yet the cold, hard truth had been real and so was the constant ache in her heart.

Several hours ago, she'd packed her bag and almost called Helen to request a ride to Knoxville to pick up a rental car. But she'd been too ashamed to admit that Helen's good advice had gone to waste. Instead, she'd thrown herself on Rita Kendrick's mercy. During the hour drive, Rita had launched into a lengthy diatribe on how Helen had "stolen" her butter-beans recipe for inclusion in the church cookbook. Fortunately, the women had made up the evening before. She wished she could say the same for her and Matt.

Though her eardrums had suffered for it, the conversation had kept her mind off her troubles. Yet the moment she'd hit the interstate for her return home, Matt's written words kept rolling through her mind.

The cabin's yours, and all that's in it. No matter what happens from this point forward, whether you find a way to forgive me or not, I still love you. I always will. M

She still loved him, too. But she didn't know if she could forgive him, even after seven hours of contemplation.

She pulled into the drive at the guesthouse at half past six, bone weary and still worried over the decision she'd made. A hot meal, a warm bath and a good book would help ease some of her suffering, at least until she climbed into bed alone.

She unlocked the door, entered the living room...and nearly jumped out of her skin when she saw the figure seated in the chair next to the floor lamp she'd left on. Her palm immediately came to rest on her hammering heart that slowed only when she identified the mystery intruder. "You almost scared me to death, Dad."

He stood. "I'm sorry, princess. I should have met you at the car when I saw you drive up."

She set her purse and keys on the coffee table and her overnight bag on the floor. "How did you know I'd be here?"

"Zelda informed me you've been living here for several weeks," he said as he stood. "And Matthew called me this morning."

She resented her father's domestic spy. She resented her husband's interference and his probable attempt to win her father over to his side. "What did he say?"

He adjusted his tie, a sure sign of discomfort, before he slipped his hands into his pockets. "He said very little other than he expected you to return this evening and requested I make certain you're all right. Are you all right?"

"No, I'm not. I'm not sure I'll ever be all right again."

"If you need to talk about it, I'm here."

As the emotional dam began to crack, one fissure at a time, she crossed the room, seeking her father's comfort as she had many times before. But rarely when it came to problems with her husband.

He opened his arms to her, held her close

as she dampened the lapels of his navy sports coat. She let it all out, cried until she felt as if she had nothing left and her tears turned to soft sobs.

When she finally lifted her head from his shoulder, he pulled a handkerchief from his inside pocket and offered it to her. "Let's have a seat and sort this out."

She wiped her eyes and nose as she joined him on the sofa. "I'm sorry," she said. "That outburst has been coming for most of the day." In reality, much longer than that.

He draped his arm over the back of the couch. "No need to apologize. I am concerned over what's causing your distress. What has Matthew done to you?"

So much for the theory Matt had tried to recruit her own flesh and blood. "It's a long story and complicated."

"I have all the time in the world to listen."

She shored up her strength and spilled the history from the past few months, covering Matt's drinking, the impending divorce, the almost reconciliation and the final blow— her husband's decision the day their son died.

When Edwin remained silent for a few moments, Rachel assumed he was about to impart words of wisdom that most likely would include leaving the man who'd married her without his permission. He shattered her assumptions when he said, "I can't fault Matthew for the choice he made. I told him that very thing when he called me that morning."

Her mouth dropped open from shock. "You knew about it?"

"Yes."

"Why didn't you tell me? Better still, why didn't you talk Matthew out of it?"

"Matthew called me after the fact. But if he had asked me, I would have supported him in the decision."

The two men she loved most had betrayed her. Their need to protect her had cost her the most precious thing in her life. "You would have agreed even if it wasn't what I wanted?"

He crossed one leg over the other and stared out the picture window toward the pool. "What I'm about to say might seem cruel, but it needs to be said."

"Go ahead. It can't be any crueler than you and my husband concealing the truth from me."

He sighed. "I never had the option to save your mother. The aneurysm ruptured during your birth, and by the time they detected it, she was already gone. And as much as I love you now, I blamed you for her death back then. So much so I didn't touch you for the first three months of your life."

Would the stunning secrets never end? "What made you finally come around?"

"Not what. Who. Your first nanny, Betty. One day she handed you to me and said it was high time I be a father to you. Then she announced she was taking Dalton to the park and she left me holding a child that I sadly resented." He paused for a moment, as if it pained him to continue. "I was certain you'd start crying to punish me for my sins. But you just stared at me with eyes that are so much like your mother's, and you smiled. In that moment, I realized I would move mountains for you."

She experienced another onslaught of emotion, coupled with the realization that maybe she'd been too hard on him. She leaned in to give him a hug and a kiss on the cheek. "Would it make you feel better if I told you that your actions left no permanent scars?"

"You'd make me feel better if you'd find some way to forgive your husband. If you'd seen him that afternoon, when we went to make arrangements for the service, you would have seen absolute torture on his face, especially when he told the funeral director he wanted the baby to be buried next to his mother."

And she'd thought she was all cried out. "I've said some terrible things to him, Dad. Things I can never take back. I've laid so much blame on him and he didn't deserve it."

"He'll let bygones be bygones because he loves you, Rachel. He, too, would do anything for you."

Except for giving her the child she wanted. But he had given her that, which led to the most compelling problem still standing in their way. "He doesn't want any more children, and I do."

"He's afraid and I can't blame him. When I learned you were pregnant, at first I was terrified something might happen to you. Matt needs time to realize that some rewards are attached to risks, yet the payoff can be worth it. Just look at what a remarkable woman you've become in spite of me."

She felt anything but remarkable at the moment. "Time is a luxury we don't have," she said. "I'm already pregnant."

It was the normally unflappable Edwin Wainwright's turn to be shocked. "Is Matthew aware of this?"

She shook her head. "Not yet. I planned to tell him last night at the cabin, but when I asked him if he'd be willing to have another child, he insisted he couldn't go through it again. That's when I basically cut him off at the knees and refused to hear anything else. I gave him back my wedding ring and told him to leave."

"You're going to have to tell him soon, princess."

"I know that. I need a few days to prepare."

"Don't wait too long. Wasted time can lead to misery."

She had the misery down pat. "How was your trip?" she asked, badly needing a lighter topic to discuss.

He grinned as she'd never seen him grin before. Even with his silver hair, he looked years younger. "Very fruitful. I purchased a condominium where I hope to retire next year."

She was quickly reaching revelation overload. "You're going to move away from Placid? And why so soon?"

His gaze drifted away. "Because I've met someone. She's the property manager at the condominium complex. Her name is June."

That certainly explained the schoolboy smile. "Is it serious?"

"You could say that. I'm going back to Florida in a couple of days and she'll be flying back with me next week."

She couldn't wait to see the woman who'd so obviously melted her father's hardened heart. "I look forward to meeting her."

"And she said the same about you." He released a brief laugh. "Rather ironic it took me thirty-one years to fall in love again, isn't it?"

"I'm thrilled for you, Dad. After everything that's happened, you deserve some happiness."

He regained his patented solemn demeanor. "A few people around here would firmly disagree, and justifiably so. I spent most of my adult life buying up the town in an attempt to fill the void that remained after I lost your mother. I've left quite a few casualties in my wake, and I'm going to try to rectify that before I leave Placid."

If love could give a jaded millionaire back his humanity, anything was possible. "Are you going to sell the bank?"

"No. I want to keep it for my future grandchildren. But I do hope you'll consider overseeing the operations as president."

She'd never even considered running the bank. The task seemed extremely daunting, even if she hadn't been facing the possibility of divorce and a very real pregnancy. "Dad, I worked as a teller the summer before college, and that's the sum total of my banking experience. I'm just not qualified to do that."

"You're my daughter, Rachel," he said. "You have a minor in accounting and a head for good business. I have no doubt you'll catch on."

For the time being, she'd bring out a good excuse before she refused him altogether. "Right now I have to concentrate on the baby."

He took her hand into his. "Of course you do. You also need to concentrate on repairing your marriage. As much as I despised that young man for taking you away from me before I was ready, he's proven through the years how much he loves you. He'll love his child, too, the minute he holds him or her in his arms. It only takes one smile to win a man's heart."

That deserved another hug. "Thank you, Daddy."

He look totally taken aback. "I believe the

last time you called me 'Daddy' you were still wearing braces."

She smiled. "Sometimes little girls need their daddies, even when they're grown."

And sometimes grown women needed their husbands, whether they wanted to or not. She had the urge to run to Matt now. To tell him about their baby and that she was sorry. But she had something she needed to do first. Somewhere she needed to be. A place where she'd learned to cope with loss. She needed to relearn those lessons tonight, in case she lost her husband for good.

AFTER DRIVING ALL NIGHT, Matt had spent most of the day trying to get some sleep. But as soon as he'd dozed off, thoughts of Rachel and her condemnation had jarred him awake. So had the dreams that had plagued him for months. Images of his son that he would never forget.

After calling the sheriff's department to say he'd be coming by soon, Matt took a hot shower and choked down a peanut-butter sandwich. The bottle of whiskey called to him like a bad-intentioned friend, but he managed to ignore it. He couldn't confront his father with booze on his breath while he lectured on the evils of alcohol.

By the time he pulled into the county jail's parking lot, he'd pretty much rehearsed what he wanted to say. He had a list of demands for his dad, along with one major ultimatum—get clean or get out of his life.

He opened the glass door to find the sheriff waiting for him at the front desk. "Sorry to see you under these circumstances, Matt," Buck said as he stuck out his beefy hand for a shake.

Not as sorry as he was. "Where is he?"

Buck pointed toward a hall to Matt's right. "In the visitors' room. Not much going on here, so you should have some privacy."

"And he's okay?"

"Better than he's been in a long time. He had a few rough patches, but he survived them."

"Chase told me about that. I appreciate the two of you looking after him."

"You can thank my son for that. Chase watched him like a hawk for a good twenty-four hours."

It gave him some comfort to know he could still rely on his friends, and he'd damn sure need them in the days to come after the divorce was final. "Can I see him now?"

"Sure thing."

He followed Buck to a heavy door where he keyed in a code. But before they walked into the hall beyond that door, the sheriff faced Matt again. "The tough part's only beginning. He's going to need a lot of support from here on out. He needs to attend AA meetings on a regular basis and he'll need a sponsor. I'd be willing to take that on."

As far as he knew, a sponsor usually came in the form of another recovering alcoholic. "I don't mean to offend you, but are you qualified to do that?"

"More than qualified." Buck passed a hand over the back of his neck. "When I was in the army, I injured my back during a training exercise. After I came home, they gave me some newfangled painkillers and I got hooked. I knew I had to stop, but I sure as hell didn't know how. Luckily, I had a best friend who made me see the light and helped me get clean and sober. He's an arrogant son of a bitch now, but he wasn't always that way. After his wife died, he got high on power. He got worse when his baby girl ran off and married a down-home country boy."

Surely he didn't mean… "Are you talking about my father-in-law?"

Buck opened the door. "The one and only. He helped me organize meetings, and to this day, he still lets the former addicts meet in a back room at the bank."

"I'll be damned. I never knew any of that was going on."

"And I'm going to trust you won't say anything to anyone. We've got a close-knit bunch of people who've been gathering for a while now. We rely on each other as a group, and I wouldn't want to have to disband after all this time if word got out."

Hell, he wondered how many addicts resided in Placid, right under his nose. Then again, maybe he didn't want to know. "It's a small world in this small town."

Buck grinned. "You've got that right. We're twined together as tightly as barbed wire. So much so I refuse to look into my family tree for fear my wife could be a first cousin."

He had to laugh over that one. "No way that's the case with me and Rachel. My blood's red where hers is blue."

"You're both lucky that social divide hasn't been a problem for the two of you. It takes a solid marital foundation to support those differences. I'm proud of you kids."

It was fairly obvious Buck didn't know about their recent situation, and he wasn't going to enlighten him now. "So the group thing works, huh?"

"Yeah, it does," he said. "Nothing better than commiserating with people who personally know the hell you've been through."

In that moment Matt gained some understanding as to why Rachel had gone the grief-support route. He still wasn't convinced it would work for him. "I'm going to do my best to persuade Ben to give it a try. And speaking of Ben, let's get this over with."

Buck led him through the corridor and opened a door to his left. "I'll be outside if you need me, but I doubt he'll give you any trouble."

That remained to be seen. He entered the room where his father sat at a small table, his hands folded on the metal surface, head lowered. Matt took the chair opposite him and decided to go slowly with the lecture. "How are you feeling?"

"I've been better, but I've been worse, too." When his dad finally looked up, Matt was shocked to say the least. His blue eyes were clearer than they'd been in years, but not exactly bright. "I don't blame you if you hate me, son."

Funny, he'd figured his dad would hate him for not bailing him out. "I don't hate you, Dad. But I can't do this anymore. I won't stand by and watch while you kill yourself."

"I know," he said quietly. "Your mama wouldn't want that, either."

That was a good sign of progress. "No, she wouldn't. Not when she struggled every day to live."

"Until the last day when she finally gave up and left me."

Of all the self-absorbed… "She was sick, Dad. She had the worst form of MS and no control over it whatsoever."

"She took control over the disease, son, when she…" He rubbed both hands over his face.

It wasn't like his dad not to complete a sentence when he was sober. "When she what?"

"It doesn't matter. It's done. I couldn't stop her."

Matt took a minute to process what Ben could be hinting at. "And you can't stop there and leave me hanging. You finish what you were going to say, dammit."

His dad leaned back in the chair, that same old sorrow in his eyes. "When she asked me to leave the pills on the nightstand with the top off, I knew what she was going to do. God help me, I knew when I got home that afternoon she'd be gone."

Suicide? The concept was too unbelievable, too staggering for Matt to grab on to. "You're wrong, Dad. She wouldn't have taken her own life. She wouldn't have done that to us."

"She did, Matt. She'd begged me a few weeks before to help her end the suffering. Like the selfish bastard I was, I kept clinging to her because I couldn't stand the thought of living without her. But that morning, when she couldn't even be touched without crying out, I knew it was only a matter of time before she was gone anyway. So I kissed her goodbye, told her I loved her and I let her go."

And since that day, the guilt had been eating at his dad like acid. A guilt no bottle of booze could ever erase. He knew that from personal experience. "Why didn't you tell me this before?"

"Because I didn't want you to think less of your mama for leaving you. Because you were just a kid and I wanted to protect you from the truth."

The only protection his father had afforded him since his mother's death. "I swear I wish I'd stayed home from camp that summer," he said when regret came calling again. "Maybe then I could've changed Mom's mind." Question was, would that have been fair? On one hand, he wanted to blame Ben for not fighting harder for his wife's survival. On the other, he understood why his mother had chosen to take back her control by ending her life, even if he didn't necessarily agree with it. Even if knowing what she'd done cut to the core of his soul.

His dad's burden had been a lot to bear, and he worried that burden might prevent him from getting help so he could get better. "I understand that what you went through with Mom was rough, but it's time to get back on track. Buck's going to tell you about the local AA meetings and I'm going to make sure you stay off the stuff, even if I have to police you every day." Hell, he didn't have any better way to spend his time. "If I let you out today, do you think you can go back into the house and not want to return to your old ways?"

"I don't want you to let me out. I want to serve my time."

He hadn't anticipated that would be his father's response. "That could be weeks spent in a cell, Dad."

"Maybe so, but I'll be sober."

And he could be avoiding reality. "You can't hide from your problems forever by staying locked up. You're going to have to face them eventually, unless you decide to become a permanent resident here."

"Nope, just long enough to get my head on straight so I can find a steady job. I imagine Buck will let me out for the meetings. And you can bring Rachel to visit me. I miss seeing that little gal."

He didn't have the heart—or maybe the guts—to tell his dad they weren't together anymore. "I'll let her know you're here, but it'll be up to her if she wants to visit."

"Is she having a tough time over losing the baby?"

He was surprised Ben even remembered that. "Yeah, a real tough time."

"I know how she feels, but Rachel's a strong lady. She'll get through this. And someday you two will have the young 'un you deserve."

Matt didn't feel he deserved a damn thing, let alone another child. "We'll have to see about that."

"You should see to it and soon. I tell you right now, I've done a lot of bad things over the years, but you're not one of them. Thank you for being a good son and hangin' in there with your old man. I love you, boy."

It all came back to Matt then, the father Ben used to be. The father he could be again if he stayed sober. Now that the secret was out, he hoped that might finally be the case. "You're welcome, and I love you, too, Dad."

It occurred to him that everyone had secrets, to protect others or to protect themselves. He'd revealed most of his own, but he still had one left to disclose. An important secret that could be the answer to winning back his wife. But when it came down to it, Rachel might not allow him the opportunity.

Nothing better than commiserating with people who personally know the hell you've been through....

When Matt recalled Buck's recent statement, he racked his brain for information that Rachel had given him about the support group. He remembered Trimble Oaks Community Center one county over, Monday-night meetings. He wasn't sure about the time, but he'd do his best to find out.

He took a quick check of his watch and realized he had little time to spare or to prepare. He had no idea if Rachel had made it back to town, and if she had, if she'd even be there. No clue what he would say or if he'd say anything at all. Maybe he'd just listen and learn and someday be able to talk about those last few moments, the ones he'd barely been able to think about, much less voice. Regardless, he needed to do this not only for Rachel, but for himself.

Tonight could prove to be his salvation... or his ultimate downfall.

CHAPTER THIRTEEN

AFTER ARRIVING A few minutes early, Rachel set her folding chair in the center of the room, facing the chair reserved for the facilitator. Other participants soon joined her, taking their places beside her and behind her, a random seating configuration that symbolized the chaos their life had become. Some couples came together, others came alone, as she always did. Some attended on a regular basis, others had come once or twice and moved on. In this particular refuge, social status, race or background didn't matter. They were all connected by one common goal—to restore some normality in their lives after losing a loved one.

During her tenure, Rachel had learned a lot about navigating the grief process, that it could be a dance—two steps forward, three steps back. She'd also learned that no two people grieved the same, and hearts mended at differing rates, some slow, some never, she supposed. She'd discovered she could come here and laugh without feeling guilty. She could cry without fear of judgment. She could speak or simply listen. Tonight she was in a listening mood, and crying certainly wasn't out of the question.

While waiting for everyone to settle in, she opened her journal across her lap and began jotting down her thoughts about the past few days. She recorded her feelings over her father's revelation and the tenuous state of her marriage.

She glanced up to see April, the forty-something leader of the group, take her seat. "Welcome, everyone," she began. "We'll start tonight's meeting with sharing time. Everyone will have the opportunity to talk openly for five minutes before we move on to the next person. As always, I request that you withhold all comments and suggestions until cross-discussion. Rachel, you're first."

She could think of so many things she could share. She simply didn't have the energy or enough time to share them all. "I went away for the weekend and saw a few old friends. I did manage to talk about what happened to Caleb without completely falling apart. I consider that good progress." Even if the relationship with her husband had deteriorated. "That's all."

April smiled before she moved on to the woman seated next to Rachel. "Nancy, how about you?"

Rachel found herself unable to concentrate on the discourse surrounding her as others spoke about their recent trials and minor victories. Her thoughts kept going back to the last conversation with Matt, the hurtful words and accusations. The pain in his eyes before he walked out the door. She needed to make amends. She needed to tell him she was pregnant. She'd do that tomorrow, when she'd had a good night's sleep and had fewer thoughts cluttering her mind.

"We have a new member tonight," April said, regaining Rachel's attention. "Could you introduce yourself and tell us a little about why you're here?"

"My name is Matt, and I lost my newborn son a few months ago."

Rachel gripped the pen so hard she thought it might snap in two. She'd recognize the voice without knowing the name. Without even looking.

She had no idea what he would say or if

he'd say anything else. It didn't matter. She was grateful that he'd come. That he was making an effort, though she questioned why he had.

"We're listening, Matt," April encouraged him. "Feel free to say as much or as little as you'd like."

Rachel ventured a glance over her shoulder to see Matt had his head lowered, his hands tightly clasped on his thighs. She faced forward and waited for what would come next. Prayed she might finally know what had happened to Matt that morning.

"He was born in a county hospital that wasn't equipped to handle premature infants," he continued. "The air ambulance had been delayed for some reason. A multivehicle accident on the freeway, I think they said. The medical staff tried to help him, but he was too sick. After they told me there wasn't any hope, a nurse brought me a chair and asked me if I wanted to hold him. As much as I wanted to refuse and get away from there as fast as I could, I didn't want my son to die in the hands of strangers. I owed his mother that much. I owed him that much."

Rachel's tears began to fall like raindrops on the journal's pages as Matt went on. "After she handed him to me, she told me what would happen next, that he would stop breathing first, then his heart would stop beating. I placed my hand over his chest and I remember thinking how little he was. But he looked perfect. He had dark hair like his mom and a dimple in his chin like his grand-dad."

He drew in a deep breath and let it out slowly. "I talked to him about what I'd teach him, like how to carve a horse out of an old piece of wood and how to rope a calf. I said we'd have to sneak that one past his mom."

He laughed then. A small, sad laugh that packed a powerful emotional punch. "I called him 'buddy,' like my dad used to call me. I told him I'd take him fishing down at the pond and I'd show him how to throw a curve-ball. And even when I realized his heart had stopped, I kept talking to him. I needed him to know that his life meant something, no matter how brief it might have been. I told him how much his mother wanted him and how much she loved him. I told him I loved him, too."

Rachel was vaguely aware of the sniffs echoing in the room and very aware of the anguish she'd heard in Matt's voice. A pain that shot straight to her heart.

After a span of silence, April cleared her throat. "Thank you, Matt."

Rachel remained completely immobilized, torn between running to Matt or giving him—and her—time to recover. Yet knowing her husband had held their baby boy in his final moments gave her the comfort she'd craved for months. She also experienced a measure of shame.

She had completely misjudged Matt by believing the decision he'd made had somehow been easy. She should have realized that the man who would give his last dime to someone in need, who'd spend however long it took to comfort a child when they'd lost a cherished pet would never, ever reject his own son. She'd been so caught up in her own anger and resentment that she hadn't taken the time to understand her husband had been guilty only of protecting her. She'd failed to recognize his struggle to come to terms with his grief in order to reach this breakthrough. And he'd managed to do that without her help.

"I believe we'll take a break now before we have our group discussion."

April's voice jolted Rachel back to the present. The overwhelming urge to find her husband sent her to her feet. She wanted to have some alone time with him, to thank him for being there for their baby when she hadn't been able to. To tell him she was so, so sorry and that she'd never loved him more.

She craned her neck to search the back of the room where people had gathered at the refreshment table. Yet she saw no sign of him.

Rachel dropped the journal into her bag and strode to the table, where she caught April's arm to garner her attention. "The new member? Do you know where he went?"

April pushed her glasses up on the bridge of her nose. "No, I'm sorry, I don't, Rachel. He called me about twenty minutes before the meeting to confirm the time. Normally I would have insisted he talk at length with me before he attended his first meeting. But he sounded so urgent, I was afraid he might be having a crisis, so I bent the rules. And since he didn't fill out the usual forms, I don't know how to reach him."

"I do."

April lifted a brow. "You know him?"

"Yes. He's my husband." And he was definitely in crisis.

Rachel didn't wait for April's reaction. She simply rushed through the center's double doors and walked into the warm, humid night. She scanned the parking lot, and when she didn't locate his truck, she made her way to the car and climbed inside. She could think of several places he might be. Places she'd usually go out of her way to avoid. But she'd do whatever she had to do to find him, scour every county-line dive, if that's what it took. She had to tell him what was on her mind and in her heart.

"You couldn't have waited until I got here?"

He'd checked on the mare before he'd left to visit his dad and figured she was getting close to foaling. Obviously she'd been closer than he'd thought, he realized when he caught sight of the foal. A jet-black, spindly-legged foal that was completely dry and nursing, which led him to believe she'd been born at least two hours ago without his assistance. Nature had a way of taking care of these things, usually without his help.

As Matt swung open the stall door and stepped inside, the broodmare nickered twice as if to say, "Who needs you?" He'd asked himself that same question on the way to the clinic. He'd like to believe Rachel still needed him as much as he needed her, but that was probably wishful thinking.

He examined the foal more closely and drew some blood to send to the lab the following day, relieved to have something to keep his mind off what had transpired throughout the day. But the memories were still fresh in his mind, the feelings still raw. Once he'd started talking, he hadn't been able to stop. And he'd intentionally left before Rachel had had a chance to seek him out. He wasn't ready to face her yet. Not until he regained his emotional bearings. Not until he knew exactly what he would say to her.

Once he'd finished tending to the filly, Matt grabbed a push broom and began to sweep the asphalt aisle that didn't really need sweeping. He thought about changing out the stalls' shavings, reorganizing the feed room, maybe even going into the office to check his schedule for tomorrow one more time. Anything to avoid walking back into an empty house, alone with only his memories and the temptation to drink away his troubles.

When he saw the flash of headlights through the open double doors, he wondered who might be coming by this time of night.

He didn't recognize the sedan, but he had no problem recognizing the driver when she slid out the door. So much for waiting to have this unavoidable discussion with his wife.

Even though it was warm outside, Rachel wore a lightweight white sweater over her blue blouse, along with an uncomfortable expression as she stepped inside. "Hi."

"Hey." He had a lot he needed to say to her, but he was going to let her lead the discussion, at least the important part. "New car?"

"Rental car. I decided to get my money's worth before I have to turn it in tomorrow."

He set the broom aside and rested a shoulder against the wall next to the feed room. "Your dad called and said you'd made it back from Wayhurst okay."

"Yes. I also made good time. The drive wasn't bad at all."

"Good." They'd covered the generalities. Now what?

She leaned back against the opposite wall and folded the sweater's hem, back and forth. "I'm glad you came to the meeting. It was a nice surprise."

He hadn't found anything nice about it. Necessary, but not nice. "I decided it was time, after I talked to my dad earlier today."

"How is he?"

"Still in jail, by his own choice. He wants to serve out his sentence and stay sober for a while before he enters the real world."

"What exactly did he say to you?"

He instinctively recoiled from telling her the whole story. He'd wait until another time, since he'd already been put through the revelation wringer tonight. "As usual, he talked about my mom and what happened the day she died. I began to understand why he started drinking, and I realized you were right."

"About the importance of dealing with your grief?"

"Yeah, and about me heading down the same path as my dad. The night after Caleb died, I went to my father's favorite hangout and tied one on. Sam had to drive me home from the bar and put me to bed, the same way I've been putting Ben to bed for years. I just wanted to be numb. But eventually that numbness wears off, and you still have to face the reasons behind the drinking when you sober up."

"You faced those reasons tonight, Matt, and I know how much that cost you. But maybe now you're ready to move forward."

He stared at the ceiling and geared up for one final admission. "I don't know how to do that without you, Rachel. Am I just supposed to forget our life together?"

"I don't believe we can forget that," she said. "But we're both capable of going on without each other. We have to decide if that's what we want to do."

That was the last thing he wanted, but he couldn't be completely selfish in this case. "I want to work this out between us. But I love you enough to let you go, if that's what you want."

"I don't want that at all." She strode across the aisle and threw her arms around him. "I'm so sorry I doubted you."

He held her close for a time before he pulled back and studied her eyes. "I love you so damn much, baby. I can't imagine not having you in my life."

"I love you, too, Matt. I love you for saying goodbye to our son when I couldn't."

"As hard as it was to do that, I don't regret those last few minutes. But I'll always regret I couldn't do more to save him. Fathers are supposed to protect their children. That day, I felt like I'd failed you both."

"You didn't fail us, Matt. My body failed

for whatever reason. But I've made a conscious effort to stop blaming myself, and I want you to do the same."

"I'm trying, sweetheart." He was about to commit to something he hadn't been able to commit to until now. "And I want to do everything possible to make you happy. That means giving you the one thing you want more than anything."

She attempted a shaky smile. "Another closet for my shoes?"

He kissed her damp cheek and smiled back. "A baby. I figure if you're willing to take the chance after everything you went through, then I should be willing to do the same. I've finally convinced myself that with your help, I can be a good father. I want to try."

The light that had been missing in her eyes finally returned. "Are you absolutely sure?"

"Yeah, I am. If you think I'm still worthy."

"You're more than worthy. But you might question my worthiness after what I've done."

He couldn't come up with one instance where he wouldn't forgive her. "What do you mean?"

She looked away for a second before bringing her gaze back to his. "When I became pregnant with Caleb, it wasn't an accident. I intentionally missed a few pills."

He'd suspected as much. "I thought that might've been the case."

"You did?"

"Yeah, and I didn't really care at the time. If you hadn't forced the issue, I would've kept putting it off. I was a little stunned at first, but watching the baby grow in your belly and seeing how happy you were, I started to get used to the idea. I even found myself imagining what he would be like."

She framed his jaw in her palm. "He would have been just like you. Strong. Compassionate. And, of course, incredibly cute."

"Cute, huh?"

"Yes, cute."

He brushed a kiss across her lips. "Why don't we go back to the cabin this weekend and get started on the baby making?"

"Well, first of all, Sam and Savannah are getting married this weekend."

Damn his friends' poor timing. "Guess we can't bow out, since we're in the wedding party."

"No, we can't. And secondly, we already have a head start on the baby making."

He wasn't exactly sure what she was getting at, but he had his suspicions. "Do you think you might be pregnant?"

"No, I don't think I am. I know I am. I took the test the day before we left for Wayhurst. I planned to tell you the other night at the cabin, but when you said—"

"I couldn't go through it again." He waited for the initial fear to subside before calm took its place. "Not only can I go through it again, I want to do it. But I've got to warn you, I'm going to worry you to death the whole time. And you're going to see a doctor in Jackson."

"I plan to schedule an appointment first thing in the morning, as soon as I'm back at work at the clinic."

"You don't have to go back to work."

She frowned. "Don't go all archaic on me. I want to go back to work."

"Then let me keep Tina on staff to help you out."

"You just like having a blonde gracing the office."

"Not a chance, sweetheart. I prefer brunettes. Actually, only one brunette, and she just made me one damn happy man."

He kissed her to demonstrate his gratitude. To let her know that even after all this time, she was the only woman he'd ever wanted. The only woman he'd ever want.

"I have another question," Rachel said when they broke the kiss. "Can we get another dog?"

Matt grinned. "I'll do one better than that." He took her by the hand and led her to the foaling stall. "This little filly was supposed to be your birthday present, but since you're coming back here, I probably couldn't keep her hidden for the next month."

Her eyes went wide with wonder. "She's absolutely beautiful, Matt. What's her name?"

"We'll have to give her the fancy name when we register her, but I figure we can decide on a barn name now. If she turns out to be like her mother, we should probably call her Mouthy. That mare can talk up a blue streak, and she's loud."

"That gives me a great idea," she said. "Since her coat is black and since she could very well be a talker, we can call her Rita."

Matt let go a laugh that echoed in the barn and caused the foal to skitter around to the opposite side of her mother. "Rita it is."

Rachel laid a quick, light kiss on his lips

and smiled. "Now that we have that cleared up, what's next?"

"Let's go home."

RACHEL WAS SO GLAD to be home, back in her own bed. Back in the arms of the man she loved.

A slight breeze filtered through the open window, lightly touching her bare skin as softly as Matt had touched her only moments ago. They'd made love so slowly and sweetly, as if they had all the time in the world. She felt as if they did, though they still had a long way to go to right the wrongs. To heal the hurts.

The bedside lamp they'd left on allowed Rachel to see her husband's beautiful face turned profile to her. And from the way he was staring at the ceiling, she sensed something was still on his mind. "A quarter for your thoughts."

"Not a penny?"

"I'm accounting for inflation."

He smiled slightly, but it quickly dropped out of sight. "I was just thinking about everything that went down today. The planets that rule confessions must've been perfectly aligned."

That reminded Rachel of another confession, one that would definitely lighten the mood. "I forgot to tell you that my father has a lady friend."

His smile returned full force. "Oh, yeah?"

"Yeah. Believe me, I was more than a little stunned to hear it. But after thirty-one years, he deserves to have someone special in his life."

"She's got to be pretty special to put up with Edwin Wainwright."

She playfully punched his arm. "Be nice."

She then recapped the rest of the father-daughter conversation, from her dad's impending move to Florida and support of Matt's decision to his determination to make amends to the townsfolk he'd mistreated through his financial dealings. She closed with the offer that could send her husband back over the edge. "He wants me to take over as bank president."

"Are you going to do it?" he asked with unusual calm.

"Not in the foreseeable future with a baby on the way."

"If you decide to go through with it, we'll work it out. The good citizens of Placid would be glad to have someone like you on their side."

Rachel was glad to have his support. She lifted her head from the pillow and laid it on his chest. "Thank you for understanding, but taking care of myself and this baby will be my number one priority for the next eight months. And I'll manage to take care of your needs, as well."

"We'll take care of each other." He sighed. "If you think about it, my dad and yours aren't all that different. Mine dealt with losing his wife by taking up residence in a bottle, and yours dealt with his loss by trying to buy every resident in town."

"So true. But you can't deny they loved the women in their lives. And they both love us, too."

"My father did love my mother to a fault. So much so he did something I never imagined he could do."

To say she was only mildly curious would be a grave understatement. Yet she knew better than to pressure him as she had over the past few months. "If you want to talk about it, I'm listening."

"It's pretty tough to hear. At least it was for me."

"I can handle it." But could he handle telling her after what he'd already been through tonight?

"He gave me the details about the day she died," he went on to say. "All the details he'd left out for years. Then again, I hadn't asked. I think somehow I knew there was more to the story."

She had a sickening feeling she might already know the rest of the story. "Go ahead."

He waited a few moments before he continued. "My mother took her own life, and he knew she was going to do it. In fact, he helped by leaving an open bottle of painkillers so she'd have access."

And she'd just thought he couldn't be hurt any worse. "Oh, Matt. Why did he wait all this time to tell you something like that?"

"He told me he was trying to protect me."

Yet Ben had failed to protect his son from becoming an adult too soon. "Do you believe him?"

"Yeah, I do, because that's what I thought I was doing for you. Protecting you from the truth."

"And you were trying to protect yourself from the pain, as well. I understand that now."

"You're right. And honestly, I'm glad he waited. I'm not sure I would've taken that truth all that well at thirteen. Hell, it's not easy to take it at thirty-two."

The despair in his voice clearly pointed to that. She pressed a kiss on his jaw. "Now that you know, how do you feel about her decision?"

"It's hard to say. I'm in a line of work where it's acceptable to put a sick animal out of its misery to end its suffering. At one time I even believed that maybe it would be better if terminally ill people had that same choice."

"But not now?"

"As selfish as it seems, I can't wrap my mind around someone intentionally ending their life. Not after watching my son draw his last breath when all I wanted was for him to live. When all I ever wanted was to have my mom back."

As he closed his eyes, Rachel witnessed something she'd never seen before. A single teardrop slid down his cheek, followed by another and then another. When he rolled toward her, she cocooned him in her arms while he cried, her tears mixed with his.

Her heart broke for the little boy who'd

never really mourned his mother's passing.
For the man who was finally mourning his
son.

She continued to hold him long after their
tears subsided and sleep began to settle over
her. She could rest easily now knowing that
her husband was going to be okay.

They were going to be okay.

Dressed in a lilac satin bridesmaid dress,
Rachel linked her arm with Matt's as they
followed the bride and groom across the
wooden bridge and headed to the newly re-
furbished farmhouse for the reception.

"Who gets married on a bridge in the middle of nowhere?" her husband muttered as
they picked their way down the grassy path
leading to their final destination.

"Two people who met for the first time on
that bridge," Rachel answered. "Besides, it
was beautiful." And it had been. White satin
streamers and purple orchids had been woven
through the railing and a white canopy had
provided protection against the possibility of
rain that fortunately hadn't come. "I swear,
sometimes men are so obtuse when it comes
to romance."

He grinned. "Yeah. We're a regular bunch

of clueless buffoons when it comes to that kind of thing."

She paused to give him a quick kiss. "But you're my clueless buffoon."

By the time they made it to the front yard where a massive tent had been set up for the after-wedding party, Rachel wanted only a large glass of water and a place to rest her aching arches.

She didn't have the opportunity for either when Jess wrenched her arm from Matt's and started dragging her toward the house. "Come with me and make it quick."

Her fellow matron of honor didn't know any other speed than quick. But when they started up the stairs, Rachel pulled her arm out of her grasp for fear she might tumble backward. "Slow down, Jess. We're both pregnant and wearing heels. That's a recipe for disaster."

"Fine." She tossed the word back over a shoulder as she continued to climb. "But we don't have a lot of time."

Was something on fire other than Jess's auburn hair? "Time for what?"

"You'll see."

Once they reached the landing, Jess took

a right down the hall and opened the door to Savannah's old bedroom. "Come in."

Rachel peeked around Jess to see Savannah standing by the bed, holding a garment bag draped over one arm. Apparently the bride needed help changing out of her wedding gown and into her second outfit specially designed for the reception.

As soon as Rachel entered the room, Savannah laid the bag on the bed and unzipped it, revealing a long white chiffon gown with tiny pearls sewn randomly into the bodice. "Put down the bouquet, take off your bridesmaid's dress and put this on," she said as she held it up.

Huh? "I'm not quite following you, Savannah."

Jess walked to Savannah's side, presenting a united front. "No arguments. You're getting married in a few minutes. Again."

Serious concerns overrode Rachel's common sense as she regarded her erstwhile attorney. "Savannah, didn't you tear up the divorce papers?"

That earned her a hearty laugh from both her gal pals. "Of course I did," Savannah said. "This is something someone wants to do for you."

"Who?"

Jess rolled her eyes. "The caterer. She wanted to bake two cakes and really rake in the dough, pun intended."

Savannah sent Jess a frustrated look before bringing her attention back to Rachel. "Your husband arranged the whole thing. He wanted you to finally have a real wedding, complete with the dress and the flowers and, yes, the cake. When he talked to me about it, I suggested we share our wedding day with you. Everything's already set up and all our friends are here, so why not?"

To think she'd recently accused her husband of being dense when it came to romance. However, once again they'd be reaping the rewards of someone else's hard work. "But this is supposed to be Sam's and your day. Won't this take away from that?"

"Look at it this way," Jess said. "We're recycling one bridesmaid dress and the decorations. In this day and time, it's good to go green."

Savannah gave Rachel a heartfelt look. "Aside from that, I can't think of anything more special than sharing this time with two of the people I care about most. Two people who came so close to losing each other."

"Chase and I would join in the fun, too, and renew our vows," Jess added, lightening the mood. "But since we had our wedding less than six months ago and I'm already knocked up, it's probably better we didn't try that. Besides, too many brides spoil the wedding stew."

They all laughed then. Crazy, loud laughter reminiscent of their youth when they'd been three young girls who'd only dreamed of finding the loves of their life. Luckily, they'd all found their true loves, not in some exotic place, but among their little group known as the six-pack.

Jess pulled the dress off the hanger and handed it to Rachel. "Let's get this party started so I can eat. The flowers were starting to look good during the bridge bash."

Rachel examined the fabric and found it to be vaguely familiar. "Did this come from the boutique where we got our dresses, Savannah?"

"It came from your father's closet," she said. "It's your mother's gown. Jess and I had it altered to make it a little more modern. And since it's an empire waist, it should fit you fine."

Lately she'd been a hormonal wreck, either

crying or on the verge of crying. She'd shed a few tears during Sam and Savannah's vows, but now she felt as if the waterworks might begin in earnest. "You guys are the best."

After a brief group hug, Jess helped Rachel into the gown while Savannah changed into a short white cocktail dress. Rachel walked to the floor-length mirror to inspect the fit and immediately recalled her parents' wedding photograph. The dress's long lace sleeves had been removed, but the rest of the gown remained intact, from the sweetheart neckline to the lengthy train. Overall, she felt like a beautiful bride, thankful that she would finally have a part of her mother with her when she repeated her vows a second time.

Satisfied everything was in place, Rachel turned and pronounced, "I'm ready."

"Not quite," Savannah said as she opened the jewelry box on the bureau and withdrew a string of pearls. "These were my grandmother's and should fulfill the something borrowed, as well as the something old."

"And we can't forget that blue requirement." Jess rifled through a plastic bag sitting on the end of the bed, pulled out a garter and shot it at Rachel like a rubber band. "Put this on."

After Savannah secured the necklace, Rachel sat on the edge of the mattress, slipped the garter on and stood. "Now are we ready?"

"One more thing," Savannah said as she opened a white box resting on the nightstand. She took out a bouquet crafted from magnolias, Rachel's favorite flowers. "Matt wanted you to have your own one of these."

If she didn't stop the urge to cry, she'd surely risk tripping from blurred vision as she strolled down the aisle. "They're wonderful."

Following a series of raps, Jess walked to the door. "If that's who I think it is, we're definitely ready to roll."

When Jess pulled the door open, Rachel expected to see Matt on the other side, but her expectations weren't met. Still, she was both thrilled and amazed to find her father standing in the hallway, looking debonair in his dark silk suit and a little misty when he surveyed her gown and sent her a sincere smile.

"You look beautiful, princess," he said. "Your mother would be so proud of you. I only wish she were here to see you."

So did Rachel. She crossed the room and

hugged him hard. "And you're supposed to be in Florida."

He straightened his tie and smoothed his lapels. "I flew back this morning after Matt called and told me what he was planning."

"I'm so glad you're here, Dad." And very appreciative of her husband for so many reasons. "But I really hate that you had to interrupt your trip."

"I wouldn't have missed finally giving my daughter away," he said. "I did tell Matthew that I'd only agree as long as he promised to treat you well and not to give you back."

"Not to worry," she said. "He's stuck with me now."

He held out his arm for her. "Shall we?"

"Yes, we shall."

As they traveled down the hall toward the staircase, Rachel noticed a brown-haired, blue-eyed woman waiting at the top of the landing. She wore a pale yellow linen suit, impressive diamond earrings and a soft, sincere smile.

Her dad paused immediately in front of the lady and grinned like a teenager on his way to the prom. "June, this is my daughter, Rachel."

She held out her hand to Rachel for a gentle shake. "It's so nice to finally meet you, sweetie. I hope you don't mind that I'm here."

How could she mind when she'd been so curious about her? "I'm very happy you're here, June. I've been looking forward to meeting you, too."

June's smile expanded. "Well, I'll go on downstairs and take my seat."

After June descended the stairs, Rachel and her father followed suit, with Savannah and Jess trailing behind them. And when they reached the front porch, the matrons of honor walked ahead toward the tent. She could hear the sounds of a piano playing Pachelbel's Canon as they walked the rock path, just as it had been the day she and Matt had married for the first time.

Her husband had definitely thought of everything, right down to the last detail. And when she entered the tent, she understood exactly how thoughtful he'd been. A silver-haired, stately man stood at the end of the makeshift aisle flanked by rows of white chairs decorated with more magnolias. The same man who'd united them in marriage all those years ago. And to the judge's left, his beloved Helen sat at the piano, expertly playing the favorite song.

When Rachel caught Matt's gaze, he gave her a wink and a slight grin. If she'd had her way, she'd have ditched the heels and taken off toward him on a dead run. Instead, she tempered her steps and held back the tears as she and her dad continued forward.

Rachel handed off the bouquet to Savannah as soon as they stopped in front of the judge.

Jack slipped on a pair of glasses and removed a folded piece of paper from his suit pocket. "Ladies and gentlemen, welcome to the second feature of today's double wedding presentation," he said, eliciting a few chuckles from the crowd. "Who presents this woman as she recommits to her husband?"

"Her mother, God rest her soul, and I do." Her father then kissed her cheek and placed her hand in Matt's before joining the new woman in his life in the first row.

Jack unfolded the paper and studied it for a few moments before putting it away again. "I tend to forget things now and then," he said as he looked over the crowd. "But I'll never forget these two young people who walked into my chapel some thirteen years ago. They were very young and broke and clearly in love with each other. It's apparent that still holds true today, and I'm more than happy to reaffirm that love." He gestured Rachel and Matt forward. "Please face each other as you once again pledge your devotion to one another."

After they complied, the judge continued in a voice as clear as a church bell. "You've already vowed to take each other in holy matrimony, through better and worse, good times and bad, in sickness and in health. Now will you both reaffirm those vows in front of the witnesses?"

Matt and Rachel exchanged a look and a smile before saying, "We will."

"It's now time to exchange the rings."

Only one ring. Though Rachel respected Matt's reasoning for never wearing one, she couldn't deny she'd been disappointed. But she wouldn't let that derail these happy moments.

Sam handed the wedding band Rachel had worn throughout the marriage to Matt. When she'd asked him about it only two days ago, he'd claimed he'd taken it to the jeweler's to be cleaned. Perhaps only a partial truth, but she could live with that little white lie.

"Matthew, repeat after me," Jack said as Matt slipped the band onto her left ring finger, where it belonged. "I give you this symbol in honor of all that you are and always will be to me."

After Matt repeated the vow, Rachel assumed they were finished. She realized she was mistaken when Savannah leaned over, took her hand and dropped a wide silver band into her palm. When she turned back to her husband, he whispered, "It's about time, huh?"

"Rachel, repeat after me," Jack said. "I give you this symbol of my love, a never-ending circle that knows no end."

Her hand trembled as she slid the band onto Matt's finger. Her voice shook as well as she recited the vow. Never before had she felt so much love for the man standing in front of her.

"Matt, Rachel," Jack began. "Before I officially pronounce you wife and husband again, I'd like to remind you that marriage is not about giving up yourselves, but giving the best part of yourselves to each other. You may now kiss your bride, Matthew."

Matt kissed her perhaps a little longer than might be deemed appropriate. Kissed her until a round of noisy applause rang out, along with a few hoots and hollers, compliments of the groomsmen.

"I love you, Rachel Ellen."

"I love you, too, Matthew Benjamin."

Jack placed his palm over their joined hands and smiled. "Now go forth, be fruitful and multiply, while you're still young enough to enjoy the process."

Matthew gave her another wink and a smile. "We've already got that covered."

EPILOGUE

HE SAT IN A CHAIR in the ornate nursery, only this time he wasn't alone. He had a toddler with soft dark curls and even darker eyes tucked in the crook of one arm and a fairer-haired, blue-eyed newborn cradled in the other arm. He visually tracked the multicolored wild horses that ran along the pale lilac walls, each one enthusiastically painted by his wife. Then his gaze came to rest on the black letters stenciled above the matching cribs carefully crafted by his father—Meg and Ellie—the names bestowed upon his baby girls in honor of their grandmothers.

Eighteen months ago they'd welcomed Ellie after a tense but uneventful birth, following a stressful pregnancy fraught with both joys and worries, plus several trips to a specialist. Neither he nor Rachel had been able to relax until they'd heard that first remarkable cry and caught the first glimpse of their baby's eyes. Five weeks ago, after a not-quite-planned pregnancy and a fairly fast birth, Meg had joined the family as the quiet one of the bunch.

Even now she slept peacefully, while her big sister moved restlessly against her father's side, repeating her new favorite word over and over. "Book, book, book..."

He looked down on Ellie's angelic face and saw a little devil in those big brown eyes. "We'll read a book at bedtime. First, we're going to go outside and play in a bit. How does that sound?"

She popped two fingers into her mouth and smiled around them. A smile that had hog-tied his heart from the first time he'd seen it. Fortunately for his wife, he'd taken to fatherhood like a duck to water, and although he'd spent a good deal of her first months watching every move Ellie made, he'd finally learned to relax. Sort of.

He heard the doorbell ring, followed by the sound of approaching footsteps. Soon after, in walked his third favorite girl. His very favorite woman.

Ellie pulled the fingers from her mouth with an audible pop and pointed at Rachel as if she'd come upon a new discovery. "Mama."

"Yep, that's your mama." And a damn good-looking mama at that.

As she approached them, Rachel touched the plaque situated on the shelf right next to the miniature baseball glove. A plaque that read "Our angel, Caleb," and served as a forever reminder of the little boy who'd briefly been in their lives, but had left a lasting impression. "The first of the usual suspects has arrived," she said as she smiled down on the trio. "You ought to see Sam and Savannah's baby. He looks just like her."

He'd rather look at his wife. He'd like to do more than look. "What did the doctor say today?"

"He said I'm perfectly fine to resume all prebirth activity." She grinned. "But I really need to be careful so I can rest my uterus."

"He said that, too?"

"Actually, no. That's my contribution. As much as I love these two, I wouldn't mind a little time to lose some of my baby weight before we dive in again."

As far as he was concerned, she still looked incredible, especially this evening. She had on a flowing summer-weight yellow top covering her white shorts that revealed a good deal of her long, toned, tanned legs.

Man, oh, man, she was still his walking, talking dream girl.

"Well, you know how it is with us, sweetheart," he said. "We're like theater popcorn when it comes to making babies. Once we get started, we can't seem to stop."

"Very true." She lifted Meg into her arms and rested the baby on her shoulder. "Now, if Daddy and his pretty little shadow would kindly get up to help greet the guests, I'd appreciate it. In the meantime, I'm going to feed this little one, provided I can get her to wake up."

Matt came to his feet with Ellie propped on his hip. "How long is this shindig going to last?"

"Until everyone leaves." She dropped into the rocker and tried on an innocent look. "Why? Do you have other plans?"

Oh, yeah. "Between the hours of eleven and 2:00 a.m., I plan to have you all to myself."

"That sounds like a good plan. It's important to spend whatever time we can together, since it's such a precious commodity."

Her suddenly wistful tone concerned Matt. "Something wrong?"

"I spoke to Helen today," she said. "I told her we'd be there in two weeks."

That explained the mood change. "How's Jack doing?"

"As well as can be expected, I guess. Helen said they've learned to live with quieter days. Sometimes he doesn't remember people, including the grandkids and J.W. But so far, he hasn't forgotten her."

"I doubt he ever will," he said. "If it were me, I'd never forget you."

She smiled a sad smile. "Even if I still forget to put up my shoes?"

He bent down and kissed her. "Even if you left every pair you own scattered in every room in the house."

When Meg released a quiet little hungry cry, Rachel began unbuttoning her blouse. "That's my cue. Now, the two of you scoot. I'll see you in a few minutes."

Matt carried his daughter down the hall and into the great room where his friends waited. "Rachel's on feeding duty," he announced. "She'll be out in a while."

The minute Ellie caught sight of Sam's daughter, Jamie, Savannah and two-month-old Ethan, the newest McBriar, she wriggled in his arms. After he set her on her feet, she practically rushed the trio, chanting, "Baby, baby, baby!" Her dark curls bounced in time with her rapid gait.

As Ellie settled in beside Jamie, Matt walked into the adjacent kitchen where Sam sat at the island, drinking a beer. A nonalcoholic beer. "I brought a twelve-pack," he said as he held up the bottle. "We can consume the whole thing without worrying that Chase is going to arrest us."

Matt had been able to count on his friends to respect his nonalcohol policy. He took a bottle from the fridge, twisted off the cap and leaned against the counter. "Anyone know when Jess and Chase are supposed to get here?"

"Jess phoned a minute ago and said they're on their way," Savannah called from the couch. "Apparently Jake poured a bottle of syrup on his head before they could get him into the truck. Can't wait for Ethan to enter those terrible twos."

Matt wandered over to the sofa to sneak a quick look at the newest McBriar. "Man, Rachel's right. He looks just like you, Savannah."

"But he has Sam's impatience gene," she said.

"I'm patient," Sam shot back as he joined

them in the living area. "I waited a dozen years for you, didn't I?"

"Yes, you did, and it was quite worth the wait."

"Can I take Ellie into the backyard to play?" Jamie asked as she stood.

Savannah rose and picked up the baby carrier containing their son. "I believe I'll join you." She pointed at Sam and Matt. "Sam, fire up the grill. Matt, you bring out the burgers. And tell Jess when she gets here to grab some food or a kid and meet me out back."

"Bossy attorney," Sam muttered as his wife walked away. "But let me tell you, I like her to be bossy in bed."

"Hell, I'd just like to get my wife in bed."

Sam grinned. "How's that celibacy thing been treating you?"

Matt scowled. "It's over as of tonight. So as soon as we're done with dinner and the girls catch up, get the hell out of here and go home."

"You don't have to tell me twice."

When the doorbell rang, Matt answered the summons and let the last of the stragglers inside. Jess looked frazzled and Chase looked frustrated when Jake zoomed by and proceeded to climb underneath the coffee table.

"Get out of there, young man," Jess called as she handed off the diaper bag to her husband, but the boy didn't budge.

Chase set the bag on a chair and calmly walked to the table. "On the count of ten… One, two, three…"

The toddler scurried from beneath and grinned up at his dad. "I wanna play."

Jess crossed the room and took Jake by the hand. "Works every time. Where is everyone?"

"Savannah's out back with Ellie, Jamie and the baby," Matt said. "Rachel's feeding Meg and should be out shortly."

"Then outside we shall go to expend some energy."

After Jess left, Matt turned to Chase. "How do you get him to mind you?"

Chase looked a little sheepish for a sheriff. "I bribe him. If he does what he's told by the time I reach five, I let him have an extra cookie after dinner. But don't tell my wife."

Danny wandered into the kitchen, arms full of sacks that he set down on the counter. "I brought my ball and glove so we can all play some catch."

Matt immediately noticed the boy's voice had lowered since he'd seen him last, and he looked as if he'd grown an inch. He ruffled the kid's blond hair. "Man, Danny, you're going to be as tall as your dad before you turn thirteen."

Danny shrugged. "I plan to be taller than him before I turn eighteen."

"You wish," Chase said. "Now, go out and help your mom corral your baby brother."

Danny frowned. "Do I have to, Dad?"

"Yeah, if you want to play catch."

"Okay."

After Danny walked away, Chase grabbed a beer, joined Sam and Matt at the kitchen bar and held up the bottle for a toast. "Here's to beautiful wives and summer barbecues. And last, but never least, to our three boys and three girls, the future six-pack."

"To the future six-pack," Sam and Matt repeated as they clinked their amber bottles together.

After they retired to the backyard to begin the festivities, Matt opted to man the grill while his guests concentrated on visiting. He soon had trouble keeping his mind on his business when two arms circled his waist from behind. "I just love a man who wields a mean spatula."

He flipped a burger, then turned his wife's

arms. "Did you sell our baby when I wasn't looking?"

She nodded to his left. "Jess would probably make an offer if Chase let her."

From the nervous look on Chase's face, Matt figured his friend wouldn't be putting in a bid. "Everyone needs a girl or two."

Her expression went serious. "If you want to try for a boy in a couple of years, I'm game. My uterus should be rested by then."

"Even if we do decide to have another baby, I wouldn't mind having another girl. Besides, I've already had a boy." A son who had left an indelible mark on his soul. "No one could ever replace Caleb." Rachel gave him a kiss, taking him by surprise. "What was that for?"

"Just because you mean more to me than you'll ever know."

And he loved her more with each passing day.

He lowered the cover on the grill and walked his wife, arms around waists, back to their group of friends.

As the sun began to set, they all shared good food and great stories from the past. They celebrated Rachel's upcoming return to college as well as Sam's bumper crops and

Chase's recent victory as the county's most recent Reed son to be elected sheriff. They congratulated themselves on adding to the population of Placid, where their journeys had all begun. They tossed horseshoes and baseballs and played with the kids until the kids were all played out.

When everyone had left and the babies were tucked into their cribs for the time being, Matt took Rachel to bed and made sweet love to her. And as they settled down in each other's arms, he counted his blessings instead of sheep.

He had a gorgeous wife, two beautiful, healthy daughters and an appreciation for all the little things, like a baby's first steps and the sound of "Dada" coming from their sweet mouths. His dad was clean for the first time in twenty years, and his father-in-law was happily married and living large in sunny Florida.

Most important, Matt had learned to grant grace not only to others, but also to himself. He'd learned to be a little more open with a little less prodding. He'd also discovered that shedding a tear now and then—as he had when his children were born—didn't make him less of a man. Just the opposite.

He'd come to understand that each moment was a gift, a sad lesson learned from a prestigious judge whose life would probably end way too soon. Just as both his and Rachel's mothers' lives had ended too soon.

He didn't need riches or fame—only a front porch with rocking chairs for when he retired in thirty years or so, and the love of a family that had been a long time coming. He definitely didn't need a bottle to cover his pain or to enhance his joy. He was already high on life.

But he did need to be the man Rachel had always believed him to be. The man he'd always wanted to be for her. The only man his remarkable, loving wife would ever need.

* * * * *

LARGER-PRINT BOOKS!
GET 2 FREE LARGER-PRINT NOVELS PLUS
2 FREE GIFTS!

Harlequin®

Super Romance®

Exciting, emotional, unexpected!

YES! Please send me 2 FREE LARGER-PRINT Harlequin® Superromance® novels and my 2 FREE gifts (gifts are worth about $10). After receiving them, if I don't wish to receive any more books, I can return the shipping statement marked "cancel." If I don't cancel, I will receive 6 brand-new novels every month and be billed just $5.44 per book in the U.S. or $5.99 per book in Canada. That's a saving of at least 16% off the cover price! It's quite a bargain! Shipping and handling is just 50¢ per book in the U.S. or 75¢ per book in Canada.* I understand that accepting the 2 free books and gifts places me under no obligation to buy anything. I can always return a shipment and cancel at any time. Even if I never buy another book, the two free books and gifts are mine to keep forever.

139/339 HDN FEFF

Name	(PLEASE PRINT)	

Address		Apt. #

City	State/Prov.	Zip/Postal Code

Signature (if under 18, a parent or guardian must sign)

Mail to the Reader Service:
IN U.S.A.: P.O. Box 1867, Buffalo, NY 14240-1867
IN CANADA: P.O. Box 609, Fort Erie, Ontario L2A 5X3

Not valid for current subscribers to Harlequin Superromance Larger-Print books.

**Are you a current subscriber to Harlequin Superromance books
and want to receive the larger-print edition?
Call 1-800-873-8635 today or visit www.ReaderService.com.**

* Terms and prices subject to change without notice. Prices do not include applicable taxes. Sales tax applicable in N.Y. Canadian residents will be charged applicable taxes. Offer not valid in Quebec. This offer is limited to one order per household. All orders subject to credit approval. Credit or debit balances in a customer's account(s) may be offset by any other outstanding balance owed by or to the customer. Please allow 4 to 6 weeks for delivery. Offer available while quantities last.

Your Privacy—The Reader Service is committed to protecting your privacy. Our Privacy Policy is available online at www.ReaderService.com or upon request from the Reader Service.

We make a portion of our mailing list available to reputable third parties that offer products we believe may interest you. If you prefer that we not exchange your name with third parties, or if you wish to clarify or modify your communication preferences, please visit us at www.ReaderService.com/consumerschoice or write to us at Reader Service Preference Service, P.O. Box 9062, Buffalo, NY 14269. Include your complete name and address.

HSRLP11B